HEARTS OF STEEL

GERI

GUILLAUME

ARABESQUE

BET BOOKS

BET Publications, LLC

ARABESQUE BOOKS are published by

BET Publications, LLC
c/o BET BOOKS
One BET Plaza
1900 W Place NE
Washington, DC 20018-1211

ISBN 0-7394-2704-0

Printed in the United States of America

DESCENDANTS OF GEORGE JOHNSON

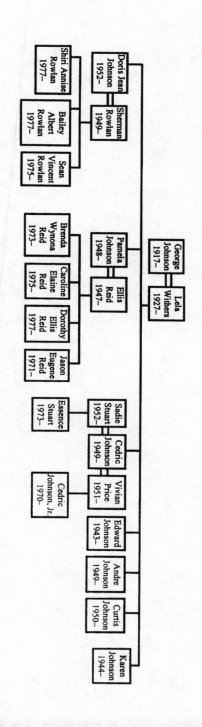

PROLOGUE

Football sucks. It has to be the most idiotic game ever invented. No, I take that back. I think that game where the moderator in black leather exclaims "You are the weakest link!" takes the prize for idiocy. But football runs a close second.

I'm not talking about *fútbol,* otherwise known as soccer. Noted players like Pelé can make even bouncing a ball on top of their heads look sophisticated.

I'm not talking about Australian-rules football, either. Given a hundred years and a book of the rules, I won't ever be able to figure that one out. I just like watching the referees in their cute white coats and fedoras perform what looks suspiciously like a Wild West fast draw to authenticate a score.

I'm talking about good, old-fashioned, Monday-night, Hank Williams, Jr., caterwauling "Are You Ready for Some Football?" turkey-day marathon, American-style football.

Am I ready for some football? No. Never. Not even if you paid me.

Before you jump to any conclusions, let me be the first to say that I *know* what the game is all about. Nobody can accuse me, Shiri Rowlan, of letting ignorance prejudice my thinking. That is, I know how the game is played.

I know how many players are supposed to be on the field. I know the player positions (mostly prone, since those behemoths can eat their weight in food). I understand the mechanics of the game. How many downs you get to score? Four. How many points you get when you score? That depends on how you get the ball across the goal line. Field goal. Touchback. Touchdown. Who cares?

I can even tell you what the Icky Shuffle is all about. Trust me, you don't want to know. What I don't get is what makes otherwise sane individuals run full tilt toward each other, deliberately trying to bash each other's brains out for temporary possession of the stuffed hide of some poor animal. It's ridiculous.

And the people who dress up, parading around in feathers or face paints, all in the name of supporting their team, ought to be looked up as well. For real! If you saw a grown man on the street, in a giant chicken costume, flapping his arms and clucking in your face, wouldn't that make you want to call the local law enforcement?

I wasn't always this way. I wasn't always a player hater. Before I saw the light, I enjoyed a rousing game of football, just as much as the next girl. There was something about sitting on the huge, sectional couch with my father and older brothers, scarfing down snacks, yelling at the television, cursing or blessing the team, that was as close to heaven as I could get on a Sunday afternoon.

I *had* to like football. If a girl following behind two big brothers wanted any attention at all from her father, she had better learn to like what he liked. So I did. When my dad cheered for a play, I cheered for a play. When my dad cursed the coach, I cursed the coach. That is, for some of my dad's more colorful epithets I substituted my own. ''Son of a rock-sucking witch'' was one of my more careful substitutions. Still, if I shouted it loud enough, it sounded very close to the real thing.

But I remember, almost to the day, the very hour, when

I came to my senses. It was the summer of '89. If my math is correct, that means I've been carrying a grudge against that stupid game for thirteen years now. I'd almost forgotten about my conversion, or rather . . . the birth of my aversion.

What suddenly reminded me just how much I disliked that game? When the little boy sitting directly across from me launched a grapefruit-size football at my head to get my attention.

Yeah, that's the way to make me a fan. Go team.

ONE

"I want it, Mommy! Please . . . please . . . pleeeeeeeze!"
I pretended that I couldn't see or hear the little boy sitting across from me in his mama's lap, squirming and begging to be set free. He'd already broken the child safety harness that was supposed to rein him in. As the plastic toy football sailed past my head yet a third time, I turned up the volume on my MP3 player and tried not to glare at him.

Now, where was that magazine I'd picked up at the airport gift shop? I'd better not have lost it. The thing must've cost me three times the regular newsstand price. Where do they get off charging that much for a magazine? For that kinda money, the pages had better be edged in gold.

Maybe they were. That article about the rise of black women in the business world looked interesting. I could use some extra pointers to help me get ahead. Recent college graduate, dewy-eyed intern. I felt like I had a FRESH MEAT sign on my back for all the employees at the consulting firm of Watkins, Smith & Cohn, Inc., to take advantage of.

Shiri can you deliver this package for me?
Shiri, can you sort and deliver this mail for me?
Shiri this. Shiri that.

Lift that barge; tote that bale. I was going to be *sooooo* glad when my internship was over and I could walk through that door as a full-fledged employee.

I opened the magazine to the table of contents, licking my thumb, and leisurely flipped through the pages. The airport monitor said that my flight out of Jackson, Mississippi, to Birmingham, Alabama, was delayed, so I took my time, letting my eyes scan the pages for articles of interest.

"Now, Geoffrey. What has Mommy told you about whining? You know Mommy's very unhappy when you whine."

Even though I'd turned up the volume, risking permanent eardrum damage, I still heard them, even over the smooth sounds of sultry India Arie jamming in my ears.

"But I want it. I want it now. Please? Please let me have the big bears. Please. *Pleeeeeeze?* I promise I won't ask for anything else."

The kid begged pretty hard. So I knew what was coming next. The mother had no choice. She was going to crack. My mama used to get that look sometimes, when she'd had just about enough of me and my brothers, Bailey and Sean.

Actually, when she'd had enough of them. I was such an angelic child. Never gave her a moment's peace . . . I mean problem. Because I was so well behaved as a child, I didn't understand how Geoffrey's mother could tolerate that behavior. I had no sympathy for her.

Well, not much.

Please don't let her look at me. Please, I silently prayed. I didn't want to see that look of quiet desperation in her eyes.

Don't look at her. Don't you dare look at her, Shiri Annise Rowlan.

Oh! Too late. I looked at her. What did I have to do that for? I think she took my sympathetic gaze as permission to allow Geoffrey to continue to annoy me.

"I promise I won't ask for anything else," Geoffrey pleaded. "Pinkie promise. That means I mean it."

"You said *that* when I bought you that GameBoy that you permanently loaned to your friends, Geoffrey. And when

I bought you those sneaker skates that are sitting and rotting in the bottom of your toy chest and those disappearing ink markers with all of the caps left off of them. No more toys, Geoffrey. *I* mean it this time.''

She sounded tough, shaking her finger at her son, but I don't think she really meant it. She was going to crack. I could tell by the look in her eyes—somewhere between maternal and murderous instinct. Geoffrey was going to wear her down until he got what he wanted.

Speaking of wants, that was a *baaaaad* suit that sister girl was working in my magazine. I flipped another page to continue the article. Said that she was the CEO of her own interior design business.

You go, girl!

That'll be me someday. I just know it. I may be a lowly WSC intern now. But a few more years, impressing the right people, taking on key assignments, and before I can say six-figure salary, I'll have one.

I paused in midflip when a shadow fell across the page. Without lifting my head, I raised my eyes. I didn't have to guess who that was. It was the mother, with bratty Geoffrey not so silently in tow. That must be some kind of record. Two minutes, three, before she went back on her word?

I looked up into two red-rimmed eyes. Either she'd been crying or drinking or badly in need of both. Geoffrey was tugging on her arm and yelling at the top of his lungs that she never got him anything he wanted. It was *sooo* unfair. And why was she being *sooo* mean to him? And he was going to run away.

I almost laughed out loud. My mama had a saying to bust up our threats to run away. When I'd threatened to do it once when she wouldn't let me go to some concert for some group that isn't even in existence anymore, she'd said, "Don't run, walk. You'll last longer and you'll get farther.''

That had certainly put the running fire right out of me.

"Uh . . . excuse me. I hate to bother you. . . .''

Then why are you? The words were held firmly in check in my mind by pressing my lips together.

"I was wondering. . . ." the woman continued.

"Yes?"

"Those bears." She gestured with her free hand toward the oversize teddy bears sitting on either side of me.

"I want one, Mommy!"

"Son, what has Mommy told you about interrupting? Do you want me to put you in time-out?"

It was on the tip of my tongue to say that if little Geoffrey had been cutting up that way in front of my mama, there wouldn't be any time-out business. Uh-uh. No way. It would be time up—and with the business end of a switch.

But these days, you can't tell people that. You know how funny people get when you try to tell them how to raise their kids. Somebody had better tell this woman that if she lets that little boy put his grubby fingers on my bears just one more time. *Just one more time . . .*

"I was wondering about your bears. They're beautiful. Where'd you get that suit for the papa bear? And those spats on his shoes are simply adorable. Are those real pearls around the mama bear's neck? Geoffrey! Don't touch that!"

I cut my eyes just in time to see Geoffrey pulling at the mama bear's clutch purse.

"Would you be interested in selling your bears to me? Or one of them?"

"I'm sorry, but they're not for sale," I said, using my most polite but insistent voice. All the while, I eyeballed the kid. Just as soon as I went back to my magazine, that red-haired, freckle-faced spawn of Satan was going to try to make off with one of my bears.

"They're an anniversary present for my grandparents. I had them custom-made. They've been married for sixty years. You understand why I don't want to sell them, don't you?" I leaned forward and tried to convince the boy with the reasonableness of my tone.

Geoffrey was starting to get the idea that he would not get his way this time. His ears perked up as he looked back and forth from his mother to me, then back to his mother again. One of us was going to have to back down, and it wasn't going to be me.

"Come on, Geoffrey. Let's not bother the nice lady anymore." The woman's face crumbled. That high-pitched, make-your-spine-curl, nails-on-the-blackboard keen of Geoffrey's had made her desperate.

"Lady, I'll pay you twice what you paid. Just name your price."

"They're not for sale." My lips were tight. My eyes weren't smiling.

My mama used to say that when my lip curled up and my eyes squinched up at the corners, I looked just like Clint Eastwood in those spaghetti western movies. That should have been enough of a warning to make this woman back up.

It wasn't. She started to rummage around in her oversize straw bag. She wasn't going to buy me off. Why didn't she tell the little hellion to shut up or get his butt whupped?

There was no way my parents would have let this go on for this long. All they had to do was give us the look and me and my brothers straightened up and flew right. I could still hear Sean's and Bailey's howls that day after church when Mama had warned us to stop passing licks.

I'd had to watch my back for months after that. Of course they'd insisted that I was the one who'd started it. It didn't matter. When Mama said no, she meant exactly that.

"I'm sorry. I really can't. But I can give you the card of the woman who made them for me. She lives here in Jackson."

"But we don't live here. This is just a stopover for us."

I shrugged, truly sympathetic. That wasn't my problem. I didn't know what else to tell her. It had taken two months and a good chunk out of my paycheck to have these bears custom-designed. An intern doesn't make much to begin with. Even if she offered me three times what I paid for them, I couldn't sell them. The look on my grandparents' faces when I dragged them through the door at their anniversary party was going to be priceless.

"I'm sorry," I said again. Hopefully for the last time.

"No, I'm sorry. Sorry to have bothered you."

"No bother." I smiled and crossed my fingers underneath the magazine against the little white lie. Okay, big, fat, hairy lie. But I didn't have the heart to make her feel any worse than she already did.

That little Geoffrey was a migraine in the making. I wouldn't have him next to me on this flight for all of the available CEO positions for black women in the world.

There was nobody sitting next to me on this flight. No one was getting near these bears. I'd made sure of that. I'd had to purchase all three seats—row, middle, and aisle. A little expensive for a couple of stuffed animals, but it was going to be so totally worth it when I saw my grandma Lela's face. She and I have a contest going.

She'd been collecting teddy bears since she was a little girl. Her sitting room was filled to bursting with every type of bear. None, I'm sure, could compare to this one. I hoped she would like them.

When I'd ordered them, I was very specific about my instructions as I sat in the little pink room in the rear of Marguerite's House of Dolls, sipping mint chamomile tea and going over my spec sheet. Marguerite was as sweet as her ultrafrilly sitting room. But she drove a hard bargain and haggled over every stitch, every detail. In the end, I got what I wanted.

Both bears were just a few inches shorter than I was, and I'm a good five-foot-four in heels. The mother bear was honey brown in color, with big brown eyes just like my grandmother's. Her skirt and jacket were bright red, my grandmother's favorite color, with a white lace blouse. A jaunty little hat sat on top of her head. Actually, it sat on top of a sleek, stylishly cut, iron-gray wig.

Grandpa Bear was taller than Grandma Bear. I'd had to put a little extra padding around the middle for Grandpa George. Everybody knew how Grandpa George liked to eat. If I walked up in there with a skinny bear, they'd tell me that I didn't get my money's worth. My cousins Essence and Brenda, who were consummate bargain hunters, would tell me that I'd been taken. I'd spent a lot of money for just the weekend trip. One small part of me wondered if it was worth it.

I had to shake myself out of it. Of course it was worth it. I was going back to see my family. I hadn't been back to Alabama in a while. Too busy on the job, I guess. I didn't mean to be so out-of-pocket. It's just those folks on the job never give you a moment's peace. I hadn't known being an intern would be so hard. The woman who recruited me right out of college had made corporate life sound so easy. Looking at my high grades, my extracurricular activities, she'd said that it would be like a walk in the park for me.

What park was she talking about? Central Park? Every day I went to work, I felt like I was being mugged. Not literally—mentally. There are some days when I feel like I can't do anything right. As soon as I do screw up, as soon as I let down my guard, some pushy upstart wants to grab what's mine.

Just like little Geoffrey over there.

"I'm watching you."

I said it loud enough for his mama to hear. If I found one bear hair out of place, one plucked button eye, one ruffle deflounced I was going straight to Geoffrey with my size-six shoe up against his bare bottom.

That's right. I said it. I don't have any love for badass little kids. I can thank my parents for that. They were strict in their raising of us, but we always knew that we were loved. We always knew where the boundaries were—boundaries kids of today either don't have or have learned to effectively push.

My daddy says that I have an evil streak in me. Maybe I do. I just don't have time for tantrums and theatrics.

Case in point was that couple standing at the ticket check-in counter. Newlyweds, obviously. They were talking loud, smooching, and shamelessly feeling each other up so that everyone knew it, too. They couldn't keep their hands off each other.

She had big blue eyes, pouty lips, and a tanning-salon glow. He had jock written all over him. Bulging muscles, laser-white, capped-teeth smile. Even with all of their good looks, it wouldn't get them on board any faster than anybody else.

"I don't understand how this could happen." Cheerleader could barely complain through her hiccuping sobs. "We made the reservation months ago. What do you mean I don't have a seat?"

The gate attendant kept her eyes lowered. Her lacquered fingernails *clackety-click-clacked* over the terminal keyboard.

"It's all right, honey. It's only a three-hour flight." Captain was doing his best to console her. It didn't work. I think she was more interested in letting everyone know how displeased she was than listening to her hubby's pacification.

"But we're on our honeymoon!" she insisted. "I don't want to be separated."

"Oh, deal with it," I muttered under my breath and rolled my eyes. I didn't want to be unsympathetic, but we all had issues with the airlines. Longer lines, restrictions on carry-on luggage, tighter security. It was the price we paid for the convenience of being able to travel the country at will.

I didn't know what the big deal was all about. What were a few hours sitting apart when they were going to have their whole lives together? Maybe she knew something that he didn't. Maybe she didn't expect it to last. She might have something there.

They looked like a pair made in heaven. But just because they looked good together didn't mean they needed to be together. Just look at J.Lo and Puffy. Poster children for the Beautiful People but certainly about as disastrous a pair as you'd ever want to meet.

Speaking of one of the beautiful people . . .

I paused in midlick, midflip of a page. I must have looked silly, my thumb hanging in midair, my tongue poking out between my lips. It wasn't easy looking cool and sophisticated when the equivalent of an African-American Adonis graced your presence.

Presence and grace. That's exactly what *he* epitomized.

He moved through the airport waiting area, unmindful of the chaos that accompanied delayed flights. He wore a crisp, white oxford shirt, with sleeve creases that would slit a wrist if handled the wrong way. Butt-hugging, prewashed Levi's with heavy starch made that swooshing sound that only professionally pressed denim from the dry cleaners could provide. For that kind of attention to detail, he must have had one heck of a dry-cleaning bill.

His skin was taut, just the right shade between Wesley Snipes and midnight. Head shaved smooth, no stubble. A man that sharp wouldn't be caught dead with a head full of stubble. A face maybe. His face had a hint of a five o'clock shadow along his jaw and chin. The thud of his boot heels on the waiting-room floor cut through that screech of Geoffrey's wail and Cheerleader's annoying whining.

I lowered my eyes before he caught me gawking. But his image was imprinted on my eyeballs. It swam on the page in front of me, blocking out the oh-so-sensible stock listings.

"J.D! I thought you weren't going to make it, man."

Captain of the Football Team grabbed his forearm and pulled black Adonis toward him in a macho-man, half hug, half wrestling-maneuver type move.

J.D. His name was J.D. I wondered what the initials stood for. Just Divine? Juicy Dessert?

He flashed his friend a lopsided grin. Strong white teeth. Not a gold cap in the row.

"Had a little bit of car trouble." He shrugged apologetically.

He wasn't speaking very loudly. I guess my ears were just hypersensitive, straining to hear him. I almost held my breath until he spoke. I hoped that something that fine wouldn't come off sounding like a thug from a rap video or a "too, too sensitive" type with an affected lisp.

He wasn't a southern boy. He didn't speak with a drawl. Yet I thought I detected an accent of some kind.

"Let me guess. You couldn't decide between the Lexus or the Lincoln?" Miss Honeymoon Heartache pouted her lips. She had her arm around her husband's, but her eyes were all over that J.D. person.

"The flight's delayed?" he asked.

"Worse than that. The airline has screwed up our reservations."

If it weren't for the fact that she was a grown woman, I'd bet that she'd stomp her perfect feet.

"What do you mean?"

"I don't have a seat in first class, J.D. Can you believe it? I've been bumped."

She'd been bumped. I could believe it. With the way she was behaving, it might have been on purpose. If she didn't stop whining, I wouldn't be surprised to discover that she'd been bumped from the flight altogether.

I didn't know which would be worse, a seat next to Geoffrey or one next to her. Though, I could probably stand sitting in the same area with her if I was surrounded by first-class luxury.

All three turned to look at the gate attendant, who simply smiled apologetically.

"What's the ETA of our flight?" J.D. asked.

ETA? I mouthed the words without making a sound. What kind of person can use *ETA* in a sentence and not sound like a geek? My hands shook, trying to keep from laughing out loud. I raised the magazine, holding it in front of my face. It made my elbows hurt, holding it at such an awkward angle. But it was better than letting him see me poke fun at him.

"Don't worry about it, sweetness. Ain't nuthin' but a thang," J.D. said confidently.

Oh-ho . . . So there *was* a little 'hood rat in him. It came out easily, but I wasn't buying it. Not completely. Everything about him said money and class.

I know the two don't necessarily always go together. But

he was a walking embodiment of someone who had it all: wealth, position, education. If he occasionally dropped the *g*'s from the ends of his words or threw in an offhand obscenity, he did it for effect, not because he hadn't had the opportunities to learn how to express himself in better terms.

The way he slipped back and forth between personas made me believe that there was a man who was just as relaxed hanging with the brothas as taking care of business in the bedroom. . . .

Oh! Did I say bedroom? I meant boardroom. I had to get my mind out of the gutter before I got on that plane. Grandma Lela could smell sexy thoughts a thousand miles away. I stopped counting the number of times she'd called me up in the middle of the night, telling me that she'd been dreaming about fish. I think that's some kind of old-folks code word. She was the one who was fishing—trying to find out if I was pregnant . . . or at least if I would admit to having sex.

If she only knew how much she didn't have worry about that. With me focusing on my career, I hardly had time even to check out the dating material in Jackson, let alone go on an actual date. That's probably why I reacted so strongly to the black Adonis. Away from my computer terminal, my four-foot-by-four-foot cubicle, and my boss dumping projects on my desk, certain parts of my body woke up and realized what they were for.

"Why don't you take my seat, sweetness? It won't kill me not to ride in first class this once."

"You can't do that, can you, J.D?" Captain of the Football Team asked.

J.D. nodded over his shoulder. There was a ticketing kiosk midway between the waiting area and the rest room. He reached into his back pocket and pulled out a black, leather wallet. He inserted a credit card, and with a few stabs at the keypad, changed his seating assignment from first-class to coach. Hubby then stepped up, inserted his own card, and purchased a first-class ticket for his wife, since one had miraculously become available.

In admiration, I whistled low under my breath while at the same time scanning the area for a rush of security. Since that awful day in September, the airlines had been especially wary of last-minute changes to seating assignments.

Now, that was a friend for you. To give up chicken cordon bleu for chicken salad on wheat *and* to risk being detained and frisked—not many would do so.

Triumphant, the happy hubby approached the gate agent and confirmed the seat. You'd think that with all of that, Cheerleader would have turned flips. She still wasn't satisfied.

"But we're not together," she complained. "I'm sitting behind you."

"After you get on board, you can see about getting some passengers to exchange seats. I'm sure after you explain your situation, they'll be more than happy to give up their seats," J.D. suggested.

I figured out J.D. must have stood for Junior Diplomat.

She flung her arms around him, holding him a little too close, if you ask me, for someone who was supposed to be so in love with her hubby. It may have been my imagination, but I thought I saw her give him a little hip thrust.

Hmmmph! Some people have no shame. I gave my magazine a little shake and returned to my article. There was more going on in that triangle than met the eye. I didn't know. I didn't want to know. My curiosity about the black Adonis dimmed.

The air crackled for a moment and the voice of the gate agent came over the PA system announcing my flight's arrival and giving the first boarding call.

"Attention passengers. Flight four-two-seven to Atlanta, with connections for Birmingham and Orlando, is now ready for boarding. This is the first call for our Gold Pass ticket holders. We'd also like to call for passengers with small children or passengers needing assistance."

I looked to my left and to my right at the bears. If I wanted to be sleazy, I suppose I could have tried to cut ahead of the rest of the passengers. I didn't know how I was going to manage those bears on board without knocking everyone in the back of the head as I passed by.

I followed suit with the rest of the passengers as they roused themselves, waiting for the gate attendant to call their range of seating assignments.

As I stuffed my magazine into my purse, all around me were the signs of departure. Cheerful waves, tearful good-byes. I wondered about each and every one of the people around me. I wondered about their lives, their individual stories. What had brought them to this place, to this point in time? When you're forced to people-watch for an extended period of time, you wonder about these types of things.

But most of all, I wondered if I was going to be trapped in that airplane for three hours with Geoffrey.

I slung my strap over my arm. The bag pressed into my hip as I grasped one bear around the waist, twisted a little to the right, and got the bear into a comfy position before I reached for the other. Grandpa Georgy Bear leaned too far forward. His black fedora with the white band and red feather tickled my cheek and made me giggle and say, "Stop that!"

As I clutched Grandma Lela's bear against my right hip, I could hear little Geoffrey whining.

"I want one, Mommy. *Pleeeeeeze!*" He must have heard me having fun with one of the bears. That renewed his yen to possess one.

His voice wailed above the departure noise and competed with the gate agent's second call.

"Quite a handful," a smooth voice said directly behind me and above my head. I tried not to crane my neck around to see. I nearly sideswiped a college student with a ratty school athletic shirt and shorts with Rockport sandals. But it wasn't she who addressed me.

I looked up into the hazel eyes of my black Adonis. I stared openly for a moment. The contrast of the tiger eyes in the midnight face brought to my mind images of inky African jungle nights and the predator eyes that blinked ominously through the foliage.

I blinked, shaking myself from the spell of his eyes, and found a way to dismiss his inexplicable effect on me. Must be special contact lenses.

"He needs his behind tanned," I retorted.

Did I say that out loud? The look on my face must have communicated my dismay. A lot of people don't believe in corporal punishment. They say that violence perpetrated against children is inhumane and only leads to more violence. Where were those people when Geoffrey chucked a football at my head, huh? I was only offering to end what he'd started.

"That, too. But I was referring to . . . to the teddy bears."

"Oh, I knew that," I said quickly to recover my composure.

"Need some help with those?"

He reached for the bears, but I pulled away. "No. I think I've got it. Thanks."

To prove my point, I stood straighter and took a firmer grip around the bears' waists. But Grandpa George Bear didn't want to cooperate. Just like my real Grandpa George. Always pulling the unexpected prank. As I hefted him higher, his Stacy Adams–clad foot swung out and caught the college student right smack-dab in the middle of her stomach.

I don't think I hurt her. Not really. But she *oomphed* anyway and clutched her stomach like I'd just shot her with a cannonball.

"Excuse me," I said with exaggerated sweetness. "I'm so sorry."

Something told me that I was going to give out a few more *excuse me*'s and *I'm sorry*'s before this trip was over. In return for my apology, College Girl gave a smile about as thin as her bony legs.

Then the gate agent unclasped the metal ring and drew back the nylon cord blocking the entrance to the next wave of passengers. I started down the connecting tube. The blast of hot, jet-fume-smelling air made me blink. I blinked as fast as I could. I could feel my own contact lenses drying out.

Standing in the middle of the ramp, my eyes tearing, I was a human roadblock. But I couldn't do anything about that. I tried to move aside, to give the other passengers room to pass.

We'd all been waiting so long to board the plane. Everyone was getting impatient. If I had been another passenger on the plane, I probably would have cursed me by now for holding up the line. Couldn't they see that I was coping the best I could with two giant, furry bears and a set of drying contact lenses?

Hindsight is twenty-twenty. Maybe I should have boxed those bears and checked them at the ticket counter like so much excess baggage. But I hadn't. I'd thought buying them seats would deliver them to Grandma and Grandpa in the best condition. And now, the ticketing line had snaked around so long, I was afraid that I'd miss my flight if I tried to check them in. I made a command decision to carry them on board with me.

After this episode, I had to remind myself not to give myself any more orders. And if I ever forgot and tried to give myself another order, I'd have to give myself permission not to follow it.

I treated these bears like they were people or something. Enough of that. They were toys! If they were a little dusty from the trip, my grandparents would just have to understand. I moved over as far to the right as I could, dragging them with me.

With my back pressed against the wall, I dug in my bag for my bottle of contact lens solution. I searched by feel alone because I had one eye squeezed shut to keep my lens from popping out. The other eye watered just as badly.

"There you are!"

I flipped open the contact lens dropper with my thumb, tilted my head back, and squeezed a couple of drops into my eyes. A few missed the mark, streaked toward the outer corner of my eyes, collected, then ran along the bridge of my nose. Closing both eyes, I tried to wiggle my eyeballs around to get the lenses to shimmy back into position.

"Here you go."

A large hand clasped my shoulder and dabbed at my face with a soft, masculine-scented cloth.

"Hey! What do you think you're doing?"

I tried to step back, but I was as far against the wall as I could go. I cracked open one eye, staring suspiciously at whoever was bold enough to get that close to me. You just don't sneak up on a black woman like that and put your hands on her. The ramp was cramped, but I didn't make that big a target.

"Oh, it's you." It was J.D. My black Adonis.

"Are you all right?"

"Yeah. I just got a little something in my eye."

"Here. Take this."

"A handkerchief?" A cloth one, too. In the days of Handi Wipes and disposable tissues, who carried cloth hankies?

"It's clean," he promised, smiling at me. His eyes crinkled up at the corners when he smiled. I liked that. And, as close as he was standing to me, I could tell that he wasn't wearing contact lenses. His eyes were his own. Naturally beautiful. I liked that, too.

"And pressed," I remarked, noticing the neat creases in the white linen. I dried my face, then passed it back to him.

"No, that's all right. You can keep it."

"I suppose it's not so clean now." I inspected it and noticed the faint traces of mascara and face powder that I'd left on it. In the corner, in gold embroidery, were the initials J.D. Again, I wondered. J.D.? Jim Dandy?

"That's not how I meant it," he said.

"Thank you," I said, using my most gracious tone. I had to amend it after sounding like I was ready to take a swing at him before.

"My pleasure," he replied, then canted his head in a

slight bow toward me. A bow! So continental. If my hands weren't full, I'd almost expect him to kiss one like they do in those old, foreign films.

"Maybe . . . maybe I could use a hand," I relented, then stepped aside to point to Grandpa Bear.

TWO

"See you on the other side." I waved to Mike and Barb as they disappeared down the ramp. Over her shoulder, Barb blew me a kiss, then wrapped her arm around Mike. Hip-to-hip, they took their place among the other Gold Pass first-class customers. They took their seats. My first-class seat.

Why was I complaining? Let Barb have it. It was going to take more than money to bring some class to that woman. I loved Mike like a brother. He was my teammate, my drinking buddy, my confidant. There wasn't anything I wouldn't do for him . . . except tell him the truth about his lady.

Correction. His wife. Barb was his wife now. He wouldn't believe me if I told him anyway. Or maybe he would believe me and wind up hating me for forcing him to see the truth. If I were in Mike's shoes, I don't know if I could choose between my woman and my best friend.

So I was going to do what all best friends do when they know their best friend has gotten involved with a skank. I was going to keep my mouth shut and run interference the only way I knew how.

I was the best man at the wedding. Standing there, dressed

to kill in my tux, I hadn't felt like the best. I'd felt like a fraud. What else could I feel when I was burning with the secret that just the night before, the love of Mike's life had tried to hit on me? It was more than a hit. The woman had thrown herself at me like an all-out body block.

We'd all been drinking. Maybe a little too much. But Barb wasn't that drunk. I'd seen her put away more than that and still be able to walk a straight line. Hell, the fact that she could drink like a fish was one of the qualities that had attracted Mike to her.

I wonder how cute that upturned nose and upturned glass are going to be three months from now when Barb gets tired of playing the happy homemaker. She was only interested in Mike's ball-playing ability long enough to get him to the altar. After the ring was on his finger—more like through his nose—she made it clear that she wasn't going to follow the Steeldogs from city to city to support her man.

What kind of a woman who knows nothing about football and cares even less winds up marrying a football player? It was Mike's entire life. He ate, breathed, slept, and spat football. I don't know how he's going to take it when the glow of Barb's beauty wears off and he realizes that they have nothing in common.

"Quite a handful," I remarked as they were leaving—that's what Barb was going to be.

My statement drew the attention of Goldilocks and the two bears standing ahead of me in line. Well, not really golden. Her microbraids were actually a shade between honey and caramel.

"He needs his behind tanned," she snapped. Then, a funny look crossed her face. Not funny ha-ha. There was nothing amusing about her face. It was rather compelling. The kind of face that made you want to study it, to indulge in all of its nuances—from the rough heart shape to the high cheekbones and the high-arched eyebrows. Full lips painted a shade too dark with a hint of gloss. Other than that, no other makeup than I could tell. Even this early in the spring, Jackson weather was too hot for all of that foundation, mascara, eye shadow, and whatever else women were using these days to give that "unmade-up" look.

The look that crossed her face was one of disbelief. She hadn't meant to say what she'd said out loud. The way she bit her lip afterward made me think that she'd recall the words if she could. Her jaw snapped shut. I could almost hear her teeth click together, the muscles in her cheeks working in tiny spasms. She glared at the squalling kid behind us.

Now that she drew attention to him, he was loud. I guess I'm lucky. After playing in a few stadiums where the acoustics could be deafening, I've trained myself to tune out just about anything. With seconds to go, a game-breaking catch on the line, I couldn't afford to be distracted by every peep and squeak from the crowd.

When the time has ticked down to the last second and you've got the game-winning ball in your hands as you're dancing the victory dance in the end zone, that's the time to let the crowd noise wash over you. Nothing like ten thousand individuals screaming your name in frenzied adulation to get your attention.

Or the soft voice of a single, pretty woman. A pretty woman gets my attention every time—whether she is screaming my name or not.

"That, too. But I was referring to . . . to the teddy bears," I ad-libbed. I'd started to say that I was referring to my friends who'd just boarded the plane. But they were no longer my point of focus.

The café au lait beauty with the chocolate-drop eyes had my full attention. I wondered about her situation. Where was she going? Who were those bears for? Her kids?

"Oh, I knew that," she said, lifting her chin. Several stray braids fell from their clip and landed across her cheek and eyes. She blew them back, ineffectively, and tried to reach up with her shoulder to brush her hair aside. Her hands were full.

"Need some help with those?" I offered. My hand

twitched, as if fighting the urge to reach around the girl in the faded college sweats and brush at Goldilocks's cheek.

"No. I think I've got it. Thanks."

She turned her back to me, maybe too abruptly, and sucker punched the college student with the bear's foot. The student clutched her stomach and groaned.

Laughter bubbled inside me, causing my lips to twitch and my eyes to tear. I hadn't seen this good a performance since my junior high school, most losing season, basketball days.

To set a pick or try to draw an intentional foul, we'd had to put on some wonderful performances. If an offensive player came within inches of touching us, we'd had tacit permission from the coach to fall to the gym floor and writhe around as if we'd been hit by a freight train.

I'd taken a fall so many times that my junior high school photo had beside it *Jack "The Splat" Deneen.* Being big and clumsy on the basketball court wasn't an asset. It hadn't taken me long to switch teams as soon as the season changed. I'd tried out for junior varsity football and found my calling intentionally knocking the other kids flat.

Now I was a big-time star wide receiver for the Birmingham Steeldogs. No longer Jack the Splat. I'm known around Birmingham as J.D. "Flash" Deneen. And all the girls who wouldn't look my way in high school are tracking me down, giving me offers that would make Hugh Hefner blush. I can't seem to beat them off with a stick. Not even the married ones. Which is why I was in this mess in the first place.

I couldn't keep ducking Mike and Barb. How many times could I use car trouble as an excuse for running late? Trying to avoid Barb had almost made me miss my flight today. She was tenacious, insistent. She won't be satisfied until she gets into my pants. Not this time. She'll just have to settle for getting into my airplane seat.

Maybe I should thank Barb. If it hadn't been for her, I wouldn't have had the opportunity to meet Goldilocks. She played it coy. Pretending that she didn't notice me noticing her. That's fine. I'll play that game for now. We may be working from different rule books, but the game's all the same. Both of us looking to make the big score.

The gate agent moved the cords, and I inched a little closer. That is, I could have gotten closer if the college student hadn't suddenly let several of her friends cut in line. They came from out of nowhere, slinging backpacks and sporting equipment. Suddenly, I was ten people deep and I saw my chance to strike up another conversation with Goldilocks slipping away.

Goldilocks moved slowly, carefully down the ramp. Those bears must have gotten too heavy to carry. She was holding them high enough off the ground to keep the big bear feet from dragging. Her back was straight; her shoulders were slightly raised when she planted her hands on her hips. There was a slight sway to her full hips and I wondered if it was natural or whether the enticing sway was a show for my benefit.

Slinging the strap of my carry-on over my shoulder, I started down the ramp with the rest of the passengers. I didn't get very far. There was a bottleneck just before the entrance to the plane. This always happens when passengers have trouble getting settled in their seats.

I was almost willing to put money on who was holding up the line. Yep. There she was, standing with her back against the wall. The bears were sitting on either side of her like bodyguards protecting royalty. Her head was tilted back, exposing a neck adorned with a slender beaded choker made of amber and irregularly shaped natural pearls.

As I moved closer, I saw what had made her stop. She lifted a small, white vial to the corner of her eyes and allowed a few clear drops to splash against them. A few drops missed and rolled down her cheeks. She fanned her face with her hand and used the back of her wrist to dab at her eyes and cheeks.

I must be one of the few men under thirty who never leaves the house without a handkerchief. I have my grandfather to thank for that. Nobleton Deneen was a gentleman's gentleman. Born on a sugarcane plant in Puerto Rico, he'd immigrated to London in the late thirties. Even when all of London was coming down around his ears in a rain of rubble and shrapnel, he'd maintained his dignity. According to one of his wartime stories, his hanky did everything from staunch the flow of blood from a gut wound to strain the impurities from the last potable water left in the city. God's honest truth, he insisted.

If I could use my hanky to attract the attention of a pretty girl, that was good enough for me. Whatever airline fates there were gave me another chance to meet up with her again, and I wasn't going to let the opportunity pass me by a second time.

"Here you go."

I placed one hand on her shoulder and with the other dried her face with a handkerchief.

"Hey! What do you think you're doing?"

She jerked away from me. Her dark eyes flashed, warning me that perhaps I'd stepped over an invisible, but mutually understood line. I could see her position. She was a woman traveling alone. I was a strange man who'd stepped too close for comfort. I could be anyone.

Strangers flirting in line is one thing. Deliberately, openly touching without permission said something else altogether. It made her throw up her defenses.

"Oh, it's you." Relief flooded her face.

"Are you all right?"

"Yeah. I just got a little something in my eye."

"Here. Take this."

"A handkerchief?" She sounded surprised.

"It's clean," I assured her, and gave my most disarming smile.

"And pressed." She wiped away the contact lens solution, examined the handkerchief, then offered it back to me.

"No, that's all right. You can keep it."

"I suppose it's not so clean now."

"That's not how I meant it."

"Thank you." Her voice was honey sweet, with a hint

of a slow, Southern drawl. I found that some Southern women may talk slow, but don't let that fool you. Their minds are lightning quick. I believe they speak slowly, softly, to gather their thoughts. And while they're gathering themselves, they're reeling you in.

My mother is a very soft-spoken woman from Alabama. Yet, just try to beat her at a game of *Jeopardy!* She could think rings around my father and me—supplying an answer while we were still trying to figure out the question.

"My pleasure," I continued, gesturing toward her bears. "Are you sure I can't help you with those?"

"Maybe I could use a hand. They're heavier than I thought they would be."

"Birthday present for some lucky kids?" I asked, blatantly fishing.

She smiled. I noticed that she tactfully avoided answering my question. She was going to make me work for every scrap of information.

As she indicated one of the bears to pick up, I did some junior sleuthing and checked out her hands.

One gold ring with an ankh symbol was on the index finger on her right. Another ring, college graduation, was on the fourth finger of her right hand. On her left hand was a pearl-and-amber bracelet matching her choker. Nothing on the ring finger of her left hand. Perfect manicure, French tips, not too long.

All the signs of being well taken care of, but nothing to tell me if anyone, other than herself, was doing the caring. If there was a man in her life, he hadn't put a ring on her yet.

"At least we don't have to walk far. I'm in row nine," she said, squeezing through the narrow entrance.

On my left, I heard pilot activity in the cockpit. On my right was the cabin entrance through first class. Mike and Barb were sitting in their seats a few rows back. They must have convinced one of the passengers to switch, after all. Mike saw me first. His gray eyes bugged a little, giving him a deer-in-the-headlights look.

"Barb! Quick! Give me the camera," he said, jostling Barb's arm. "You wait until I tell the rest of the team about this one. They'll never believe me. I've got to have a picture of this."

He held up the small, silver-toned digital camera to his eye. The light flashed, making small dots dance before my eyes.

"I'll take my blackmail money in small bills, nothing larger than twenty-dollar denominations, if you please." Mike grinned at me and slapped me on the back as I passed by.

"Sweet J.D. Always the gentleman," Barb added. She touched the ultrasleek, sophisticated chignon coiled at the base of her slender neck. For a minute, my mind did a fast backtrack, remembering how she'd pulled the pins from her hair and tossed the peroxide platinum curls over her shoulder. The locks had tumbled down her shoulders, almost to her waist, barely covering the surgically augmented breasts she'd bared for me.

I hadn't felt very much like a gentleman, then. I'm only human. When a beautiful woman touches me with intent to arouse, I'm not going to disappoint her. But Mike had been my best friend since the third grade, since before I could fully appreciate what a woman's touch could do for me— or to me. I wasn't going to let my teammate down. When Barb threw herself at me, that was one pass I had to fumble.

"That's me. A regular Sir Galahad," I replied.

I felt Barb's eyes boring into my back. Two cold, blue pinpoints of light zeroed in on my spine and pushed me past the first-class passengers.

The line stopped moving as the passengers ahead of us stuffed their carry-on bags into overhead bins. Babies cried, cell phones rang with last-minute calls, and the warm staleness of air yet to be circulated worked its way into my head. I could feel the beginnings of a headache throbbing at my temples.

The man ahead of us tried to jam an overstuffed carrier on wheels into the overhead compartment. Goldilocks turned her head to avoid being elbowed. He continued to grunt and strain, despite the flight attendant's gentle reminder over the intercom.

"Passengers, if you have found your seat assignments, please clear the aisle so that others can pass. If you need assistance, press the call button located in the panel above your seats. Thank you for your cooperation."

The struggling passenger jostled Goldilocks, pushing her backward into me. The bear stopped our bodies from making contact. She turned her head to look back at me, her expression a delicate mixture of irritation and apology. Still, he kept cramming, ignorant that he'd nearly given her a goose egg in the middle of her forehead.

I'd had enough. I shifted the bear to my right arm, reached above both their heads, and slammed the compartment shut. The resulting sound echoed through the cabin. For a moment, it seemed as though a hush fell over the passengers. Heads turned to stare at us.

The passenger glanced up at me. Dark, red-rimmed eyes sized me up and considered whether it would be worth it to say something about me taking matters into my own hands.

I lifted my chin and narrowed my eyes, in effect issuing my own challenge. "Whassup, man?"

"Thanks, bruh," he muttered, then scooted out of the aisle. His head barely touched the button panel as he moved toward the window seat. He didn't say another word, didn't even make eye contact with me again as I continued down the aisle.

The rest of the passengers let out a collective sigh as the conversational buzz picked up again.

"Here we are," Goldilocks said. "Seats A, B, and C."

"You've taken all three?"

"Does it make sense for me, after all I've been through, to stuff those bears up there?" She lifted a finely arched eyebrow at me and I was oddly reminded of that character Spock from the original *Star Trek* series—droll, with an underrated sense of humor.

"No, I guess not," I remarked, plopping Papa Bear in a seat. She slid him over, saying, "Grandpa always gets the window seat.'' She placed the mama bear in the middle and took the aisle seat herself.

"Thanks for the help, mister.''

"Any time.'' I paused, thinking maybe I should say more. At least tell her my name. Find out hers. Find out where she's going, and how I can get there, too. I wasn't ready to leave her just yet.

The lady behind me rushed my schedule. She cleared her throat loudly and said, "Some people would like to get to their seats *before* the plane takes off.''

"See you on the other side,'' I said to Goldilocks before moving on. Hopefully, my smile and the memory of my kindness would be enough to hold her attention, her interest in me until we landed. I wanted her thinking about me the entire trip. I wanted her thinking just as hard as I knew I was going to be thinking about her. And I didn't even know her name.

Three hours to Birmingham and I was going to be fixated on a nameless woman—the woman with two tall bears and the honeyed smile.

Five rows back and one row over I found my seat. It was on the aisle. Usually, I prefer the window. I like to stare into the clouds and go over plays in my head. I couldn't be picky this time. The young man sitting in my window seat had already settled in. He leaned his head against a scrunched-up jacket and snored softly, a faint whistling through his nose and throat that was just enough noise to add to the pounding gaining strength at my temples.

I reached up and placed my own bag in an overhead compartment. As I prepared to close it, I felt several pairs of eyes staring at me, waiting to see if I would have another slamming fit.

Part of me wanted to give them the show that they wanted. After all, I was a performer. I get off on being a crowd-pleaser. The other half didn't want to give them the satisfaction of thinking that they were in the presence of yet another angry black man.

The overhead compartment closed with a barely audible

click and I took my seat. As keyed-up as I was, it would take some time to relax, so I crossed my arms. It was warm on this plane. I felt the beginnings of stickiness as my supposedly high-endurance deodorant quit. I looked over one shoulder, then over the other at the guy snoring soundly beside me.

Assuming that curiosity about me had faded, and no one was watching, I raised both arms high over my head as if to stretch, then took a quick (and hopefully unobserved) whiff. Just checking. I couldn't get close to the lady if the smell was going to drive her back. So far, so good. It was just dampness, no odor. I didn't know how much longer it would hold out, so at the first available opportunity, I meant to slip into the lavatory and see about freshening.

The flight attendants in navy blue uniforms and sensible heels sashayed past, counting heads and checking overhead bins. Sleeping Boy next to me had the right idea. My eyelids felt slightly grainy as I allowed them to close.

THREE

"See you on the other side," he said, then touched my shoulder in passing. My heart skipped up into my throat, beating so loudly that I didn't trust myself to speak. So I just nodded, and made myself extremely occupied with adjusting the seat-belt buckles on my bears.

Did he notice how he affected me? Could he tell how my fingers shook? They didn't feel like my own hands. They felt like someone had replaced them with thick, clammy, Vienna sausages like my Grandpa George likes to eat right out of the can with saltine crackers.

Come on, Shiri. Get a grip on yourself, girl. He wasn't all that. He probably didn't even mean to touch your shoulder. It was an accident, an incidental touching as he grabbed the back of the seat.

Hoping that I wasn't being too obvious, I waited until there was a small break in the flow of traffic up and down the aisle, then plucked a glossy airport merchandise magazine from the seat pocket in front of me. A simple flick of the wrist and *oops!* How clumsy I was. I reached down to retrieve it. And if I happened to catch a glimpse of those gorgeous sculpted buns as he walked way, then so much the better.

My head leaned over the armrest, turning a fraction to the left to see if I could locate where he was sitting.

"Here you go, ma'am."

Before I could get a good look, a flight attendant dropped down with his saccharine, practiced smile and blocked my view. He passed the magazine back to me.

"Thanks." My expression was as bland as my tone. I may have missed the booty shot, but my maneuver wasn't a total loss. I knew where he was sitting. Just a few rows back on the opposite side. Another quick glance back. I didn't want him to know that I knew where he was. I didn't want him to know that I was interested enough to pull a cheap stunt like butt-watching.

His long arms were folded behind his head. His eyes were closed. Could he be asleep already?

Well, there went that foolish female fantasy that I had. The one centered around the desire that he couldn't take his eyes off me. All women have had them. That magic moment when the man of your dreams, your true love, your soul mate, catches your eye from across the room. Suddenly, the rest of the room loses focus, like someone has smeared petroleum jelly all over the camera lens. Violins start to play, and you start toward each other in super-slow motion. The next thing you know, you're running hand in hand on a lush tropical island, splashing through crystal-clear waters making waves against sand so sparkling, it could be made of crushed diamonds.

Like in a Destiny's Child video, the wind machine blows your hair back in the perfect direction. You've got the perfect perm. Not even the waters of the Caribbean can kink it up. Your bathing suit is the perfect color, a perfect fit. As you run along the water's edge, the strategically placed thong stays in place, no matter how hard you jiggle. No stretch marks. No love handles. No cellulite. You don't even need a cover-up.

Ahhh . . . my perfect fantasy was blown to bits by one

simple fact. The black Adonis wasn't interested in me. He was just being polite—or, at the most, flirtatious.

I blew out a disappointed breath and tried to stare out the window to lift my spirits, so to speak. It wasn't easy being on the aisle seat. I had to crane my neck to see around the bears. I'm the opposite of most white-knuckle fliers. Most folks who are afraid of flying don't want to be reminded that they're on an airplane. They'll drink themselves into a stupor, listen to staticky headphones, or endure crappy movies to avoid feeling like they're thousands and thousands and thousands of miles above the ground.

I don't like to fly, either. To be more accurate, flying doesn't bother me nearly as much as the alternative—which is plummeting to the ground in a fiery ball. It's the fear of crashing that gets me all worked up when I get onto an airplane. I like the window seats. As long as I can see blue skies, fluffy white clouds, I'm okay. I tell myself that God's up here in Heaven. Any place He chooses to hang out is okeydokey, fine with me.

As the plane taxied to the runway, the flight attendants went through the emergency procedures in what looked like a cross between directing traffic and a Madonna "Vogueing" contest.

As if I were preparing for a test, I listened to every word, repeating them softly to myself. I wondered what the airline's policy was on women, children, and teddy bears going first if something did happen to the plane. I snickered as I imagined the faces of the emergency medical response team standing ready at the bottom of the escape chute as the bears came sliding toward them.

My grin quickly faded as the captain came over the intercom and gave us the flight expectations—travel time, arrival time, and weather conditions of the destination city. The flight was delayed, the destination time was going to be delayed, and worse than that . . . sounded like there would be rough weather ahead. A few thunder boomers, the captain told us. He had every confidence that we should be able to get through the storm by climbing above it.

Bad idea, I thought. To do that, we would have to get closer to the storm. Correct me if I'm wrong, but isn't the more prudent course of action to try to get *away* from the danger?

An hour into the flight, we hit it. The first wave of storm clouds. My fingers clasped the armrest. I gritted my teeth so tightly that my jaws ached.

The engines whined as the plane banked to the right and my cup of mostly watered-down ginger ale slid to the carpeted floor. It rolled out of sight. I think I heard a plastic crush as though it met an untimely demise beneath the heel of someone's shoe.

"Please, God."

I prayed not because I thought I was going to die. The way my stomach was heaving, I almost thought I'd prefer to die. I prayed not to be ill and embarrass myself in front of everyone. The sound of someone else on the flight retching started a chain reaction of my own gastric juices, making me clamp my hand over my mouth.

"Please, sir. You'll have to return to your seat."

Someone tried to make it to the bathroom? Barf bag wasn't good enough for him?

"For your own safety, please remain seated until the captain turns off the seat-belt-required signs."

"Please, miss. My . . . uh . . . my wife is up there, and she's deathly afraid of flying. I have to go to her."

That sounded like . . . it was! I looked over my shoulder to see J.D. skirting around the attendant. He was heading my way.

The plane took another unexpected dip, causing him to pause and hold on to the seats, one on either side of him, as he made his way toward me.

"Don't tell me that a big strong fellow like you is afraid of flying." I tried to sound flip and saucy. But I was the one who was afraid. Scared spitless. I'm sure he saw that in the creases between my brows and the hole I'd almost chewed into my bottom lip.

"Nope. Just need someone to hold the bag while I puke

my guts out. I thought since I carried your bears, you'd be willing to return the favor.''

I'm sure in the history of great pickup lines, his would never make the books. But who could be picky at a time like that?

''Are you all right?'' he asked, scooting past me. I unbuckled Grandma Lela Bear's seat belt and shoved her over to make room for him.

''Just peachy,'' I said breathlessly.

''You're a terrible liar, Peaches,'' J.D. retorted. He clasped his hand in mine and gallantly pretended not to notice that it was ice cold.

''Jack Deneen.'' He introduced himself, giving my hand a gentle squeeze. ''My friends call me J.D.''

''Shiri. Shiri Rowlan.''

''Pleasure to meet you, Shiri,'' he said, and somehow made me believe that he'd be pleased to be sitting next to me even if the plane was going down in flames. A direct look. An open, honest, appraising look that swept over me from my tinted roots to my crossed legs.

''That's a very unusual name.'' He tilted his head toward the bears. ''Then again, I'm sure it fits the subject.''

The plane jolted, sending Grandma Lela Bear *bonk*ing softly down on J.D.'s head. I tried not to giggle. This wasn't funny. We could all die. The plane could crash. If the man was going to die, let him die with some dignity.

''Not that I'm complaining, J.D., but before you buckle your seat belt, do you think you could turn the granny bear around?''

''Excuse me?''

''Reposition her,'' I continued. It's bad enough that they have to share a seat, but the way he'd placed Grandma Lela's bear on top of Grandpa George's, well . . . it looked . . . it looked . . . it looked obscene. Like the bears were trying for a membership in the mile-high club. Dressed as the bears were, looking so much like my grandparents, it hurt my brain to think that they would still be interested in sex.

"Do you want me to turn her around?" J.D. suggested, reaching for the buckle.

"No!" Grandma Lela sitting on Grandpa's lap? The plane thumping up and down like a pogo stick. No, that would be even worse. "Never mind. Just leave her where she is."

"Are you sure you're all right?" Even his frown of confusion at my obvious, nutcase ranting only enhanced his handsome face.

"Not really. I'll feel a lot better when we fly out of this storm."

"Talk to me, Shiri. Maybe that'll take your mind off of this storm."

"I really don't feel like talking," I insisted. I'd rather listen to him talk. The sound of his voice was deep and rumbling, not unlike the thunder I imagined shook the clouds. I liked the way my name looked on his lips—a soft pucker, a prelude to a kiss. I wouldn't think about the flight at all if he would just keep talking to me.

The plane banked to the left. I could hear the change in the engines as we gradually made our descent.

Too soon. The flight was over much too soon and I still didn't know any more about her than I did before. I have her name. But not much more than that. She was afraid of flying. Who wouldn't be after a bumpy, gut-wrenching flight like that?

She wore vanilla musk and minimal makeup. But there's so much more I wanted to know. If I didn't do something fast, she was going to walk off this plane and away from me forever.

A few more minutes. I just needed a few more minutes with her. My mind raced as the plane left the runway for the loading ramp. If I couldn't get much out of her in three hours of the flight, how was I going to get anything of substance from her in five minutes?

"I'm going to hang out here for a while, so if you want

to go back to your seat . . ." Shiri left the sentence unfinished, but her meaning was clear. She was dismissing me.

"Do you need any help getting your bears off the plane?" I wanted to see who was there waiting for her. A passel of kids? An anxious husband? A representative from the overstuffed toy convention?

"You don't have to do that. My relatives are waiting for me." She held out her hand. "It's been a pleasure, Jack Deneen."

Her tone was polite and dismissive at the same time. What else could I do but take what crumb she offered and move on? Chalk this up to just another chance meeting—two people who briefly touch each other's lives then move on, never to meet again.

We stood there. All around us, people prepared to leave. I heard sounds of relief that this unpleasant flight was over. But I wasn't ready to let go. Call it instinct. Call it ego. If I didn't push the bounds of the socially acceptable conventions, this woman would walk away from me.

I used the proximity of the overhead bins to lower my face toward her. Brash. Bold. I was going to kiss her goodbye. I rationalized that the illusion of the near-death experience entitled me to a kiss. A small one. A peck on the cheek.

Her dark eyes widened. Was she surprised? Maybe. Willing? I hoped so. I leaned even closer, confident that by now she knew what I wanted, what I intended to do.

But she performed an emotional reversal on me and withdrew her hand. She stepped backward across the aisle, murmuring something about not blocking the way for other passengers.

I hoped that she didn't see the disappointment in my face. No. I take it back. I hoped she *did* see. I wanted her to know how she affected me. I wished I knew why she affected me. Why was I so fixated on this one woman?

I had thousands of screaming female fans. Any one of them would give close to anything for this opportunity. Egotistical? Perhaps. Truthful? Definitely. I'm a wanted man. But not, apparently, by Shiri Rowlan.

To avoid more awkward moments for us both, I returned to my seat and retrieved my overnight bag. I toyed with the idea of waiting for her, of not leaving the plane until she did. It could have the opposite effect. It could tick her off, make her call security to detain me if she thought that I was harassing her.

Strengthening my resolve not to appear desperate and pathetic, I slung the bag's strap over my shoulder and stepped back into the aisle. The plane noise had hushed. The voices of the flight crew drifted back. I'm reminded of an old *Saturday Night Live* skit where cookie-cutter flight attendants stood by the door and vapidly waved. *"Buh-bye, now. Buh-bye."*

A few more steps and I would be even with Shiri's seat. A few more. Just a few more. Almost there. *Keep it cool. It's obvious that she's not interested, so let it go.*

"Can I have your phone number? Call you while you're here in town?"

I paused and looked around me, as if wondering if a ventriloquist had thrown his voice to come out of my mouth. I had no intention of asking her for her phone number— the last act of a desperate man, sounding *this close* to begging. Any more desperate, and I could be a character out of Spike Lee's movie *She's Gotta Have It. Please, baby, baby. Please.*

She looked at me and offered the kind of smile that someone gives when she is trying hard not to smile. "I don't think so," she said, shaking her head. But she chewed her bottom lip. A sure sign of indecision. Could she be considering it?

"Yo, man. Get your mack on some other time. I've got five minutes to catch my next flight."

Shiri turned her head at the sound of the heckler, so I moved out of the aisle to let the last of the stragglers pass. In that moment, a decision had been made. She wasn't going to give me the digits.

Knowing that she'd made up her mind, I did what any black man, mindful of his pride and ego, would do.

"Then I'll give you mine. You call me," I insisted as I unzipped my overnight bag. I found a tablet, promotional material with the team's logo on it, and a pen.

Because the cap had been left off, I made a mental note to have Soledad, my housekeeper, buy some extra stain pretreater the next time she did laundry. That should take care of the stray pen marks left on my clothes.

I scribbled small circles in the top corner of the pad and shook the pen back and forth a couple of times until the ink ran freely. Using the back of the seat to support me, I wrote down my cell phone number and my pager number.

"Here." Holding the paper between crossed fingers of my index and middle finger, I passed the slip across to her. "Here you go."

She barely glanced at it, then tucked it away into the deep recesses of her purse.

"Don't lose that now," I said, half in jest. If she was anything like my sister, once items were stuffed into the bottomless pit of a purse, nothing short of an experienced excavation team could dig them out again.

"I won't," she promised. "It's right here." Then she patted the side of her purse. I couldn't help but notice that she patted the wrong compartment. Had she done that on purpose, to mess with my head?

"You're not going to call me, are you?"

"You never know," she said, in that maddeningly non-committal voice.

"Yeah, sure."

I stepped back into the aisle, heading for the exit. Glancing over my shoulder, I placed my hand to the side of my jaw, mimicking a telephone. *Call me*, I mouthed to her.

FOUR

When I stepped off the plane, I thought about all of those comedy movies and cartoons where the frightened passenger throws himself on the ground and kisses it—promising never to fly again. It didn't seem so funny to me then, or far-fetched. If it weren't for having to lug these bears all the way down to the passenger pickup area, I would have been down on my knees, thanking the Maker for allowing me to come through in one piece.

I suppose, in a small way, I should thank Him for Jack Deneen, too. If it weren't for Jack talking to me, calming me down, and even on occasion making me laugh, I would have been a nervous wreck. Or worse, carried off the plane heavily sedated like that crazy guy from that *Twilight Zone* episode who saw a gremlin, bent on mass destruction, harassing him on the wing of the plane.

I edged my way past the milling crowd. The family hugs of greeting seemed more emotional, more heartfelt. Kisses between loved ones seemed more passionate. Embraces of friends were less restrained. It was as if getting off that plane made us all realize just how close we'd come to never getting off another plane again. Humbling thought. A near-death experience can certainly put things in perspective.

"Shiri! Shiri, baby. Over here!"

Someone called my name. I recognized the voice. It was my aunt Rosie. But I couldn't see her. I stood on tiptoe, trying to see over the crowd. But when you're only five-foot-four in heels, you've got to stand as erect as a ballerina on point to see above the heads of those who aren't vertically challenged.

"Over here, honey!"

"Aunt Rosie! What are you doing here?" I was surprised to see my aunt Rosie in the airport. She was actually my grandaunt, my grandma Lela's older sister; but she never liked the sound of the word *grandaunt*. Said it made her sound as appealing as a dried-up prune. Seeing her here now was a pleasant surprise. She almost never flew. Her motto— if God had intended her to fly, she would have been born with wings.

"I thought Uncle Edward was going to pick me up."

"He is. I just came along for the ride. Actually . . ." She looked at me and winked. "Take a look at this." She reached into her purse, pulled out a wallet, and handed me a card.

"What's this?"

"What's it look like?" she said smugly.

"It's a driver's license. Aunt Rosie! You finally learned how to drive? Oh, my God, I don't believe it."

"Your uncle Andre is still driving that old '75 Suburban."

"You mean the big yellow one with the gray primer on one door and the mismatched blue door on the other?"

"And the bobbing-head dog on the dash. Yes, that's the one. It's big enough and built like a tank. When he told me that he was coming to pick you up from the airport, I talked him into letting me drive. I figured that was the best way to break in my new license without breaking my neck."

She grasped my shoulders and squeezed with warm, brown hands.

"Let me take a look at you. Honey, what are they feeding you down in Jackson? When did you grow hips?"

"I didn't grow them," I corrected. "I think it was a drive-by 'hipping.' One night, I went to bed as a size seven. The next thing I know, I'm squeezing myself into size twelves. I try to exercise, but I spend a lot of long hours on the job, eating fast food at my desk."

"*Hmmmph.*" Aunt Rosie then pressed her lips together and folded her arms. For a moment, she looked so much like my grandma Lela that I started to hand over the bears to her.

"Don't you worry about it, honey. It looks good on you. I told your mama that you were too skinny anyway. 'Doris Jean,' I said to her, 'that child isn't going to get enough to eat out there, all by herself. Once she is out there on her own, she'll forget everything we taught her about nutrition.' "

"I didn't forget," I quipped. "I just didn't apply what I'd learned. You'd think that after sitting all those days in the kitchen, listening to you and Grandma Lela and Mama swap cooking stories, that I'd know enough to be a master chef by now. Besides, I'm not alone. I know you're just a couple of hours' drive away, Aunt Rosie, if ever I need you."

"Turn around. Let me get a good look at you."

I spun around slowly, taking the bears with me.

"You didn't call to say that you were bringing friends with you, so I can only guess that those are for Lela and George."

"Uh-huh. What do you think of them? You think Grandma Lela will like them?"

"That papa bear is a little on the thin side, don't you think?"

"Aunt Rosie!" I started to laugh.

"Come on. Let me take one of those off your hands. However did you manage on the plane with this behemoths, Shiri?"

As I touched my hand to my hair, patting it genteelly, I said in my best Southern belle, Blanche DuBois imitation, "I've always depended on the kindness of strangers."

Aunt Rosie took Grandpa Georgy bear from me. As she

turned away, heading for the parking garage, my eye caught a spot of color on her right shoulder.

"Aunt Rosie, I think you've got a smudge of something on your back." I dug inside my purse for the handkerchief that Jack had given me with the intention of wiping away the smudge.

Aunt Rosie looked over her shoulder and said, way too casually for me, "Oh . . . that. That won't rub off, honey. That's permanent."

"Permanent?" Funny. I'd never noticed before that Aunt Rosie had a birthmark on her shoulder. I peered closer, then gasped when I realized that the only thing permanent about Aunt Rosie's smudge was the ink.

"Close your mouth, honey, before you swallow a fly." She placed her index finger under my chin and lifted so vigorously my teeth clicked.

"Aunt Rosie!"

"What?" she said, sounding so innocent. But her dark brown eyes snapped and sparkled—like they always did when she was holding back a laugh at your expense.

"Don't 'what' me, missy," I said, sounding older than she ever could. "What is that on your back?"

"It's an ankh. An Egyptian cross."

"I know what an ankh is," I said, wagging my hand at her. She'd given me a silver ring with an ankh emblem as a graduation present. "What's it doing back there?"

"Healing quite nicely. Don't you think?" She paused in midstride to examine the exquisite work. I had to admit that it was lovely. The symbol was robin's-egg blue, edged in black.

"Does Grandma Lela know anything about this?"

"Not yet."

"When did you . . . how did you . . . why in the world . . . have you lost your mind?" I could only think to ask in exasperation. "Why would you put yourself at risk like that?"

"What risk?"

"You know tattoos don't just wash off. You could have gotten hepatitis, or lockjaw, or anything."

"You sound just like your mother. That Doris Jean worries about every little thing."

"I'm afraid I'm going to have to side with Mama on this one, Aunt Rosie."

"I'm not some starry-eyed sixteen-year-old, Shiri. I'm eighty years old. I knew what was I getting into. I did my homework and checked it out completely before I went. Diablo's has a very good reputation—as far as tattoo parlors go."

"Diablo? You got a tattoo from a man named Diablo?"

This was getting better by the minute. I'm sure my tone and my scrunched-up expression conveyed my disapproval. But then I had to check myself. Aunt Rosie was a grown woman. A lot "growner" than I was—and had been that way for awhile. After all, who was the one carrying on, slaving over a couple of teddy bears? I was ready to punch a kid's lights out because I thought he was thinking too hard about those bears. How adult was that?

Who was I to judge her if she wanted a tattoo? The more I looked at it, the more it grew on me. It was a work of art. An expression of Aunt Rosie's boundless free spirit— a testimony for all to see of her passion for life.

"So, did it hurt when you had it done?" I asked, curiosity getting the better of my prudish nature.

"It hurt more than a splinter and less than childbirth." Aunt Rosie tilted her head and regarded me with an impish grin. "You know, he had this cute butterfly design that would look really sweet right about there."

She jabbed at a spot on the side of my right thigh.

"No. Never. Not me," I quickly denied. "With the way I'm spreading, that cute little butterfly will look like a pterodactyl mauling my leg in six months' time."

"Shiri, you're not that big," Aunt Rosie insisted. "Don't get caught up in all of that superskinny, supermodel crap. You look good. If you're not eating right and not exercising, well . . . that I'm concerned about. With a little behavior modification, we can fix that, even if it takes me driving down to Jackson every week to check on you.''

"You don't have to do that, Aunt Rosie.''

"I love you like you were one of my own, Shiri. I want you to take care of yourself.''

"I will, Aunt Rosie,'' I said, making a mental promise to try to do better. I'd been in such a hurry to graduate and get out on my own, I'd forgotten how much strength I got from family and their support. They were always going to love me, whether I made it to the top rung of the corporate ladder or not.

We linked arms and passed through the doors leading to the parking garage

I extended my arm, aiming the garage-door remote in the direction of the control box inside. The batteries were going. It took a few seconds before the infrared beam activated the door. The door finally lifted, slowly, looking oddly like the huge maw of some prehistoric beast about to swallow me whole as I eased the nose of the Lincoln Navigator into the left parking spot of the two-car garage.

A quick flick of my wrist shut off the ignition. As much as I was glad to be home again, I just sat there, listening to the ''un-noise'' of interior of my SUV. The low whir of the radiator fan, still running to cool the engine after the drive from the airport, the subtle *tick-tick-tick* of the car keys swinging, clicking against the steering column. I could even hear the soft creak of leather under me as my weight settled into the seat. I pressed my fists to my eyes, saying a small prayer of thanks for the safe arrival from my trip.

I'd only been away for a few days, but it sure felt good to be home again. After a moment of silent reflection, centering myself, I gathered my traveling bag and my thoughts and headed inside.

Once inside, I sniffed. I could tell that Soledad had been doing a little extra cleaning. The place smelled of pine cleaner and potpourri. Automatically, my hand reached for the security control pad on the wall to enter my code and disarm the system. I threw open a couple of windows and turned on every ceiling fan in the house. The cross breeze felt good.

Soledad meant well, but to her, clean wasn't clean until your eyes burned from an infusion of cleaning chemicals. One of these days, she was going to blow my house sky-high with all of her creative mixing. I'd finally had to draw the line when I caught her trying to remove a kitchen counter stain with a noxious concoction of chlorine bleach, pine cleaner, and *un poquito* drop of ammonia. It took a while, but I'd finally convinced her that I *liked* the stain. It added character to the pristine surroundings—kept so by her vigorous attack on grime.

She'd conveniently sorted my mail into bills, junk mail, and letters from friends—which, I noticed, seemed to be getting fewer and fewer. Nobody took the time to write letters anymore. All of my friends were "Webbing" it, e-mailing me jokes, scams, and scares as fast as any Web server could handle them. I tossed the stack back onto the foyer table, resolved to go through it all, even the junk mail, after I'd settled in.

I headed for the refrigerator. Now that the contents of my stomach weren't churning around like smoothies in a Waring blender, I was ready to break the fast. Soledad had been busy in there, too.

Though I'd given her a few days off while I was away, she'd prepared a few meals for me, neatly labeled in opaque covered plasticware. She'd made the kinds of meals that always tasted better the second day as leftovers. Pasta and chicken, spaghetti, turkey meat loaf. She'd even prebagged some salad for me in zippered plastic bags.

"Thank you, Soledad. You're a true godsend." Literally. I think when God made the earth, he took whatever forces of nature were left over from the making and formed Soledad. She must be nearly a hundred years old, having been with my family for almost ninety of those years. *Crotchety* described Soledad on her best days. She was a little hard of hearing, especially when you asked her to do something that she didn't want to do or didn't think it wise to have done. You didn't give Soledad orders; you made suggestions, recommendations. Remember that, and she would take care of you with as much fierce loyalty as she had toward her own. She'd watched over my sister and me since we were old enough to pronounce her name.

I slid a casserole into the oven. The Pyrex dish scraping against the metal made the racks vibrate—like the pinging of a bell calling me in to supper. I set the temperature to a low warm. By the time I finish my workout, the scrumptious mixture of broccoli, cheese, rice, and chicken would be bubbling nice and warm, the flavors sufficiently mixed to make me want to do justice to the meal that Soledad had so lovingly prepared for me.

I then turned my attention to the business of working up a good appetite. It had taken me years to perfect my workout routine. I'd finally settled on a series of exercises that would leave perspiration streaming from every pore. Every muscle had to strain, scream for mercy. I'm not masochistic, just extremely competitive.

When I step out onto the playing field, I have to know that no one has worked harder than I have to be there. No one was better suited for the job than I was. I wasn't perfect, I knew. Just damned good.

That's why it was bugging the crud out of me trying to figure out why Shiri Rowlan wasn't more receptive to me. It was driving me even crazier to know that I couldn't stop wondering why she wasn't interested in me. I've had women walk away from me before. Not many, but enough. I couldn't shake the feeling that this time, I'd lost someone different. Someone special.

I've got to her out of my head before tomorrow's practice. I can't have my head stuck up in the clouds when my feet have to pound ground.

The next stop was my home gym. Soledad calls the room the chamber of horrors. Every device in the room looks like the instrument of choice in a Salem witch-trial torture chamber, with its assortment of carefully selected pulleys and weights, benches and racks. The left rear leads to the pool and hot tub. To my right, a small area lined with shelves holds clean towels, my workout clothes, and an assortment of natural liniment and rubs for when I overdo it. Not if, when. I always do. To my left, the entire wall is mirrored to help me monitor and correct my form. Am I vain? I don't think so. Just a consummate perfectionist.

I stripped out of my traveling clothes, down to my under-wear. That's when I caught my reflection in the mirror. I'm not a narcissist. But I do take pride in myself, in my appearance, and my abilities. As I stood there, nearly nude, I wondered what Shiri would say if she saw me now. Would she roll her eyes in feminine disgust? Would she give me that noncommittal half smile? The smile that promised nothing, revealed nothing.

I flexed my arms and ran my palms along the bulge of my biceps. I did a half turn, watching how the muted light threw shadows across the planes and valleys of my abdomen. I thought about how her small, soft fingers would feel around me, caressing my shoulders, down my back. My back arched as I imagined her perfectly manicured nails clutching me, raking across my skin as only a woman in the throes of passion would.

"Damn it, J.D. Cut it out!" I chastised myself, snatching my hands away before I could measure how aroused the very thought of her had made me. This was ridiculous. Why was I driving myself nuts? For as much as I was able to discover about her, I might as well be dreaming about a fantasy woman.

I threw myself into my workout, determined to exercise my demons way. Several reps at the lat-pull station made my shoulders ache. I bench-pressed until my pectorals burned. Then I reached for a jump rope to pump up the old cardiovascular system. The wooden handles had worn smooth through consistent use. The nylon cord was a blur as I made it hot pepper—a jump rope game my sister and her friends used to play. Sometimes I'd join in. Though admittedly at first to annoy her. Looking back on it, I suppose I have her to thank for my speed and sureness of foot. After a couple of times of having that rope, moving at lightning speed, slam against my ankles, I learned how to pick up my feet.

My feet skipped and shifted to the rhythm of a beat only they understood. My hands were held at my sides. My wrists flipped up and down to keep the momentum going. I spun the rope until every breath burned through my nostrils, until the rubber worn from the bottom of my athletic shoes threatened to make me slip.

Thwack! Thwack! Thwack! The nylon cord hit the hardwood floor until I thought I saw sparks fly.

Finally, pushed beyond an unspoken limit, I collapsed onto the floor, sucking wind and laughing aloud at my silliness. What was I doing? Getting all worked up over a woman—a woman I barely know. I hadn't been this sprung since my sophomore year in high school when I'd had a crush on a senior.

Languidly, I pulled myself to my feet, stripped out of my workout gear, and grabbed a towel. It was the hot tub for me now. The feel of the hardwood under my bare feet was replaced by the inlaid stone floor that formed a two-foot splash guard around the perimeter of the hot tub.

Good old Soledad. I could tell by the lingering scent of chlorine that she'd had the pool and hot tub serviced while I was away. I sat on the edge and adjusted the force and direction of the jet sprays churning just beneath the surface. As I treated my legs to a water massage, I stared into the boiling water and thought how adequately the water reflected how I felt.

My calm surface suddenly, explosively, was broken by inner churning. All for the want of a woman. Not just any woman. One woman. Shiri Rowlan.

I slid off the edge of the hot tub and carefully eased in.

The jet spray and heat soothed my aching muscles. Yet my mind stayed in turmoil. There was nothing that I could do about it but accept the feelings for what they were . . . whatever they were.

FIVE

It took a few minutes to figure out where I was. When I opened my eyes, I was a little disoriented. My room didn't feel like my own. It was. It was just my room of several months ago.

Without moving my head, I let my eyes scan the contents. I had to squint, because sometime during the morning, someone had drawn back the curtains and opened the miniblinds. Probably my mama. She was a firm believer in the power of fresh air to cure all ills. She'd also opened the window a crack so that a steady, whistling breeze cut through the room.

She'd been doing that since I was in junior high school, when my body had started to go through the change—during what my older brothers affectionately called "The Musty Years." Between the ages of eleven and fourteen, I went through a lot of Secret and Love's Baby Soft. We should have bought stock in those companies.

The morning breeze rattled the glossy paper of my posters dating back from before DeBarge was popular. Those posters covered almost every inch of wall space. My high-school diploma, with the cracked picture frame from when I'd thrown my size-six shoe at my brother for sneaking into my room, made a soft *thump-thump-thump* against the wall. How old was I then? Fifteen? Sixteen?

Above my head were strung several decorative fishnets that held all of my stuffed animals and baby dolls. There were so many, it was a minor miracle that they hadn't come crashing down to crush the life from me. Teddy bears won at state fairs, hearts given on Valentine's Day, Kewpie dolls and porcelain collectibles, and enough Barbie dolls to stage my own plastic beauty pageant. They all swung precariously overhead, obliviously staring out at the microcosmic world of a young girl's room through button eyes. Even the ones with the eyes that my brother Sean had poked out with a Phillips-head screwdriver seemed to be doing their best of keeping their toy vigil over me while I slept.

God, it was good to be home.

In my apartment in Jackson, I hadn't had the time, money, or inclination to decorate, to give my new place a sense of home. I had one lonely ivy plant, badly in need of water, that was sitting (wilting, actually) in the terra-cotta planter that my Uncle Curtis had given me as a going-away present. That was one of the few items in my bedroom in Jackson that gave me any indication of where I'd come from.

One of these days, I thought as I stretched languidly, I was going to repot the thing and give it a new lease on life. Or—I yawned and rolled over, pulling the covers over my head—I could wait for the last of the yellow leaves to drop off and save me the trouble.

It's not that I didn't care about the gift my uncle had given me. I did. I took very good care of the terra-cotta planter. I dusted it once a month, whether it needed it or not. Sometimes, I think I could hear his voice. "You know, a little water won't break the thing."

The elephant-ear ivy had been an afterthought when I'd been in the apartment for about a month. Before then, the planter had been a good place to keep all of my loose change.

I tried to go back to sleep, but my cousin Brenda, who'd spent the night with us, was singing in the shower softly to herself. Okay, not so softly and definitely not in key. I didn't mind listening to her caterwaul. I was surprised and pleased that she'd agreed to sleep over.

No mystery when I found out why. Her own home was full, with overflow relatives who'd come in at the last minute to attend my grandparents' anniversary party. Some folks from my grandpa George's side of the family had decided at the last minute to show. One of them, Brenda said, was a chain smoker. Another was rumored to have an overactive bladder. No, she'd said as diplomatically as she could to her parents, it was best if she found another place to crash for the weekend.

Listening to her now, I was reminded of the time we'd put on a talent show when everyone had come over to celebrate my mom's birthday. No, I take that back. We weren't really celebrating her birthday. Because if you ask my mom every year on the day rumored to be her birthday, she'll give her age as twenty-five. She's been giving that same answer for about twenty years now. Can't call it a birthday party if the responsible party won't admit to getting older.

So, on the day *rumored* to be her birthday, we'd eaten cake and ice cream (flavored shaved ice for the lactose intolerant), danced to old records, and played spades, pluck, and dominoes until the wee hours or the neighbors called the cops on us. It's not clear in my memory which event came first.

Brenda, Essence, and I had done our version of Tina Turner's theme song to the movie *Mad Max Beyond Thunderdome*. It was a routine that brought the house down.

The refrain still echoed in my head. Maybe with adequate psychotherapy I'll be able to get that song out.

We'd gelled and teased our hair so that Tina would have been jealous of our dos and sneaked fishnet stockings from my brother Bailey's room. (To this very day, he's still trying to explain—or deny—how they'd gotten in there.) Skirts pinned tight and enough lipstick to compensate for our preteen pouts, we'd sung and strutted our stuff.

Come to think of it, I don't think either of us sang very well then, either. It was the effort that we'd put into it that made Mama, Aunt Karen, and Aunt Pam clap so vigorously and hug us so tightly that we thought our ribs would crack.

I was still grinning at the memory when Brenda stepped out of the bathroom with a huge, maroon terry-cloth towel wrapped around her torso and another on her head. She'd slept in the daybed beneath the huge bay window in my room, having made enough room for herself by pushing more of my stuffed animals onto the floor. My talking Winnie the Pooh bear squeaked out a "there's a rumbly in my tumbly" as Brenda partially stepped on it crossing the room.

"You're awake now, Sleeping Beauty?" she greeted me.

"Did you save me any hot water?"

"I think I left you a couple of drops," she teased, wrinkling up that cute freckled nose of hers. She sat on the edge of the daybed, pressing her thick, auburn hair between the towel to dry it. For a moment, I experienced a moment of jealousy. You could stick a bird's nest in Brenda's hair and she would still look good—naturally.

I, on the other hand, have to work at it. Not just work. Getting my hair so that I'm happy with it is a major undertaking. It takes hours of planning, preparation, and implementation.

I have what I affectionately call "in-between hair." Not good, not bad. Not long, not short, not curly, not straight. If I'd entered my head of hair in a beauty pageant, I would probably walk away with the Miss Congeniality award. It tries so hard to be good. But every now and then, Lord help me, every now and then, it does what it wants to do no matter how I cajole and threaten to shave my head bald.

Since I'm so much on the go, I don't have time to fool with it. I pay others a tidy sum to do it. Merquitia over on Monument Street in Jackson does wonders with a human hair weave. She doesn't own a shop. She's just a lady who does hair.

I was lucky to find her. A friend of the lady who works

in the mailroom in my building told me about the cousin of the man who now sometimes does my nails about Merquitia.

She and her teenaged daughters, Jessica, Imani, and Erica, see me religiously, every eight weeks for no less than ten hours to wash, condition, tint, and braid. I go in as much for the gossip as I do for the gorgeous hair that results from the ordeal.

"Gee, thanks. You are so kind."

"Don't mention it." Brenda then reached into my nightstand drawer for the metal nail file I've always kept there. If I went to her room, I'd find one almost exactly like it by her bed. When we were kids, we'd bought matching nail files so that we could pry open each other's diaries and read them. That was, we rationalized, the best way to tell each other secrets without openly confessing. If either of us ever got caught doing something wrong, we could honestly say to our parents, "She never told me that!"

Brenda curled one long leg under her, and bent the other knee so that she could rest her finger on it while she filed. Her voice was slightly staccato, broken by the vigorous filing action.

"So, are you going shopping with the folks today?"

"Do I have a choice?" I asked, pulling a long face.

She wasn't fooled. As much as I complain about my parents—and what recently left-the-nest child doesn't?—I loved being around them.

"Of course you always could stay here," Brenda suggested. "But you know how good Aunt Doris is at finding sales. She knows how to sniff out a good bargain. If you're not there when she finds one, you're going to be kicking yourself all the way back to Mississippi."

"I know. I'm still kicking myself for the last time we went shopping. How in the world did she find that Tommy Hilfiger shirt for under fifty bucks? She must have switched the price tags."

Brenda widened her eyes as if the thought never occurred to her. "Nah. You think?"

I yawned and stretched again, thinking I'd sneak in a few extra winks before Mama came up to roust us out of bed.

"Come on, Shiri. Get up," Brenda said. "I'm ready to play."

"I'll be up in a minute."

"No, you get up now!" she said, in a voice so much like Mama's, I almost shot straight up out of bed. For a minute, I was back in high school, jumping to the drill sergeant–like command of her voice.

"I know you don't want me to come up there," she went on to threaten. Brenda could almost imitate Mama as well as I could—she'd spent the night over at my house or me at hers so many times. We were so inseparable, we were almost mistaken for sisters. Me, Brenda, and my cousin, Essence.

I sat up, stuffed a pillow under my nightgown, and then plumped it under my backside. Standing up in the bed, I put my hands on my hips and strutted up and down, exaggerating my walk by sticking my butt out even further. My feet sank ankle-deep into the mattress as I paraded up and down the bed.

I crooked my finger and shook it menacingly at Brenda. "If you girls don't get out of bed, I am not driving you to school. You can walk to school for all I care. I don't know what you think this is. If you think that I was put on this earth to chauffeur your behinds around all day, you've got another think coming. This isn't a taxi service, you know. Burn up my gas for nothing. *Hmmmph.*"

Brenda burst out laughing, trying to frown at the same time. "Oh, girl, you know your mama's behind is not that big."

"I know. I was doing your mama."

"I've got your mama for you!" Brenda leaped up and grabbed another pillow. She dove toward me, trying to swat me with it. She swung so hard, I barely got out of the way in time.

Oomph! She caught me on the side of my head, and down I went, arms flailing to keep me from tumbling off the side of the bed.

"You've been practicing," I gasped, rubbing the side of my head.

"Nuh-uh. I haven't had a good pillow fight in years. You're just getting old and tired. You're just slow."

"Who's getting old?" I said huffily. "I'm not old. And if you weren't so 'flicted yourself, you could have knocked me into next week instead of missing me by a mile. Old? I've got your old for you."

"Girl, you know I'm just playing," she mollified. She paused and grinned at me. "You look good for your age."

I was only a few months older than Brenda, and she wasn't going to let me forget it.

"Seriously, Shiri. You must be beating all of those business execs off with a stick."

"Yeah, a Popsicle stick. With all the work I have to do, I don't have time to be thinking about men."

Brenda leaped forward and clamped her hand over my mouth.

"Shhh!" she said frantically.

"What?" I asked, my words muffled by the palm of her hand.

"Do you want someone to hear that?"

"Oh, no," I groaned, realization suddenly hitting me harder than Brenda ever could in a pillow fight.

"That's right." Brenda nodded. We looked at each other and said solemnly in unison. "The target."

I slid off the bed and tiptoed to my bedroom door. As I pulled it open just a crack, I winced at the creaking sound of hinges needing a healthy dose of WD-40.

"Is anybody out there?" Brenda whispered.

I shook my head and blew out a breath with all the relief of a teenager sneaking past sleeping sentry parents after breaking curfew.

"That was too close, Shiri." She collapsed on my bed.

"This close to the family reunion planning meeting and you want to blab that you're not dating? That's like waving a red flag in front of a charging bull."

"Or a piece of cheesecake in front of Uncle Curtis." I giggled.

"You know how our folks like to single somebody out every year to get hooked up at the reunion. Last year it was our cousin, Darryl. The poor man didn't stand a chance. One minute, he was winning the prize for coming the farthest to attend the reunion; the next thing you know, Grandma Lela is throwing that registered nurse at him."

"Grandma Lela swears to this day that the woman tripped." I repeated what I'd been told.

"And you believe her?" Brenda said incredulously.

"It was kinda suspicious. Unless the woman tripped over air, I don't remember seeing anything that would make her fall on Darryl like that."

"Fall on him. Fall for him. However it happened, it was all carefully orchestrated. Our folks are the masters at it by now. Every other year, before, during, or after the reunion, you can count on a wedding."

"Or an engagement announcement," I said glumly.

"They switch off. Last reunion it was a male cousin. It's going to be a single girl this year. Boy, girl, boy, girl. That's how it goes."

"And I had to shout out that I'm not seeing anybody." I slapped my forehead. I'd even mentioned it to Aunt Rosie. It was like painting a giant bull's-eye on my forehead.

Brenda patted my shoulder as if in sympathy. "Girl, if you haven't got a man by the time you check into the hotel at the next reunion, you'd better grab one of those bellboys. Pay him a couple of extra bucks to represent until the heat is off you."

"What about you, Bren? How's your love life?"

Though we'd been as close as sisters when we were growing up, we'd sadly grown out of touch. If it weren't for the special occasions like my grandparents' anniversary, a family reunion, or a wedding, I don't think we'd make the time to have these heart-to-heart sessions like we used to do. It made me sad to think that the girl who I'd shared everything with was now a woman who I knew so little about.

Brenda lowered her eyes and blushed. When she did so, it made the freckles across her nose stand out more.

"Not really," she said, toying with the edges of my dust ruffle.

"Not really?" I repeated, mocking her. "What does that really mean?"

She shrugged. "It means I'm seeing someone but not really seeing him."

"What does that mean? Is he poking you in the eyes every time you come near or what?"

"No!" Brenda laughed. It was an infectious laugh. No one who hears it can ever resist smiling a little in sympathetic humor. She could always make me laugh—even when the occasion didn't call for laughter. Like the time we both got caught trying to sneak out of school on senior skip day— sitting in the principal's office, trying to explain to parents who were beyond furious . . . closer to nuclear meltdown. Things probably would have gone better for us if Brenda hadn't made me laugh at the wrong moment.

Three weeks' grounding is a long time when you're seventeen. I still owe Brenda for that one.

"It's a little too soon to tell right now. I don't want to jinx it," she replied quietly.

I leaned close and pried open her right eye.

"What are you doing?"

"Do you remember how Mama always said that she could look in our eyes and tell if we were sick or just faking to get out of going to school?"

"Yes, I remember. She was always especially suspicious on days she knew that we had exams. We had to be bleeding from the eyeballs before they let us stay home."

"You got to stay home with bleeding eyeballs?" I exclaimed. "My mom dropped Visine in my eyes and told me to get on to school."

"At least you didn't have to go to school with chicken pox. I *told* my mom that it wasn't an acne flare-up."

"She should have known better. You never had acne a day in your life," I grumbled. "Witch."

"It was my last day of eighth grade. Mama didn't want me to miss it. Most kids give away mementos and sign yearbooks on the last day of school. I wound up giving the entire eight-grade class chicken pox over the summer. I'm sure they loved me for that. But that doesn't explain why you're prying my eyes open."

"I'm just checking to see if you look sufficiently lovesick to keep Grandma Lela and the rest of the matchmaking militia from making you the target."

"But what about you? If they zero in on you, I'm sorry, Shiri, I can't help you. Normally, I'd have your back. You know that. But not this time. This time, I can't stop them from hooking you up with . . . with . . ." Her voice trailed off. And suddenly, I knew that she knew something. Years may have passed since we'd last spoken to each other. But I knew that look. That look that said that she'd let something slip without meaning to. All we Johnson women had that look.

I think Jack Deneen had seen that look on my face in the airport when I'd said out loud how that little Geoffrey should get his behind spanked for behaving like such a brat.

Brenda was trying to cover up that look now. I wasn't buying it.

"With who?" I demanded.

She shrugged and shook her head.

"With who? You know something, don't you, Bren?"

"Nuh-uh," she quickly denied.

"Yes, you do! You traitor! You're in on it. They got to you, didn't they? How'd they do it, Bren? What did they promise you? That you'd be safe from their plotting for at least two years?"

"I don't know anything. You're talking crazy. You'd think I'd give you up?"

"To save your unmarried hide? You'd better believe it."

"Shiri, I am so hurt," Brenda said, pressing her hand against her heart as if wounded.

"You don't know what hurt is," I contradicted. I was going to make Brenda tell me what she knew the only way I knew how. I grabbed her foot, upended it, then started to tickle her in the spot that I knew would send her into hysterical spasms of laughter.

"Cut it out, Shiri!" Brenda flipped over onto her stomach—squealing, gasping, crying, and threatening all at once.

"You'd better tell me!" I shouted as I plopped down and straddled her thighs to keep her immobile. It was like trying to hold down a bucking steer.

"I'm going to tell Aunt Doris!" she warned.

"That's not all you'd better tell, Brenda Reid."

"I told you. I don't . . . don't . . . don't know anything. Shiri, cut that out before you make me wet the bed!" Brenda shouted conveniently, as Mama had just poked her head into the room. She had the pressed-thin lip look that she always got when she tried hard not to laugh.

"If you do, you'll be stuck here doing laundry while we're all out shopping. Shiri, get off of her before you cut off her circulation or something."

"Yeah, and we have to amputate my legs," Brenda said, playing the sympathy card. "She's gotten heavy, Aunt Doris."

"Think about it this way. If we have to amputate, you could get the child's plate at the lunch today and save yourself some cash," I said with exaggerated brightness.

Brenda launched another pillow at me. I ducked and pulled on the corner of her towel. I guess I thought of it as a symbolic exposing of her meanness.

"Shiri!"

"Oh, please. Like we haven't seen those before."

"Will you two stop kidding around? That was your

grandma Lela on the phone. She'll swing by at ten o'clock to pick us up, and she expects us to be ready.''

"Shop till you drop. *Ching-ching!*" I imitated the sound of a toy cash register.

"For a man for Shiri," Brenda muttered under her breath. I narrowed my eyes à la Clint Eastwood and wiggled my index finger at her. I still had some tickle power left, my warning told her.

"Get dressed and come down to the kitchen. I'm afraid all I've got are muffins and coffee. We'll stop and have a big lunch later. I think your grandmother has a special place in mind that she wants to try."

Brenda and I exchanged concerned, knowing glances. Grandma Lela never did anything without a plan. If we weren't careful, we'd be fending off proposals from busboys.

"What was that for?" Mama asked, her lips pressed so tightly in the no-laughing line that they practically disappeared.

"What was what for?" I asked.

"That look."

"What look?"

"You know what look. That look that passed between you two."

"What look? Did you see a look, Bren?" I asked, turning to face her.

"I don't know. I wasn't looking." Brenda backed me up. Good ol' Brenda. I could always count on her, even after all of this time.

"Yeah, right. You two would back each other up if one of you said that the moon was made of blue cheese."

"That's Swiss, Aunt Doris," Brenda corrected, and planted a kiss on Mama's cheek.

"Oh, go on!" This time, Mama did laugh, and gave Brenda a crushing hug. "It's so nice to have you here, Brenda. You should visit more often."

"*Maaaah-ahhhmm!* That's not fair," I said in my whiniest voice. "You didn't tell me to visit often." I pouted.

"That's because I like her better than I like you." Mama then patted my cheek affectionately before heading out.

"So, you're finally admitting it. I always knew."

"You two go on and get dressed. You've got about fifteen minutes before they honk for us."

SIX

Fifteen yards out, I planted my foot and pivoted a hard ninety degrees to make a lateral cut toward the goalpost. As I looked over my shoulder to check my progress, I sensed the ball before I heard it whistling through the air. I could feel it before I saw it hurdling toward me—a dark speck against a cloudless cerulean sky.

Sometimes, in practice, it paid to count on more than just your physical senses to make a play. My junior high school coach imparted that bit of wisdom to me once after I'd dropped my third pass in a crucial game.

Old Coach Reeves. I wonder what ever happened to him.

"Son," Coach would say to me, patting me on my shoulder in restrained macho sympathy. He called everyone son. And he patted everyone on the shoulder. Sometimes, I think it was because it was easier than remembering our names. The way we were switching positions, it didn't do to call us by our jersey numbers. Those were just going to change again when the coaches made player and position adjustments as they did after every loss.

Sometimes, I can still hear the rattling of phlegm in Coach Reeves's throat—the sound that he made to announce that he was about to make a speech. Actually, it was the sound he made *before* he spat out a loogie and began making his speech.

"Son, my great granny, Lord rest her soul, could have caught that ball in her false teeth. This ain't rocket science. It don't make no sense for someone with as much love as you've got for the game to be so lousy at it. If you want to make it past third-string junior varsity, you'd better start using that head up there for something more than bouncing that ball off of it. It's either that, or go over and talk to Coach Thorpe about getting a spot on his soccer team."

Old Coach Reeves. I wonder what ever happened to him.

For all of the warm fuzzies he gave us during those early, insecure years, maybe he was hit by a bus. His brand of encouragement didn't make sense at the time. I'm not sure that it makes all that much sense to me now.

But I do know this. Any player who was ever worth anything, who was ever remembered for anything, had something more on the ball than being able to use his eyes, ears, and hands to handle one.

They all had that unexplainable something. A sixth sense that helped them zig when others would have zagged, leap when others would have ducked. Whatever it was they had, it made the difference between a championship year and a see-ya-next-year. I'd like to think that I have that extra something.

The sting of the leather pierced through my practice gloves, causing the centers of my palms to tingle, almost itch. I clenched my hands ever so slightly, a gentle reassurance that I'd done my job. Another pivot to turn upfield again. Simple, rote. As predictable as clockwork.

The daily drills were called that for a reason. The routines were bored into our heads. Like quicksilver, signals from my brain shot through my extremities, telling my arms and legs when to move, where to go. Fleet, fluid. Function and finesse—you needed it all in football.

Another fifteen yards up, I stopped and threw the ball to one of the trainers before jogging back to my position at the end of the drill line. It was only nine o'clock, but the day was already starting to warm. The sun made my sunglasses hot to the touch, caused beads of perspiration to collect under my bandana. The blue-and-white cloth darkened to a solid blue of wetness. I didn't mind too much.

If I concentrated really hard, I could pretend that the sound of trainer's whistles were the sounds of tropical birds, stirring the humid air with their song back on my grandfather's sugarcane farm in Puerta Rico.

I don't know why I'm so nostalgic about the place. I didn't spend much time there. I'd only visited a handful of times. My grandfather had made his home on the outskirts of London and didn't return often to the soil of his birth. Nothing nostalgic about sweating for hours in the sun, chopping cane for the enrichment of someone else.

My own father didn't even think of having ties to the island. Not that island, anyway. He even gave up his connection to the British Isles. He became a naturalized citizen when he gave in to the desire of the Yank tourist he'd met in the summer of '69 and married the following winter.

I was born on American soil—literally. My mother went into labor near the tail end of the transatlantic flight. Born in Birmingham herself, she didn't want her children growing up among foreigners.

"Move up."

Someone behind prodded me, reminding me of where I was, and what I was supposed to be doing. The drill line moved swiftly, methodically, and it was my turn again.

"I'm surprised to see you here, Flash," another team member from the drill line opposite me called out. Everybody called him the Deacon, for his fanatical drop-to-the-knee-in-prayer pose after every score—even if it was the other team's.

"What do you mean?"

"I thought you were going on the honeymoon with Mike."

I could have taken that comment to be a crack about my friendship with Mike. We hung out together so much, we were often ridiculed. In fact, sometimes we acted like an old married couple—completing each other's sentences, squabbling over things that didn't matter, or letting things that should have torn us apart slide without so much as a blink.

Too many times to count, we'd sometimes show up to practice wearing almost the same outfit. To cover, we confounded the other teammates, especially the rookies, with "Didn't you get the memo? How come you aren't properly dressed out?"

Any other time, I would have dismissed the ragging as business-as-usual jokes. But not this time. I couldn't quite shrug it off. A few snickers from other team members, sly and lascivious, made me uneasy. Judging from the harsh hazing that followed, I could tell that they hadn't all been as drunk as they'd seemed to be the night before Mike and Barb's wedding. Someone had seen what had gone on between Barb and me. Gossip could run through a team like this one quicker than athlete's foot fungus.

As I came up again in line, my turn to run the sprint pattern, I wondered if there were more than two witnesses to Barb's proposition. It was possible. There was so much confusion the night before the wedding. We'd rented out almost an entire hotel floor. Most of us needing privacy had returned to our rooms . . . or to somebody else's. The chorus of "Get the hell out!" or "Shut the damn door" had rung out more often than the chorus of "Get Me to the Church on Time."

I'd slipped away to down a couple of aspirins. The music and the mood had worn me down quicker than I'd like to admit. I remember when I could stay up all night carousing, pop a couple of Bayers, and be back on the party circuit or the job the next day without my body being the wiser for its torture.

Makes me melancholy to think that I can't handle the high life like I used to. Maybe that's why I didn't resist right away when Barb found her way into my room. I'd let myself buy her flimsy excuse of needing a quiet, private place to fix her makeup. What could be more appropriate than her own suite? I'd asked her point-blank.

"Have you seen my suite lately?" She'd laughed and jerked her thumb in a direction down the hall. "Your coach should have as much enthusiasm and attendance at practice as I've got going on in that room."

"Mike's just letting off steam. A last go-round before he has to settle down and become Mr. Responsible."

"Exactly. That's why Mike practically worships you, J.D. You understand him. And it's not as if Mike is all that deep. Don't get me wrong. I love him; but he's not exactly *Who Wants to Be a Millionaire* material, is he now? If you understand him, then you know exactly what I'm feeling. You know why it's important for me to be here."

Her voice had been too low, too deliberately pitched for that to be a simple agreement with my sentiment.

When alarm bells started going off in my head, I'd dismissed them as just the beginnings of the headache. That sinking feeling in the pit of my stomach had been just a physical reaction to the aspirin. It couldn't have had anything to do with the fact that I had a sneaking suspicion that my best friend's woman was about to come on to me.

It couldn't have been that. I simply refused to accept that it was true, and that I'd then stood by and said nothing when the time in the ceremony came for me to object to the wedding.

I suppose if I wanted to take the moral high road, if the incident ever came to the full light of day, I could say with a clear conscience that nothing really happened. Nothing had. Not really. Something had pulled me back—whether it was the fear of discovery or my sense of propriety that was stronger, it didn't matter. The end result was that disaster had been averted.

Barb was with Mike now and I wasn't. I was here, back in Birmingham. I couldn't help but feel that even with my perception of Barb's faults, she was with Mike. He had someone. Someone who he cared for deeply. And what did I have? Who did I have? No one.

The trainer yelled, "Go!" but I didn't hear him. I was too caught up in my thoughts. Too caught up in a bit of self-indulgent self-pity.

"Yo! Flash! Shake a leg!"

Coach Brodie launched a ball at me to get my attention. Instinctively, I reached for it, but it bobbled out of my hands and clipped me soundly on my shoulder to startle me back to the present.

Almost to the present. Somewhere, in the back of my mind, I could hear the phlegmatic rumble of Coach Reeves urging me to join the soccer team.

Fifteen yards out, a few steps to the right, and *whiz-wham*—the ball dropped into my hands like a toddler taking his first steps and falling into the waiting arms of a devoted parent.

Come to Papa. Get to know me, I encouraged the football. By the time we played our first game, we'd be like old friends.

A few more drills and the trainers blew their whistles, shrilly announcing the close of the morning practice session. We had a couple of hours to take care of personal business until the afternoon practice.

There was a mild stampede for the locker room. A cacophony of curses and congratulations for another good practice—hyping each other up, psyching each other out to keep the energy for the second session. Soon the shower room was misty with steam, smelly with liniment.

Someone tossed me the sports page from the newspaper.

Sweet! We'd made the front cover, along with the statistics of other arena football team rankings. I was surprised to see the heavy coverage. Arena football doesn't usually get as much press as the National Football League. The NFL has all of the major networks and the press bamboozled—like they're the only game in town. The college boys get a little respect, if they're in the top-ten ranking of their divisions.

The article generated more activity in the locker room. The paper passed from hand to hand, along with several cracks about whether or not the current holder was smart enough to read it. Looked like all of the good press and the media blitz handled by our marketing specialists had done their jobs. The Steeldogs were ranked in the top five.

I felt responsible for that ranking. Since signing with them, I'd had the unshakable feeling that a lot of the fans' hopes for a championship were riding on my shoulders.

I wasn't alone in this feeling. If you asked any team member, they'd all answer the question the same way. They'd all say that they were responsible for the team's success. Let me be clear. Individually responsible, but not solely responsible. Not one man on this team felt that he alone was responsible for the team's success. We all did our parts or we would all fall apart. Another pearl of wisdom from Coach Reeves—or any coach who'd ever had an influence on the players on this team.

"You've got my back if they team up on me, don't you, ladies?"

My cousin Essence put her hand in front of her mouth, pretending to daintily dab at her lips with her napkin, as she passed along a request for solidarity to Brenda and me.

I was in midsip of my water and had to swallow quickly to keep from choking through my laughter.

"Don't trust Brenda to hang with us, Essence," I whispered back. "I think she's already been subverted."

Essence looked askance at Brenda, who'd raised both of her hands in protest of her innocence.

"What does she know?" Essence demanded. "Who are they going after this time? Which one of us is the target?"

"She won't tell," I said in disgust.

"Not even after you tickled her?" Essence asked.

"How did you know I tickled her?" I sounded surprised.

"Oh, please. That's how you always got anything out of us, Shiri. When we were kids, all you had to do was waggle your finger at us and we spilled our guts."

"Not this time," Brenda said. "We're not kids anymore."

"And we're no spring chickens, either. That's why we're having this discussion," Essence reminded us.

"Shh! Here they come." I motioned for silence before our aunts and Grandma Lela returned from the ladies' room. We cousins weren't fooled. They couldn't all have to go at the same time. They were plotting something. I knew it.

When I'd tried to follow them into the ladies' room, to scope out their plot, they'd clammed up so quick and stared at me as oddly as if I'd walked into the wrong bathroom. I'd almost had to back up and take a second look. Yeah. I was in the ladies' room. I was in the right place.

Aunt Karen had gotten a funny look on her face. Not funny ha-ha. Funny like "I'm busted" kinda funny. She'd then turned, actually done an about-face, and said, "So, Doris, do you think that the weather should be clear on Labor Day?"

"Oh . . . oh, yes," Mama had stammered, like she couldn't get her lips to change directions fast enough. "Clear and warm. Perfect for the family reunion."

What was she? An almanac? Why in the world was she trying to predict the weather almost a year away from the event? They had changed the subject. It had been obvious on their collective guilty faces.

"What are you doing in here, Shiri?" Grandma Lela had asked bluntly.

"It's a bathroom." I'd stated the obvious. "I thought I'd take care of a little personal business before we started shopping."

"There are no more stalls," she'd then retorted and stepped into the last one. "Go on outside and wait until one is freed up."

I couldn't believe it! She'd ordered me out of the bathroom! And after all I'd gone through to bring her those bears. Of course she didn't know about them yet. The celebration dinner wasn't until tonight—which was one of the reasons we were all out shopping. It was a chance for us to spend some time together, as well as spend a little money.

"We'll be out in a minute, honey." Aunt Rosie had patted

me affectionately. At the same time, she'd steered me toward the door.

By the time I'd made it back to my seat, I'd been wearing an expression of mild irritation. They couldn't treat me like that! I was grown. I held down a job. I paid rent. But I'd just been told when to go to the bathroom like a three-year-old. What was wrong with *that* picture?

As soon as I'd resumed my seat, Brenda and Essence had pounced on me, pumping me for information.

"Well? What did they say?"

"Who's it going to be?"

"When are they going to spring a man on us?"

I'd shrugged. "You got me."

I didn't know any more than when I'd first followed them inside. All I had were my suspicions—and a suspect, long-range weather forecast.

The rest of the luncheon went relatively smoothly, with talk centered mostly on our respective jobs and the various cities to which we'd all moved. We talked about who would likely be on which reunion committee, how exciting the reunion trip should be, and how many we expected to attend.

Even though our table server was cute and attentive—and who wouldn't be with a table filled with attractive women—no one seemed to be trying to foist us off on him. Maybe my trip to the rest room had put a scare into the matchmaking militia, making them regroup, rethink their strategy.

Maybe not.

It all happened so fast, my head reeled from the shock. One moment I was reaching for a credit card, offering to pick up the tab for lunch; the next, I was instantly transformed into the "target."

It all happened in the blink of an eye. Or rather, in the fluttering of a paper. I'd almost forgotten that I had it. Jack Deneen's telephone number. But as I pulled my wallet from my purse, the paper drifted to the floor and made all the impact of an atomic bomb.

"You dropped something, Shiri," Essence said, reaching for the traitorous scrap.

"Oh!" I bent down to reach for it, but Essence was halfway there. As I leaned over to snatch it up before anyone could spy the contents, our heads collided.

"Ow!"

"Careful!"

"Watch it."

That split-second delay in grabbing it made all the difference. Brenda's sharp eyes noticed the Steeldogs logo and the handwritten note with the request for me to call Jack. It wasn't as if she had supersharp sight. She was able to notice it because she was faster than both Essence and me combined.

Brenda managed to scoop the note from both our grasps. She was so fast, it reminded me of a scene from that old *Kung Fu* series. *Snatch the pebble from my hand, Grasshopper.*

"Shiri!" she said, looking up at me with shining eyes. "Where'd you get this?"

"What is it?" Mama asked, wanting to know what kind of dropped paper, short of a C-note, could cause so much commotion at the restaurant table.

"Nothing," I said hastily and held out my hand for Brenda to return it. You should have seen how easily the shining in her eyes turned to the glimmer of sweet revenge. This was her payback for my tickling her.

"Nothing," Brenda echoed, mimicking me, then waved the paper in front of everyone's noses, gloating. "Nothing but the phone number of one of the sexiest men in the entire state of Alabama! Sexy and unmarried. Did I mention that he wasn't married?"

Her admission was like waving raw meat in front of a pack of pit bulls. "It's from Jack The Flash Deneen of the Birmingham Steeldogs."

"What?"

"Who?"

"How did you get that?"

"What's a Steeldog?"

Questions from my relatives came from every corner.

"It says here that he wants Shiri to call him at her earliest convenience. And he's underlined *earliest*." She turned the note around for the others to see, show-and-tell style.

"Where did you get that?" Aunt Rosie asked, then snapped her fingers in remembrance. "Wait a minute. . . . I think I saw him. He was on the flight from Jackson, wasn't he? I saw a man—a long, tall, gorgeous drink of water—coming off the plane. He was literally mobbed, people asking for autographs. I knew he was some kind of celebrity, but I couldn't connect the face with the name. So that was Jack Deneen, huh?"

"Shiri, have you been holding out on us?" Essence wanted to know.

"No, of course not. There's nothing to tell."

"Maybe I should tickle you until *you* 'fess up," Brenda suggested, raising a finely arched eyebrow at me. "It would serve you right."

"There's nothing to confess," I insisted. It was my turn to raise my hands in protest of my innocence.

"Uh-huh," Grandma Lela said, narrowing her eyes at me.

Suddenly, she broke into a wide smile and nudged my aunt Karen. Aunt Karen nudged Aunt Pam, who sort of winked at Aunt Rosie. It looked like a human version of a domino rally.

The only thing I could do was put my head in my hands. That was it. My fate was sealed. If it hadn't been decided among them who would be the "target" when they all went into the ladies' room, the traitorous scrap of paper had made the decision for them. There was no question now. I was it. The target.

"Let me see that," Aunt Pam said, holding out her hand across the table. I had to resist the urge to snatch it out of Brenda's hand as she held it out for them.

"You know, there's been a lot of buzz in the local sports news about that man. They say he's pretty good."

"I wouldn't know," I said stiffly. "I don't follow football."

"Yeah, I hear he's supposed to be some kind of superstar at that, too," Essence said slyly. "I was at a club once, where a bunch of those Steeldogs were supposed to hang out."

"And what were you doing at a club, missy?" I asked, trying to throw the heat off of me.

"Uh-huh. Don't even try it, *missy*," Essence stressed in return. "I was there for a bridal shower for a friend of mine. Anyway, someone yelled out, 'Steeldogs in the house!' The next thing you know, the place is a zoo. You've never seen so many women lose their minds all at once. Screaming. Running. Dropping their own dates like they were bad pennies. It was ridiculous. There were so many bras and panties with telephone numbers thrown at those poor players that it looked like an explosion at a lingerie factory."

"What's the matter, Essence? Couldn't get yours off fast enough?" I said snidely.

"You hear that, Aunt Doris, Shiri is being ugly to me."

"Play nice, girls," Mama said automatically, sounding as she had when we were kids growing up together.

Aunt Pam scanned the note, shaking her head.

From there, things went from bad to worse. Grandma Lela peered over Aunt Pam's shoulder, reading the note aloud to herself.

"This is a cryin' shame," she said softly. "In my day, when a man wanted to spark a woman, he did so with respect. He came to her parents' house and courted openly, like a nice girl deserved."

"George was over at our house so much, we started to adopt him," Aunt Rosie remembered. "Lela, remember that time our folks were out and he came over with that wilted bunch of daisies?"

"They were not wilted," Grandma Lela said quietly. Her eyes softened. "At least, they didn't start out that way. It was one of the hottest summers in Alabama history. And he came over to ask my father if he could escort me to a church social."

"I love this story." Mama sighed. Resting one elbow on the table and propping her chin on her hand, her eyes turned just as misty as she listened.

"Don't interrupt, Doris," Aunt Karen chastised.

"He stood out on the front porch, dressed in a brand-new black suit that he'd borrowed from his brother," Grandma Lela continued.

"The jacket too long in the sleeves and the pants were too short in the leg, as I recall," Aunt Rosie said. "Looked like that goofy kid from that TV show. What's that kid's name?"

"Steve Urkel," Essence and Brenda answered in unison.

"Oh, yeah. That's his name. I love that show. That Reginald VelJohnson is one hunk of a man."

"Hunk of something," I muttered, secretly questioning my aunt's taste in men and television.

"You should have seen the look on Lela's face. She thought he was the most dapper young man in the world," Aunt Rosie continued.

Dapper? Brenda and I mouthed and grinned at each other. But we knew better than to interrupt.

"It must have been over a hundred degrees in the shade. Poor dear. He was perspiring so badly, clutching those daisies as if his life depended on it. All I could do was offer him a drink of lemonade through the screen door. I didn't dare let him in. Not with my parents out of the house," Grandma Lela recalled.

"He kept dabbing his forehead with that hanky. It must have been wringing wet. I think it was more in fear of what my father would say when George asked him to take Lela to the social. I finally took pity on him and let him into the front sitting room," Rosie teased. "But I sat with him, watched him like a hawk."

Grandma laughed out loud. It was a wonderful laugh, sort of like Brenda's. It made me think that humor was as hereditary as the color of our eyes.

"She certainly did. She didn't leave us alone for a minute."

"Yes, I did," Rosie corrected. She shook her finger at Lela. "I went back into the kitchen to refill our glasses."

"You made an awful lot of noise, rattling those glasses around, Rosie."

"I wanted you to hear me when I came back. I certainly heard you . . . or rather, heard George asking you for a little kiss."

"Grandma!" Essence teased.

"It was only a polite peck on the cheek," she replied, blushing, and touched her index finger to the spot as if she could still feel the imprint of it on her face.

She then turned her piercing gaze to me. "That's how we did it in those days, Shiri. Respectfully." She placed her palms flat on the table and leaned forward so that her face almost brushed the floral centerpiece. "You *are* a nice girl, aren't you, Shiri? You didn't do anything to give that man the impression that you weren't?"

"Grandma!" I squeaked, my face as red as the cherry glaze on my cheesecake. I could feel waves of heat wafting from my face, threatening to wilt the flowers of the floral arrangement.

"Of course she's a nice girl, Grandma." Essence stepped in smoothly. "Shiri probably wouldn't give that dog the time of day. That's why he had to push his telephone number on her. Otherwise, he'd have hers and we wouldn't be having this conversation right now. Isn't that right, Shiri?"

Sweet Essence. I should have known that she'd back me up. My head bobbed up and down in agreement, like a cork.

"Well, we'll just see about that. Somebody give me one of those cell phone thingamajigs."

Quicker than lightning, four different telephones appeared on the table in front of my grandmother. Analog. Digital. Miniature. Some with customized face plates. She had her pick.

She adjusted her glasses and said, "Read that number out to me, Pammie."

"What? What did she say? Mama, what did she say?" I asked.

My breath came out in a breathy whisper. Panic had closed my throat, making it difficult to speak, even breathe.

"She asked your aunt Pam to read that man's number out loud to her," Mama said calmly. She took a sip from her coffee as casually as if my grandmother had asked someone to read a selection from the menu to her.

Grandma Lela held the telephone almost at arm's length, trying to read the small numbers on the handset as Aunt Pam called out the numbers.

I turned pleading eyes to Aunt Rosie. It was her sister. Couldn't she do something to stop her? But Aunt Rosie only gave me that *it's going to be all right* look.

Grandma put the telephone up to her ear and cleared her throat delicately, waiting for someone to pick up on the other end—while I waited for a miracle to end this. A bolt of lightning. A herd of wild elephants. Abduction by aliens. I wasn't choosy, just as long as I didn't have to be conscious for what could very well turn out to be the most embarrassing moment of my life.

Second only to the time in the second grade when that snotty Lois Magee passed me a note that said that DeAndre Jenkins, the cutest boy in the school, liked me. She double-dog-dared me to go up to him and tell him that I liked him, too.

And gullible me, falling for the oldest trick in the book, wound up standing there, stammering, nearly in tears while he called me a stupid, stinky, sissy-girl and chased me all the way home with his notorious rock-throwing ability. Every year after that until the fifth grade, I could always count on at least one sneak attack from that brat.

I wonder what ever happened to good old DeAndre? Someone once told me that he was once a candidate for the Heisman Trophy, some sort of hotshot quarterback attending a Big Ten school. Another reason to detest the game of football. He probably got his skill chuckin' stones at me all those years.

"Yes, hello. May I speak with Jack Deneen, please?"

"Tell me this is a sick joke," I whispered to Brenda, tugging on her sleeve.

"Shh!" she shushed me and brushed my hand off of her. "I can't hear."

"This is going to be delicious," Essence said, rubbing her hands together. I had a sneaking suspicion that she wasn't talking about the desserts.

"Mr. Deneen, my name is Mrs. Lela Johnson." She paused, then said acerbically, "Never you mind how I got this number. What I want to know is what intentions you have for my granddaughter."

She paused, waiting for the response, then said, "You mean you make it a habit of passing your private number out indiscriminately, sir?"

Another pause. "Let me refresh your memory, Mr. Deneen. Shiri Rowlan is my granddaughter. She's a nice girl—a good girl."

I grimaced, fearful of what Jack must have been thinking. He'd been unexpectedly kind by keeping me company on the plane. After the brush-off signals that I'd given him at the airport, he hadn't had to do it.

Grandma then lifted her eyes to the ceiling as if listening very carefully to the response. "I see." Another pause. "*Hmmm*. I see."

"What? What does she see?" I asked aloud to no one in particular. No one was listening to me, anyway. Their eyes and ears were all glued to Grandma's lips.

"Is that a fact?" Grandma continued, then looked curiously at me.

"What's a fact?" I demanded but respectfully, because you didn't use that tone with Grandma Lela. Not unless you wanted your lips knocked into next week from a lightning-fast, backhanded slap. I personally had never received such treatment. But I'd heard things.

"Well, sir, in that case you can tell her yourself tonight over dinner. Do you like Thai food?"

"Tell me what? What is she doing?"

"Why are you so interested?" Brenda wanted to know.

"You don't follow football. Remember?" Essence put in her two cents.

My own words had come back to haunt me.

"Sounds to me like she's just invited him to dinner," Aunt Rosie said, winking at me.

I shook my head, not comprehending. The setup couldn't be as simple as that. These women were masters at it, often taking weeks of planning to arrange a meeting between the "target" and the "intended." They'd been in the matchmaking business for years, for as long as I could remember them planning family reunions. By producing that phone number, I'd made it too easy for them. I'd taken all of the fun out of their matrimonial machinations.

Grandma said with finality, "Eight o'clock sharp at the Surin West restaurant. Do you need directions? No, I don't imagine that you do. It's my anniversary, Mr. Deneen. A very special one, so please dress accordingly."

She then closed the phone and handed it back to Aunt Pam.

The table was silent for a moment. All eyes turned toward me. Then, an explosion of laughter had more than a few patrons staring at us.

SEVEN

I heard the cell phone ringing, but couldn't find it right away. It was stuffed in the bottom of my bag, wedged somewhere beneath my sweaty workout gear. My first inclination was to let it ring. I had voice mail. Whoever it was could wait. But something, loud and unwilling to be ignored, in my mind said, "You'd better answer that. It could be Shiri."

Instinct, maybe. Or wishful thinking. I didn't remember being this impatient waiting for a woman to call since high school. I congratulated myself. Somehow, I'd almost managed to get through the entire practice without thinking about Shiri Rowlan, and wondering whether or not she was thinking about me.

As the telephone continued to ring, I flipped it open and checked the caller ID before answering. It was a number that I didn't recognize. Usually, I don't answer those kinds of calls. There are so many scams out there. You answer a call from someone you don't know, accept long-distance charges from an unfamiliar area, the next thing you know, you're fighting a *gazillion*-dollar bill with little recourse because you were the idiot who took the call.

The number was unfamiliar, but the area code said that it was a local call. I took a chance.

"Hello?"

"Yes, hello. May I speak with Jack Deneen, please."

"Speaking." I paused in midstride. It was a voice that I didn't recognize. Feminine. Elderly. There was the tiniest bit of treble, indicating advanced age. And it was colored by a soft, cultured drawl. At the same time, it was an authoritative voice. The way she asked for me made me believe that she knew that she was speaking to me before I'd confirmed it.

"Mr. Deneen, my name is Mrs. Lela Johnson."

I didn't recognize the name. If this was another telemarketer trying to get me to change my long-distance service, I was going to be very perturbed. "How did you get this number, Mrs. Johnson?"

"Never you mind how I got this number. What I want to know is what intentions you have for my granddaughter."

I could have dismissed her as a crank caller—simply hung up the phone and turned off the ringer. After repeatedly getting my voice mail, crank callers usually give up. Yet something about this call didn't feel like a crank. Most cranks that stumble on my cell phone number don't know that it's mine. That is, they don't ask for me directly. This woman had.

"You mean you make it a habit of passing your private number out indiscriminately, sir?"

That struck a raw nerve. I should have hung up. I could have hung up. But I didn't. Instead, I stood out there in the parking lot, tired, baking, wondering who this was and what they wanted. If curiosity killed the cat, what was it going to do to this Steeldog?

I cradled the phone between my ear and shoulder as I climbed into my SUV and started the engine. I adjusted the air-conditioning to full-blast cold, thinking that the jolt of cool air would also cool my temper. I was too tired, too hot for guessing games.

"There is nothing indiscriminate about my behavior, madam," I said, adopting her formal tone. It was indeed formal, almost regal. This was the tone of a woman who commanded respect.

"I can't answer your question because I'm not sure who your granddaughter is and how she got my—"

She cut me off, even as the realization of who this woman might be hit me. An image of Shiri, adjusting those ludicrous bears on the airplane seat, saying almost in chagrin, "Grandpa always gets the window seat."

Those bears were presents for her grandparents. This must be Shiri's grandmother.

"Let me refresh your memory, Mr. Deneen. Shiri Rowlan is my granddaughter. She's a nice girl—a good girl."

Shiri! She'd contacted me. Correction—it was her grandmother who'd called. I couldn't even begin to imagine how she'd gotten my number. What would possess her to call me? Overprotectiveness, obviously. Somehow, she'd found the number and was now rushing to her granddaughter's defense of what her tone suggested was an evil, immoral, callow fellow.

It almost made me want to laugh. If only she knew how unnecessary her defensive response was. Shiri was quite capable of fending off any unwanted advances. As easily as she could draw me to her with her reluctant smile, she could also chill me with a disapproving frown and a toss of her head.

"More than nice, Mrs. Johnson. The very essence of proper civility," I said, and hoped that she didn't hear the humor I tried to squelch from my tone.

"I see."

I couldn't tell by her tone if she was mollified or if she thought that I was full of it.

I forged ahead, unmindful of the verbal roadblocks the grandmother was throwing in front of me. It must be genetic, this coolness of verbal response. Shiri was loaded with it.

"In fact, Mrs. Johnson, I'm surprised that she kept the number at all. She was very reluctant to take it. I think she did it to humor me, to get me to stop bothering her with my completely unsolicited conversation."

"Hmmm. I see."

Again, the noncommittal response. Was she giving me monosyllabic replies to keep Shiri from knowing what was going on?

I took a chance and asked, "Is she there with you now? She can tell you for herself."

Either Mrs. Johnson didn't fall for it or Shiri wasn't there with her. I kept talking, quickly, trying to erase whatever negative impression she had of me.

If I had to guess at Mrs. Johnson's age, I would wager that she had been raised in a time when people valued manners over expediency. I wasn't going to find out what I wanted to know by bombarding her with prying questions. It was going to take gentility. Finesse.

"Mrs. Johnson, it's obvious that you care very much for Shiri. I can hear the concern in your voice. You can rest assured that my, uh . . . intentions are completely honorable. If you know her so well, then you also know what an attractive, intelligent, well-bred young woman she is."

Was I laying it on too thick? Was I smothering my chances of ever getting to see Shiri again? If Mrs. Johnson didn't think I was sincere, she could end this conversation just as quickly as I could—with the press of a button. Click. Dial tone. No more Shiri.

If Shiri was as close to her family as the conversation led me to believe, then I wasn't going to get very far with her without going through the grandmother first. I had to keep her talking.

"Is that a fact?" she said, in a curious mixture of maternal pride and condescension of my obvious flattery. But hey, if it worked, I'd lay it on as thick as Betty Crocker's best frosting.

"An undisputed fact, madam. I'd be a sorry spectacle of a man—stone-blind, deaf in one ear, and dumb as a brick— if I didn't at least try to get to know her better. I'd like another opportunity to try, if that meets with your approval, Mrs. Johnson." I felt a little like Eddie Haskell, trying to convince the Beaver's mom that I was a stand-up guy.

"Well, sir, in that case you can tell her yourself tonight over dinner."

Victory! Something had worked. Either that, or she was luring me in to do me in, to make sure that I never bothered her granddaughter again.

"Do you like Thai food?"

"I love Thai food," I said enthusiastically, though I wasn't sure if I did or didn't. I hadn't tried it since I was a young boy. I had a vague recollection of needing lots and lots of water. But for the chance to see Shiri again, I'd eat a platter of molten lava.

"Eight o'clock sharp at the Surin West restaurant. Do you need directions?"

"I've lived in Birmingham almost all my life," I said solemnly, assuming that a woman like Mrs. Johnson would appreciate the appearance of stability.

"No, I don't imagine that you do." She used that tone again that felt oddly like a slap on the wrist—as if admitting that I knew my way around the city was like admitting that I got around.

What could Shiri have told her about me to give her that negative impression? There wasn't much she could have said. I thought I'd been on my best behavior at the airport.

"May I ask the occasion, Mrs. Johnson?" My mind raced ahead to figure out what I had in my closet to pull together appropriate attire.

"It's my anniversary, Mr. Deneen. A very special one, so please dress accordingly."

The phone line went dead. And just like that, I had a date. I had a date!

I slapped the steering column and crowed triumphantly to the roof of the SUV. Suddenly, I paused. Doubt crowded in. I had a date, but with which one? Shiri or her grandmother?

It didn't take a Rhodes scholar to figure out which woman I preferred. But if I had to charm the older one to get to the other, well . . . a man had to do what a man had to do.

And the first thing I had to do was get the feel of the

football practice off me. Even though I'd taken a brief shower after the drills, my grandfather would have called it "a lick and a promise." I needed hygiene fortification. I needed charm power. That meant the works: haircut, manicure.

Somehow before eight o'clock, I had to squeeze in the second practice session, buy an anniversary gift for the grandparents, buy flowers for Shiri, wash myself, get my truck detailed, select an outfit, find the restaurant . . .

If Mrs. Johnson was as discerning a woman as she sounded over the phone, then she would scrutinize me from head to toe. Normally, I wouldn't have worried. I am a man of discerning taste—a little gift from my mother. She would scrimp and save to purchase something of quality that she wanted, rather than settle for something of lesser value.

Sometimes that meant extravagance. But not always. She taught me the value of caring for the few quality items we had. The alternative was not caring for the cheaper items because we knew they were easily replaceable. Mother was not one for waste. Now, I choose my clothes and accessories carefully, paying as much attention to quality and style as I do to the price tag.

My grandfather taught me a long time ago that money couldn't buy class. Class came from within. It was conveyed by the way you conducted yourself.

"Keep your head unbowed, Jackie boy. There's nothing wrong with a long day's honest work. A little dirt under your fingernails won't kill you. And that's the God's honest truth."

Then he'd sent me off with a pat on the back, saying, "But your mother will kill you if you come to the supper table without washing your hands."

Let Mrs. Johnson use the white-glove test on me. I was going to pass the inspection with flying colors.

As I pulled out of the parking lot, I considered the possibility of blowing off the afternoon practice session. Maybe I was taking an awful chance, jeopardizing my good standing with the coaching staff and team owner by going AWOL. We had a scrimmage game next week.

What if this night turned out to be disastrous? What if I got to the restaurant and found that I couldn't stand to be around Shiri Rowlan and her intrusive, if well-meaning, family?

I paused at a red light, my fingers nervously drumming on the steering wheel.

Why was I doing this again? I tried to rationalize why I was having recurring thoughts about a woman I barely knew. I played over in my mind our chance meeting at the airport— from my first glance at the full-lipped, full-hipped, honey-dripping woman nestled between the two bears, to the last look as I left her struggling with those toy monstrosities on the plane.

We had only been together three hours. Not much time. But packed within that three hours, I'd shared with her a gamut of emotions that left me wanting to laugh with her and love with her. In reliving those three hours, my hands tingled when I remembered the strength of her fingers as she clasped my hand in fright.

The plane had dipped unexpectedly, raising a cry from the passengers. She'd stopped in midsentence, and her hand had flown out to grab mine. It had been an instinctual response. One human being seeking out another when one believes that death is imminent. We were not-so-perfect strangers, sharing a less-than-ideal situation. The brush of her fingertips against my palms had sent a jolt up my arm, made me want to wrap it around her tense shoulders and draw her close to me.

They say that adversity brings people together, forges an undeniable bond. Could my attraction for Shiri be a by-product of that experience? Could I, in seeking her out, subconsciously be seeking the closeness we'd shared, if only for a while?

I shook my head at my foolishness. Psychobabble. I'd wanted to get to know her before I ever stepped foot on that plane—before the forces of nature ever forced us into each other's company. Nature had played a part in guiding me to her before the storm.

My mouth turned up into a smile, remembering how she'd reluctantly laughed in polite tolerance of my jokes. I appreciated the depth of her commitment to her family. I was given a glimpse into her upbringing by her open expression of irritation at the airport hellion.

Only three hours. Three lifetimes' worth of emotion crammed into that short span of time. I don't remember ever before meeting a woman so open, so passionate about life.

Open is such a funny word to think of in terms of Shiri Rowlan. Because if you'd asked her, I'd bet that she'd say that she hadn't revealed a thing about herself to me. Her carefully modulated responses to my questions might have deterred a less persistent man.

I can attest that you don't get far in this world giving up at the first, halfhearted block. If you wanted something, really wanted it, you kept at it.

"Keep those legs churning," Coach Reeves used to roar at us, through summer heat practices and muddy, half-frozen soil during the games. "Dig! Dig! Dig!"

I was going to keep digging at Shiri until the proverbial whistle blew. The more she resisted, the harder I was going to pursue. Natural, male instinct or an unwillingness to be defeated. I have to believe that it's more than that. I have to believe that it's more than physical attraction and a desire for conquest that would make me want to risk benching and a hefty fine during the game.

If I was willing to brave the perils of a family in full force on a first date, then I was going to make it worth my while. Maybe I'm just crazy. One too many shots to the head without my helmet. Call me crazy, then.

I wasn't going back this afternoon to practice. There was just too much at stake.

"Vamp," Brenda said, shaking her head. Her expression was my prime factor in deciding against one of two dresses that I'd bought to wear to my grandparents' anniversary dinner. We sat in my room, comparing our purchases and catching up on old times.

"Who asked you?" I muttered, holding the dress in front of me as I checked out the effect in the mirror. Traffic-stopping red. It had a high collar, but was shorter than I remembered. Its hemline was definitely nearer to my waist than it was to my knees. My mother wouldn't approve, but I was sure Jack Deneen would. After the verbal lashing my grandmother had given him, I wanted him to know that at least one Johnson woman was on his side.

"You did," Essence reminded me. "You asked. And I'm here to tell you, that dress says *hoochie mama* to me," she concurred. "All you need now is six-inch nail tips and sparkling gold shoes."

"To match the gold tooth you'd need right up in front for all the world to see when you skin and grin at that football player."

"You ladies are nothing nice," I chastised.

"Trust me, you don't want to wear that one," Brenda said. She pulled off the plastic store covering protecting the second dress. That dress was more demure, but I had to admit, I liked the way it fit me better than the first dress. When I sat down in it, I wouldn't have to worry about whether my hemline would crawl up my thigh with all the vigor of a salmon heading upstream to spawn.

The dress was black suede, and slightly off the shoulder. The hemline was longer, falling just below my knees, but a kick pleat in the rear gave a tantalizing glimpse of my thigh when I walked. I ought to know. When I bought it in the store, I'd paraded up and down in stocking feet in front of the dressing room for a full ten minutes before taking it off. It had only taken me a split second to decide that was the dress I wanted—even when I saw the hefty price tag.

The fact that it appeared to slim my hips and lift my bust line was enough to blind me to the cost. Together with the open-toed, black suede pumps and the eight-inch pearl strand necklace that I'd borrowed from my mother (that is, that she didn't know I'd borrowed), the outfit made me feel very sophisticated.

Standing in front of the full-length mirror in my room, I held the dress up to me and pulled my hair high, off my neck. Turning my head to the left and to the right, I considered the possibility that my cousins were right. This was a better choice. More appropriate for the evening. I'd feel more comfortable in this dress, more confident.

"I look good," I lifted my chin and announced to the room.

That sent Essence and Brenda into spasms of laughter.

"Oh, you're just jealous!" I accused them.

"I've got to go before Shiri's head swells, sucks up all of the oxygen from the room, and pulls us into the resulting vacuum." Brenda stood as if to leave.

"Spoken like a true college professor," I teased.

But before she left, she kissed me on the cheek. "You know that I'm just messing with you, Shiri. You sure do look good, girlfriend," she whispered. "Now, you go get that man."

Essence made gagging noises. "Oh, brother. With all of this saccharine-sweet sentiment flying around, I'd better go before I need an insulin shot."

"Come here, girl. Show us some love," I called out to her.

We opened our arms and drew Essence into our circle. For a moment, we were kids again, swearing to be best friends forever—to never let anything come between us. And nothing did. Except, of course, life itself.

Suddenly, I felt ashamed for every cursory e-mail I'd ever sent them in my halfhearted, family-obligated effort to stay in touch. I regretted the missed birthdays, graduations, and promotions. I lamented over tears we'd never shed together, losses we'd never helped each other to bear. I wanted to recant every broken promise to call, every unanswered Christmas or birthday card.

And at that moment, I resolved to try harder. To be a better cousin, a better friend.

"Get out of my room," I said, through a throat tightening with emotion.

"See you tonight, Shiri," Brenda promised.

"Later, cuz." Essence planted a peck on my cheek and followed Brenda down.

I moved to the window, drew the curtains back, and waved at them from the window. The sound of their car engines, fading as they headed down the road, was an eerie reminder of just how easy it was to lose sight of what really mattered to me.

There was a time when there had been nothing I didn't know about my cousins. Now, they were virtual strangers to me.

"Not again." I made a solemn promise, one that I intended to keep this time. I turned to my stuffed animals. With them as my witness, I would have to stick to it. "I'll never let them out of my life again."

EIGHT

I couldn't take my eyes off him. This was worse than it had been at the airport. When I'd first caught sight of him, striding through the terminal, I had what I'd considered to be a mild case of curiosity. It had been just an exercise in people-watching to help pass the time. The way he carried himself would have drawn my eyes to him—even if I'd been in a committed relationship. After all, I am a woman. I've got eyes.

I used them to their full effect, zeroing in on him with laser-beam accuracy. This time, I didn't have a magazine to hide behind. This time, when he saw me, he knew that I was watching him. My appraisal was open, unfiltered.

I wanted to speak with him again in the worst kind of way. Not at all like when we were on the plane. Then, I'd kept the conversation going because it kept me distracted. He'd prevented me from making a total fool of myself— shrieking in unadulterated terror each time the airplane rode the wave of another air pocket.

But this . . . this was something entirely different. As he stood in the foyer of the restaurant, I knew beyond a shadow of a doubt that he was waiting there for me. No chance meeting. No happened-to-be-going-my-way. He was there, with an invitation from my grandmother, but with an inclination to be there that was all his own.

As soon as he saw me, his entire face lit up with a smile. His eyes, both feral and gentle, swept over me. I closed my eyes for a moment, thankful for the fashion fates that had guided me in the choice of this outfit.

I'd read romance novels where the heroine claimed to be floored at the sight of the romantic interest. I'd always passed that off as a crock of horse spit—often quickly flipping past those initial meeting pages to get to the "good part." The happily-ever-after part.

If a man wanted to quicken my breath, let him touch me. Pleasure me. None of this eyes-meeting-across-a-crowded-room business. You couldn't pay me to believe that a simple look could make my heart pound and my breath freeze.

I renege. I recant. I take it all back. Jack Deneen's gaze could—and did. If I had ten thousand years and just as many words, I don't think I could ever explain it—how I felt both cherished and challenged. How he, without saying a single word, could make my backbone straighten and my knees weaken. I felt my face flush and hypersensitive nipples pucker as if brushed by a bracing wind.

The very pit of my stomach churned, not unlike the feeling I got every time I stepped onto an airplane. This time, it wasn't a knot of fear but an expanding, volcanic flash of desire. I doubted, in my state, if I could eat a single bite of dinner tonight.

At the same time, I wanted to nibble along his freshly shaved jawline. I wanted to sample the delicious curve of his full lips. I could spend the entire evening touching my tongue to each of his fingertips and watching his response each time I tasted another digit.

The pressure of my brother's hand against the small of my back as he steered me to our private dining area jolted me back to reality. I had better get a grip on myself before I entered the dining area. Grandma Lela, Mama, and my aunts would be watching me like a hawk. I could almost see my grandmother sniffing the air, and instantly determining from the changing scent of my pheromones that I wasn't thinking "nice girl" thoughts about Jack Deneen.

"Shiri," Bailey said, squeezing my elbow. "We'd better hop to it, girl. You know how Grandpa George doesn't like to be kept waiting, especially when there's food involved."

"I'll be there in a minute," I said, not taking my eyes from Jack.

"Who's that?" Bailey demanded, and indicated by the sudden addition of bass in his voice that he didn't take too kindly to the towering Adonis in the Armani suit visually feeling up his little sister.

Working with my father in our family roofing business had given Bailey his own share of sculpting. He wasn't as tall as Jack, but I think they matched each other, inch for inch, in the width of their shoulders.

"Grandma Lela invited him," I said quickly, disengaging my elbow from his possessive grip. More of my relatives had started to pour into the foyer. If I didn't move quickly, I wouldn't get a chance to talk to Jack privately before dinner. I'd be too overwhelmed with multiple versions of "long time, no see" greetings, wet kisses of welcome, and exclamations of how I'd grown.

"Go on in. I'll be there," I promised, pulling away from him.

"Grandma Lela invited him, huh?" he said, suspiciously. "I don't think he's a relative. I would have remembered him. Though something about him is kinda familiar. He wouldn't be from Grandpa George's side of the family, would he? Cousins from out of state?"

More like out of this world! Jack's gaze was sending me reeling to the stars. "He's Jack Deneen." I refreshed my brother's memory.

Bailey snapped his fingers in recognition. "That's right! He's that receiver for the Birmingham Steeldogs. *Dang!* I didn't know Grandma Lela had that kind of stroke to get that hotshot receiver to come to her dinner party."

He started toward Jack.

"Where do you think you're going?" I put my hand in the middle of his chest to stop his progress.

"To talk football, maybe get his autograph. What do you think?"

"Oh, no, you don't."

"Why not? He's a football player. That's his job. He's not going to mind me talking a little shop with him. Maybe give him some pointers to improve his game."

I glanced back at J.D. where he stood patiently. From this distance, his game looked pretty good to me. In the back of my mind, I wondered why he hadn't approached me yet.

"Listen, Bailey, you are not going to ruin this night for me . . . that is, I mean . . . for Grandma Lela with talk about that stupid game."

I kept my voice low and tight, tapping my index finger into his chest for emphasis. I could hear them now, monopolizing the conversation with football stats and predictions for the games to come. I didn't want to hear it. I had issues with the game. But that didn't mean I wanted to insult the man who played it.

"Go on, now. Get to gettin'. I'll be in to dinner in a minute."

"Oh, all right," Bailey grumbled. "But I don't see why I just can't talk to the man." It was like sticking a plate of his favorite dessert, peach cobbler, in front of him, handing him a spoon, and telling him that he'd better not touch a crumb.

I waited until he was almost out of sight, smoothed my hands over my dress, then started toward Jack. Just as I'd feared, I had to wade through a wall of well-meaning relatives before I could cross the twelve feet that separated us.

"Hi," I said a little breathlessly, and felt a little foolish for the inadequate greeting.

"Hello, Shiri Rowlan. I was wondering whether I'd have to send a search party out to rescue you."

God, how I loved the way he said my name—as soft as a kiss. Possessive and familiar, formal and respectful. We didn't speak for several heartbeats, letting our eyes communicate privately what curious onlookers had no right to hear.

I pulled another handkerchief from my inner jacket pocket and dabbed at Shiri's cheek. It gave me an excuse to move closer to her.

"A present from one of your relatives," I said and wiped away a smudge of lipstick, undoubtedly left by one of her female kin. At least, I hoped it was a female.

Pressing the handkerchief into her palm for safekeeping, I took the opportunity to squeeze her hand in silent welcome.

"If this keeps up, I can start a collection of Jack Deneen memorabilia," she said, lowering her eyes. She then noticed the flowers that I'd completely forgotten I'd brought for her.

"Are those for me?" She sounded pleased, even surprised. It made me wonder what kind of men she'd been dating to be so astonished by an old-fashioned, yet effective, means of showing interest.

"That depends," I said, holding them toward her, then pulling back just as she reached for the gold cellophane wrapper.

"On what?"

"On whether or not you think these are good enough to convince your grandmother that my intentions are completely honorable."

Shiri's laugh hinted at her embarrassment, but she said, "You have to convince me first, Jack Deneen."

"And how do I do that?" I asked, leaning toward her.

She didn't step away, but met my gaze head on. "You can start by handing over those lovely flowers."

"Do you like them? They're yours, then."

"Mama volunteers at the Birmingham Botanical Gardens," she told me. "Sometimes, she catches the lead horticulturist when it's time to trim back wild growth and takes some cuttings home with her. Or, when they have auctions, she's always bringing home pottery filled with blossoms. The house is always filled with the scent of flowers."

"Nothing like natural beauty to lift a spirit," I replied, touching my finger to her cheek. In doing so, I noticed the time. Ten minutes until eight o'clock. I'd been waiting at the restaurant, determined to be on time, since 7:25.

Since I wasn't sure about Thai food, I'd requested a menu and a few minutes of the maître d's time to figure out what I could tolerate and what I'd better steer clear of. Whether the supper tonight was buffet style, order from the menu, or preplanned courses, I was going to make sure that I wouldn't embarrass myself in front of Shiri's family.

"Shall we go in?" I suggested, crooking my arm. She slipped her arm through mine. Her hand rested on my forearm.

"Do me a favor, will you, Jack?" she asked, looking up at me.

What? Anything for you, Shiri. You name it. Walk barefoot over a bed of hot coals? Bring you the moon? Develop a cure for the common cold? If you ask it, I'll do it.

"What is it? What can I do for you?"

"Try not to talk about football tonight," she pleaded with concerned eyes.

Oh, woman! Anything but that!

I looked at her. "Are you serious?"

"Very," she said, pressing her lips together.

"May I ask why?"

"It's my grandparents' sixtieth anniversary. That's quite an accomplishment, especially these days when couples are lucky if they last five years without tearing each other apart. It's a special night for them. I just don't want anyone to steal their thunder."

"You mean me?"

She nodded. "Something tells me that you're going to be a very hot topic of conversation at tonight's dinner table."

"Why do you think your grandmother invited me if she was concerned about anyone taking away her limelight?"

"That's another long story. For another time," Shiri promised.

"So, what do I do if someone asks me a football-related question?"

"Punt," she suggested, with a raised eyebrow.

"Unlike the NFL, there is no punting in arena football."

"I know that," she said in the same prickly tone as when I'd caught her offering child-rearing advice—or rather paddling-to-the-rear advice—to the airport hellion. "I meant it figuratively."

"I see," I said slowly. "I'll do my best, Shiri. But I can't promise if your grandmother pins me down with threats to my person if I don't explain the difference between a touchback and a touchdown, that I won't cave in."

"I couldn't ask for anything less than that, Jack Deneen," she said wryly.

Together, as close to hand in hand as we could manage, we entered the area reserved for Shiri's grandparents' anniversary dinner.

In all, there were about thirty of the Johnson family who had gathered.

"There certainly are a lot of your relatives here tonight," I murmured out of the corner of my mouth.

Normally, crowds didn't bother me. I was used to the pressure of their scrutiny. But this was different. I didn't have my teammates with me, sharing the responsibility of success or failure. I had Shiri; but I wasn't completely sure what team she was on. She seemed pleased to see me. But if Mrs. Johnson gave me the thumbs-down, would she side with her?

"Oh, this is nothing, just a fraction of my family. You should see us in about a year."

"What happens then?"

"That's when our family reunion is scheduled. My mother and aunts are doing the planning this year. Tomorrow, we'll meet and have the official kickoff planning session."

"You need an official meeting to figure out when you all want to meet again?" I sounded incredulous.

"Have you ever been to a family reunion, Jack?"

I shook my head. "I get together with my relatives during

all the major holidays when time allows. But we've never had an official reunion.''

"You don't know what you've been missing!'' she exclaimed. ''It's like having a huge party with hundreds of your closest friends. No two reunions are ever alike, because each year there's a different set of planners. One year, we held the reunion on a cruise to Jamaica. Another year we all met in New York. We've been in Texas twice, here several times, of course. All of that effort to coordinate so many people takes careful planning, lots of money, and lots of support.''

"Where will you be the next time?''

"I don't think my mom and aunts have decided. But the last I heard, it was a toss-up between Orlando or Nashville.''

"Pick Orlando,'' I suggested. I wasn't a big fan of country-and-western music. If I intended to ingratiate myself into this family, I at least wanted to do it where I could have some fun. I'd visited Orlando a couple of times, traveling with the team. Sea World was always a big draw. I could see myself, walking hand in hand with Shiri, snapping pictures with those giant, costumed cartoon characters—as much a part of this sprawling family as her closest cousins.

It didn't bother me a bit to think that I'd still be with Shiri in a year's time. What bothered me more was the here and now. We approached the dining table.

I took a mental deep breath and gave myself a rousing pep talk. *All right, Jack. Here you go. Don't fumble this one.*

There were five round tables in the room, each able to seat seven or eight people. She steered me toward the head table, to a woman I knew had to be Mrs. Lela Johnson, a striking woman of indeterminate age and timeless grace. I thought I'd had her pegged until I noticed a woman who might have been her twin sister sitting just a couple seats over. They were involved in a lively discussion. Their voices rose slightly above the rest of the family's.

At one point, the rest of the room quieted, until everyone

realized that they weren't the target of the elder Johnson sister's wrath. I couldn't make out exactly what the conversation was about. But the words *mark of the devil, juvenile tendencies,* and *laser peel* made their way across the room.

"My grandmother's sister must have told her about her tattoo. And now Grandmother has hit the roof. I knew she would. I told my aunt Rosie that she would."

"Are they twins?"

"No. My aunt Rosie is older; but you'd never know it the way my grandmother behaves."

"Bossy?"

"I wouldn't say that." She looked up at me, wrinkling her nose at my choice of words. I could tell that she was searching for a diplomatic way of rephrasing my assessment of her grandmother.

"It's just that she knows what's best and likes to tell you in no uncertain terms. She's strict, but fair. Come on. Let me introduce you to her."

"Are you sure that's a good idea, Shiri? They seem to be a little preoccupied."

"Don't tell me that a big, strong athlete like you is afraid of a couple of little God-fearing, churchgoing ladies?"

"Your grandmother has all the gentility of a Bengal tiger," I remarked. "And I mean that respectfully."

She squeezed my arm. "Come on, Jack. Don't be afraid. I won't let anything happen to you."

I stopped. "You heard me?"

"Of course I heard you. I know I seemed scared out of my wits, but I was listening to you, Jack. I heard every word you said."

As we approached the table, the conversation dropped off bit by bit. It seemed as though all eyes swiveled toward us.

"Grandma," Shiri said, loud enough to be heard, but not so loud as to appear to talk over the conversation between the sisters. "I have someone that I want you to meet. Grandma, this is Jack Deneen. Jack, this is my grandmother, Lela Johnson."

Mrs. Johnson looked up at me for what seemed like several

minutes and didn't say a word. Then she held out her slender hand.

"How do you do, Mr. Deneen."

"Pleasure to meet you, Mrs. Johnson."

"Thank you for coming on such short notice. I hope we didn't inconvenience you."

"Not at all," I replied, and mentally crossed my fingers against the small stretch of the truth.

"Your seat is there, Mr. Deneen," Mrs. Johnson indicated. "Next to my sister, Rosie Kincaid."

"Mrs. Kincaid." I extended my hand to her, but she stood instead and clasped me warmly to her.

"Shiri told me how you kept her company on the plane, Mr. Deneen. Not being a big fan of air travel myself, I can appreciate how much comfort a friend can be. Thank you."

I think I said something equally gracious to Shiri's aunt. But inside, I was soaring. So far, so good. They hadn't dismissed me outright. I'd been a bundle of nerves, waiting for Shiri and her relatives to arrive. Scenarios of varying degrees, from mildly embarrassing to the unforgivably uncouth, had flown through my mind as I'd used the Global Positioning System in my car to get to the restaurant.

I could only imagine what kind of silly grin I had on my face at the time. My motives for sitting next to Shiri on the plane had been purely selfish. But if by being so, I could win one more Johnson over to my side, I'd take the praise.

"So, you're with the Birmingham Steeldogs?" A tall, elderly gentleman dressed in a dark, three-piece suit stood and held out his hand to me. A large, rawboned man, he looked uncomfortable in the fancy surroundings. His hands, large and gnarled, spoke of advanced age, failing strength, but uncommon endurance as he patted at his shining, perspiring forehead with a handkerchief.

"This is my grandfather, George Johnson," Shiri introduced. "Grandpa, this is my friend Jack Deneen."

"Pleasure to meet you, sir," I said, shaking his hand. "Congratulations on your wedding anniversary."

"Thank you, thank you. Yes, I'm feeling mightily

blessed.'' Once the pleasantries were over with, he thrust his hands in his pockets, leaned close, and said, ''So, son, what do you think of your chances this year to take it all?''

I shrugged, pressing my lips together and shaking my head.

He stood, staring at me, watery brown eyes blinking periodically, as if he expected me to say more. I didn't. I'd promised Shiri that I wouldn't.

I glanced at Shiri and responded carefully. ''I . . . uh . . . I really couldn't say.''

''What do you mean you can't say? You tryin' to tell me that you're sworn to secrecy about whether or not you're going to make it to the ArenaCup championship?''

Rosie Kincaid caught the look that passed between Shiri and me, then chuckled softly. ''You poor boy. Shiri, tell me that you didn't put a gag order on our guest.''

''Aunt Rosie, you know me better than that,'' Shiri dissembled.

How could she have sounded so innocent knowing fully well that's exactly what she'd done?

''Uh-huh. It's because I know you that I'm hereby overruling you.'' She looked up at me with a conspiratorial wink. ''I'm sure Shiri meant well. But I'm here to tell ya, the child has some major issues with the game of football. But that doesn't mean it has to ruin your evening, does it, Jack?''

''No, but I promised that I'll try not to bore anyone with my stories.''

''Maybe you could tell the one about you when you were playing for the University of Alabama and the mascot for Louisiana State. That one isn't boring,'' Aunt Rosie suggested. ''You could tell that one.''

I think she was laughing at me, enjoying my discomfort.

''Not in polite company,'' I declined.

''What about you and the mascot?'' Shiri wanted to know.

''That's definitely a story for another time.'' I tried to kill the interest before it got out of hand. I didn't want to be judged tonight for some misspent reckless antics in college.

"Let's just say that our friend Jack found some very creative uses for duct tape and stink bombs," her aunt Rosie continued.

"You heard about that?" I asked in chagrin.

"Oh, I can't wait to hear this one," Shiri said.

"Sure you can," I said, patting her shoulder. "I think a more interesting story is what turned you off football." I turned the conversation back to her. "You didn't tell me that you didn't like the game."

"Oh, well . . . I guess the subject never came up," she said and winced. We both knew that wasn't exactly true. She'd had plenty of opportunity to tell me to stop running my mouth about the game. It had been mostly all I talked about on the flight from Jackson to Birmingham.

From the way she'd responded, I'd thought she was a dedicated fan. She'd nodded at all the right moments, asked questions at all the appropriate intervals. I looked at her now with a grudging respect. She must have been in agony the entire trip—between the threat of imminent death on one hand and my boring her to death with my stories on the other. I wouldn't be surprised if she hadn't entertained thoughts of jumping out of the plane to put an end to her misery.

"Is everyone here? I'm ready to eat now," Shiri's grandfather announced to the room.

"Please join us at our table, Mr. Deneen." Shiri's grandmother indicated a couple of seats.

"Oh, goody! We get to sit at the grown-up table," Shiri said in mock awe.

"You won't be so pleased when you find out about all of the embarrassing stories I'm going to tell Jack all evening," Aunt Rosie predicted.

"Aunt Rosie," Shiri began in warning.

"Don't sound so surprised, honey. You know we were not going to let this evening slip by without trying to totally humiliate you."

"Grandma, you're not going to let her do that, are you?"

"You mean totally humiliate you?"

"Yes."

"Well, not totally," Mrs. Johnson promised.

"Exactly," Mr. Johnson added. "I mean, what kind of loving, supportive grandparents would we be if we went around telling all your friends that when you were nine years old you put Vaseline on your chest to encourage your bust to grow?"

"George, leave the girl alone. Don't embarrass her in front of her friend."

"Thank you, Grandma," Shiri said in relief.

"Besides, she wasn't nine—she was twelve and still flat as a pancake."

Shiri put her elbows on the table and hid her head in her hands. "Times like these I almost wish I was adopted."

"*We* won't have to embarrass her," Mrs. Johnson said, lifting a disapproving eyebrow. "I'm certain her questionable table manners will do the job for us."

She jerked her arms back, then folded her hands primly in her lap. I leaned over and whispered loudly so that almost everyone at the table could hear, "If you can remember to keep your elbows off of the table, I'll try to remember not to chew with my mouth open."

"Can we order now?" Mr. Johnson insisted.

"In a minute, George. Wait until the whole family is here," Rosie said.

"If some folks want to travel on CP time, that's their business. We told them what time dinner would start." He waved over one of the table servers and indicated to start taking drink orders.

I was glad that I had arrived a good twenty minutes early. Seemed like running late was an unpardonable sin in this family. Moments later, a couple who I assumed were Shiri's parents walked briskly into the dining area.

I might have passed the father on the street and not recognized him as being related to her. He stood about five-foot-eight or -nine, with the build of a pro wrestler: wide shoulders and long arms, barrel-chested. His dark hair was speckled with gray, bristly, and shaved close to his head. Though the suit he wore was well tailored, probably altered to fit his irregular features, subtle body movements led me to believe that he'd rather be wearing something else, something that allowed him a greater range of motion.

He tugged at his tie as if to adjust it and he walked with his hand near the buttons on his jacket, as if he wanted at any moment to rip the confining cloth away. When he came over to shake my hand in introduction, his grip was firm, sure, and callused—the mark of years of hard labor.

The woman who walked in on his arm was definitely Shiri's mother. They say that eventually all daughters turn into their mothers. I couldn't help staring. That was going to be Shiri in twenty years or so. My head swiveled back and forth, noting the similarities between the two women. They had the same heart-shaped face, the same deep-set, almond eyes.

"Sorry I'm late, Mama," Shiri's mother said as she leaned down to kiss Mrs. Johnson on the cheek. "Happy anniversary."

Mrs. Johnson reached up and patted her daughter affectionately, then sniffed delicately.

"You smell like gasoline," she noted.

"We had a flat tire. I helped Sherman change it."

I also noted the obvious differences. Mrs. Rowlan had a few more lines around the mouth and eyes, a touch of gray in her hair. She was somewhere between stout and Rubenesque, but wore her weight comfortably, as if she'd stopped worrying about conforming to what the fashion industry pushed as the perfect size.

She exercised to maintain good health, I could tell that from the firm tone of her bared arms. But she wasn't going to starve herself or squeeze into too-small clothes or shoes. That I noticed by the light gray silk, free-flowing, two-piece tunic and pants and low-heeled shoes that she'd selected.

Also, unlike Shiri, she wore her obvious affection for and devotion to her husband openly. Shiri still sought her relatives' approval before emotionally investing in a relationship. Doris Johnson Rowlan may have once had to go through a similar approval process, but she had passed through. Sherman Rowlan was now a member of the family—and the one and only man in her life.

During the course of the evening, I don't think Mrs. Rowlan realized how often she showed to the world how much she loved—and was still in love with—Sherman Rowlan. From the time the first course was served, they shared from each other's plate, offering tender morsels. They participated in the table conversation, yet at the same time managed to convey to the room that they were wrapped up in each other. He held her hand, she leaned her head on his shoulder. He laughed at her jokes; she kept his plate full.

The more I watched them, the more encouraged I became. In a few years, that could be us. If Shiri and I could make it past these crucial, beginning stages of desire cooled by doubt, romance tempered by rationalizations, we had a chance.

If—and what a huge if—we were willing to accept the unexplainable pull toward each other, celebrate rather than condemn our differences, we, too, might find that once-in-a-lifetime love.

NINE

"Don't lose them," Shiri said and grasped my arm. An early spring rain fell in steady sheets, but the wipers kept our vision clear with a steady *swish-swish* rhythm.

"I won't," I promised. "Don't worry."

"There!" she pointed excitedly. "They're turning off there."

A flash of red brake lights and the amber blinking of turn signals pointed the way to the caravan of cars that had left the restaurant.

"I see them, Shiri. Relax. Even if they do get ahead of us, I know what hospital they're going to."

"I don't believe this," Shiri muttered. "All we wanted was a quiet evening with the family."

"I did my part," I replied, trying to ease her fears with a little humor. Very little. "I didn't talk about football tonight."

She returned a reluctant smile.

"At least your grandmother liked her bears. That's something to be thankful for, huh?"

"Her face did kinda light up when we brought them in," she remembered.

"That's better." I squeezed her hand.

"I'm sorry I'm not being better company. I'm just a little worried about my cousin Brittany."

"She'll be all right."

"How do you know?" she demanded. "She could have brain damage."

"I doubt it!" I laughed at Shiri.

When she made a huffing noise at me and folded her arms, I patted her reassuringly.

"They were just being kids, Shiri," I continued. "They're extremely resilient. The doctors will be able to take care of her just like that."

"Snow peas?" she said incredulously. "What normal kid sticks snow peas up her nose?"

"Could have been worse," I offered.

"I don't see how."

"It could have been brussels sprouts. Brittany told me at dinner that she hates brussels sprouts."

Shiri's smile widened. "She told you that?"

"Uh-huh. Made me swear that I wouldn't tell anyone. She's got everyone fooled into thinking that she's a good girl who always cleans her plate."

"Yeah, right. Did she tell you about the time that she hid her brussels sprouts in a pair of tennis shoes in the back of her brother's closet?"

"No, I don't think she got around to that."

"We were used to Brandon's room smelling; but seven-day-old brussels sprouts stench beat Brandon's worst pair of smelly socks or shoes hands down."

"Maybe she started hiding vegetables up her nose because her family discovered her best hiding place?" I suggested.

She looked at me, pursed her lips, and shook her head. "You're on her side, aren't you?"

"Whew . . . boy . . . the rain really is coming down," I said, deliberately sidestepping the question. "Here, put this on."

I handed Shiri my jacket to throw over her as she opened the car door. I tried to find a parking spot close to the emergency-room entrance. The best that I could do was about fifteen yards away. The parking lot was full tonight.

Shiri stepped out and down into a puddle of standing water. I heard her curse under her breath and wondered whether she could still take her brand-new shoes back, as long as she kept the receipt.

I placed my arm around her waist, guiding her as we headed for the emergency-room doors. The doors slid open as soon as we stepped under the cover of the awning.

Shiri slid the jacket off her shoulders, shook some of the raindrops off, and handed it back to me. She did all of this with barely a break in her stride. She'd caught sight of Brittany's parents talking to the triage nurse.

"Uncle Anthony," she called out, and clasped him warmly to her in a supportive hug.

I turned my eyes away so that she would not see the surge of jealousy. I didn't mean to feel petty. It was just that I had been looking forward to spending this time with her. Having to spend it in the emergency room of a hospital, instead of over a candlelight dinner, did something to me. Emotionally, I was somewhere between pissed that I'd skipped practice for this, relieved that little Brittany seemed to be all right, and pleased that Shiri had chosen to ride to the hospital with me instead of abandoning me at the restaurant with the remainder of her family.

Something in me kinda snapped. Before I'd gotten a chance to get close to her, I was upstaged by a nine-year-old with snow peas crammed up her nose. At some level, I felt about as childish as Brittany. I was three times her age, but was behaving, in my opinion, half her age.

While Shiri tried to get information from her relatives, all I could do was stand by and try to look as if I was being supportive. A person could only stand around for so long without feeling about as functional and uplifting as the reproductions of artistic prints adorning the hospital walls.

I touched Shiri lightly on the shoulder and said, "If you need me, I'll be over there." I indicated a row of chairs across the room.

"Uh-huh. Okay," she replied, though I wasn't entirely convinced that she was talking to me. She could have been responding to her uncle, for all of the attention that she gave me. She never quite looked directly at me, just sort of turned her head toward the direction of my voice.

I took a seat and tried to find a way to look sympathetic, yet supportive. It's possible, though I put a cramp in my facial muscles like you wouldn't believe. The muscles that controlled my eyebrows alone went through some serious contortions: furrowed with concern, raised with sincerity, then arched in sympathetic support.

It wasn't that my sentiments weren't sincere. They were. No one could have foreseen how events would have turned out tonight. No one. I'd prepared for grilling from the parents, maybe even scorn from the grandparents. I hadn't figured on having to dust off my old CPR skills.

I emphasized my emotions because I knew that everyone would be watching me. Shiri came from a large family, but it was an extremely close-knit family that jealously guarded against any rivals for affection. All I had done was give Shiri my phone number. You'd think, from her grandmother's reaction, that I had passed on the plague.

No self-respecting mack would have let an opportunity for getting to know a beautiful woman pass by. As I sat in the hospital waiting area, I thought about what I might have done to change the progression of events that had brought me here.

"What are you in for?"

A voice, gravelly and demanding, accosted me as if I were an unwelcome guest at the county correctional facility.

I looked to my left, then to my right, and twisted around to try to find the interrogator. A little boy, who couldn't have been more than eight years old, sat cross-legged on a chair behind me and four seats over.

His arms were folded, his chin resting on his forearms as he peered back at me with two of the oldest eyes that I'd ever seen in a child. Curious and suspicious at the same time.

"Are you talking to me?" I pointed to myself.

"Yeah, I'm talking to you," he responded. He had an old man's voice, too. I didn't get that much bass in my voice until long after puberty.

"I'm not sick," I said. "I'm here for a friend of mine."

"The fine lady in the black dress." He nodded his approval to me. I wasn't quite sure how to respond to that. They say that kids are brutally honest. And it was obvious that he had good taste in women. So I let that one go unchallenged.

"What are you in for?" I asked.

"I'm not here for me, this time. I was here last week. For this."

He held up his arm and I noticed that it was encased in a cast from elbow to wrist. The cast was covered with signatures in various inks, various colors.

"I'm here for my sister. You hear that screaming?"

I lifted my head, training my ears in the direction of one of the triage rooms.

"I don't want a shot! I don't want a shot!" It was a childish treble, rising in pitch, intensity, and frequency, followed by the crash of something loud and metallic.

"That's her. She's gotta get stitches. Flipped off the bed and busted her fat head wide open. Mama told her to stop jumping in the bed. That's what she gets for not minding."

"Stitches. Man, that's rough."

"She'll be all right," he said knowingly. "When they strap her down, if they don't give her a shot, they'll pack her head with some kinda smelly gel and gauze."

"How do you know so much about the emergency room? Do you want to be a doctor when you grow up?"

He gave me a look that said, *Oh, please!*

"What's your name, son?"

"Mama said that while she's in there with Bianca, that I shouldn't talk to strangers. I shouldn't tell them anything. Not my name. Not where I live. Or nothing."

"That's good advice that your mother gave you." I extended my hand to him. "Just so we're not complete strangers, name is Jack. Jack Deneen. My friends call me J.D.''

"Nuh-uh," he contradicted with all of the enthusiasm of a child catching an adult in an untruth. "Everybody calls you Flash."

"Now, just how do you know that?"

"My daddy saw your picture in the paper and told my mom that you might just do some good for football if your ego didn't get as big as your head. What's an ego, Flash?"

"You tell your father . . ." I began, then quickly checked myself. This was a kid, even if he did have an old man's mouth. "You tell your father thanks for the advice," I amended.

"Do you want to sign my cast, J.D.?" he asked, holding it up again.

"Sure. If you can find some room for me."

"Mrs. Lentschke's whole second-grade class signed it. Even Tyler Duncan. And he's the one who pushed me off the monkey bars in the first place. See? He signed it right there and drew the broken bones with the blood gushing out of it."

"A veritable Vincent van Gogh," I remarked.

"A very who?"

"Van Gogh. He was a famous artist back in the day."

"Tyler's not going to be an artist when he grows up. My mom says that he's going to be a sociopath. What's a sociopath, J.D.?"

"You'd better have your folks explain that one," I deferred.

He tossed a dark blue pen to me from his stash of crayons, markers, and gel pens crammed conveniently, if not orderly, into a zippered plastic bag.

"I think I see a spot right here," I said. "It's just below the elbow." He turned his back and extended his arms as best he could. I signed my name with a flourish and drew a flattened oval with cross-hatching. That was my rendition of a football. In the center of the oval, I penned my jersey number. Not exactly worth displaying in the Smithsonian, but the artistic attempt brought a smile to his face.

"Thanks, J.D. I guess this means we're not strangers anymore. So I'll tell you my name. My name is Casey. But I'm not going to tell you where I live. I don't want Mama to get my behind."

"Pleasure to meet you, Casey. And you're welcome." I resisted the urge to reach out and pat him on his head. It would have felt too much like a saccharine-sweet soda commercial. I settled for balling up my fist and holding it out to him for a little dap. He clenched his own fist and tapped it once on top of mine.

"There you go," I encouraged. It struck me as oddly sentimental, how small his hand looked on top of mine. For a moment, I could almost imagine that this wasn't a stranger's hand. Instead it was the hand of my own son, sharing a special moment with me despite the grimness of our surroundings.

When who I presumed to be his parents came out to collect Casey, he ran up to them, shouting at the top of his lungs that I'd signed his cast. My signature had been elevated in importance over Tyler Duncan's gore-gushing bone drawing. A proud moment for me—to go from booger-picker to best ball player all in one evening.

"Looks like you've made a new friend." Shiri settled into the seat next to me.

"He's a good kid," I assessed.

"If a little loud," she observed.

"You have issues with kids?" I asked, partially to tease her about the comment she'd made about the kid in the airport. The other part of me wanted to feel her out. I wanted to know her feelings about kids in general.

Myself, I can see an entire carload of kids. I want enough to start my own football team, offense, defense, and coaching staff included. Sounds impractical, maybe even like the ramblings of a madman. But that's what I want. And I want a woman who shares that vision. Or nightmare. It all depends on how you looked at it.

So far, Shiri seemed two for two against children. She loved the kids in her own family. Her panic when Brittany had fallen back in her chair, choking and grasping at her throat, told me that she had the capacity within her to love. But it's different when they're your relatives or someone else's kids. You could love them as much as you want to, then give them back when it's inconvenient for you to have them around.

I still didn't have a good clue of where she stood on having children of her own. That reminded me of how little I actually knew about her. Did she want kids? Could her thinly disguised dislike of children be a symptom of sour grapes? Maybe she wanted kids but couldn't have them.

Though I couldn't help but notice that she had what my grandfather called baby-bearing hips. Her hips were wide enough to handle the load of the last stages of pregnancy. Yet they were not so wide that I couldn't wrap my arms around her. They weren't so unwieldy that I didn't want to put my hands on either side of her and pull her toward me.

"Look, Daddy! Look who signed my cast!" Casey turned around so that his father could get a good look. "Jack 'The Flash' Deneen. You were wrong, Dad. He's not a stuck-up pretty boy with washed-up dreams of ever playing in the NFL. He's good people."

Shiri and I exchanged glances. I don't know who started laughing first. The gleam of amusement in her eyes might have been sparked by the quirky twitching of my lips. She laughed until tears came to her eyes, then rested her head on my shoulder to gasp for breath. I kissed the top of her head.

"How's Brittany?" I asked.

"She's going to be all right. She's more scared than hurt and more embarrassed than scared. Thanks for acting so fast, Jack."

"I'm glad I was there to help."

"Don't be so modest. You know that you picked up a few brownie points with my family, don't you? They'll be talking about you for weeks to come."

"Really?" I asked, toying with a few strands of braids that had worked themselves loose from her French twist. My index finger traced the line of her jaw and followed along the outline of her full lower lip.

"And what about you, Shiri? Will you be talking about me, too?"

She pulled her head away, coy. "I can talk about you now, if that's what you want," she replied, lifting one eyebrow in mock annoyance. "Let me see. What's an old standby? Oh, yes. You're ugly and your mother dresses you funny."

"That's not what I meant and you know it."

"I know," she said, turning serious in an instant. "And I can't say what I'll be thinking about in the weeks to come, Jack. I haven't planned that far ahead."

"Then why don't you let me put something on your mind now?" I asked tacit permission for something I'd pretty much made up my mind I'd do from the moment I saw her at the restaurant: I was going to kiss her. I had to. There was no way that I wasn't going to try.

As I leaned forward, I hovered just a fraction before moving in. I wanted to give her the chance to change the direction of the conversation. She didn't pull way. Instead, she closed her eyes.

"Hey, Flash! My dad wants to shake your hand."

Casey popped up between us, yelling his father's offer to make introductions.

"Hold that thought," I murmured to Shiri, and forcibly pulled myself away.

There he goes, I sighed in both relief and resignation. I watched as he chatted with the little boy's family. The Flash was charming, gracious, as smooth as fresh-spun silk. He certainly had a way with people. His popularity had something to do with being some kind of hotshot athlete. But I was equally sure that Jack Deneen would be just as charismatic flipping patties at some burger joint.

He was a force unto himself, drawing everyone in and

around him with all of the intensity of a tornado during the play-by-play reconstruction of a Steeldog glory game. As the gathering around Jack grew larger, I felt my patience growing thinner. This wasn't the time or place for gridiron grandstanding. This was a hospital. There were sick people here. People on their deathbeds. The feats of an athlete seemed inconsequential in comparison to the life-and-death battles going on all around us.

Not everyone agreed with my sense of propriety. When a young woman resident in too-tight scrubs stood too close, laughing a little too loud at one of Jack's corny jokes, I felt my waning patience come to an abrupt end. I'd had just about all I could take of Jack Deneen and his entourage of devoted fans for one night.

Yes, I was grateful for his quick thinking and his knowledge of CPR. Because of his efforts, my cousin Brittany would live to hate and hide another brussels sprout. And yes, I had to admit that we made a good-looking couple, walking arm in arm into the restaurant. Heads had turned as we'd walked by, practically swiveled three-sixty *Exorcist* style. The way my family responded favorably to him, I had private, fleeting fantasies of seeing him as a permanent addition. If he looked at me one more time with heat in those tiger eyes, I was going to melt into a messy puddle.

But the more time I spent in his company, the more I realized how much I didn't know about him. I see the public face that he puts forward, the crowd-pleaser, the female magnet. Judging by the quick way he'd dumped me for the willing ear of an audience, it made me rethink how much I wanted to know him.

I hoped that it wasn't jealousy. Could I be that petty, that selfish? He was a man of the public. His profession counted on his being able to please the people. So he wasn't doing anything. Not really. He was just being Jack. If I couldn't handle who and what he was, then the fault was mine. It was better that I found out now, before I allowed myself to get emotionally invested in him.

I told myself that it really didn't matter. I was only going to be in town a few more hours anyway. I might as well enjoy his company for the little time we had left. I stood up, physically pulling myself away from the negative feelings that were starting to bring me down. A few words to my aunt and uncle to check on Brittany, make my excuses. Said my good nights. Then I raised my hand to vie for Jack's attention.

When I knew that he was watching, I held my hand up in the shape of a *T*. Time out. Game over.

He nodded and mouthed over the heads of his fans, *Sorry*. He tried to pull away, but not before signing a few more autographs, shaking a few more hands.

"Time to go now, Jack."

"Is everything all right?"

"Uh-huh. They're taking Brittany home tonight."

"Some crazy night, eh, Shiri?"

"Absolutely insane. I'm exhausted."

"Then let me give you a lift home."

"Do you mind? I've got to get out of here. I can't stand being in hospitals."

"Come on then." He placed his arm around my shoulders. And in that moment, all of my irritation fell away. He felt so right, like he should have been at my side all along. As if he'd always be there.

Still, I couldn't bring myself to trust those feelings. So much had happened this weekend. My emotions had gotten a total working over.

"The rain's stopped," he said as we stood under the awning of the emergency-room entrance.

"Uh-huh," I responded, and congratulated myself on what a witty conversationalist I'd turned out to be tonight. I looked out onto the parking lot, shaking my head. "Some date this turned out to be."

"Thank you," Jack said, with a wry twist of a smile.

"Why are you thanking me? It was horrible! First, you're raked over the proverbial coals by my family. Then you have to dredge vegetables out of my cousin's nose and wind up driving through a spring monsoon to get to the emergency room. Please, Jack. You don't have to be kind.''

"I wasn't being kind, Shiri," he gallantly denied. At least, I thought he was being gallant. "Trust me," he replied. "I was being completely selfish. My actions were motivated by my own self-interests.''

"I don't believe you." I shook my head slowly back and forth. "I don't think you have a selfish bone in your body.''

At that, he laughed loud enough to draw the attention of several of the waiting-room occupants still inside. He bit his lip to stem the laughter, leaned close, and whispered.

"Yes, I do, Shiri Rowlan. And one of these days, when we get to know each other more intimately than we do now, I'll show you." He raised my hand to his lips and kissed it. His eyes never left mine. And before I knew it, the words popped out.

"I don't want the evening to end like this." They flew out of my mouth before the wisdom of revealing my innermost thoughts could prevent them. I think that I surprised him as much as I did myself. He took a startled step back and didn't speak for a couple of seconds.

"In that case, darlin', what would you suggest?''

I shrugged my shoulders. "I don't know. I just know that we can't let the date end on this note. Maybe we could go out for coffee or something? To talk, rationally, normally, without the fear of a fiery airplane crash or being under the watchful eye of my relatives.''

"Sure. I'd like that. And I know the perfect place. A coffee shop not far from UAB.''

"What are we waiting for?" In my mind, I reasoned that I had one more chance to correct the karma between us. If we couldn't make an honest connection sitting and talking over a cup of coffee, then there was no hope for us. None at all.

I had a two-o'clock flight tomorrow out of Birmingham back to my safe, predictable life in Jackson. Here was my chance to step out, to take a chance. A little voice in the back of my mind kept urging, egging me on. *Go for it, Shiri. You go, girl.*

"I'm going, I'm going," I said out loud in response to the voice, and ignored the strange look that Jack threw in my direction. I had to make myself take this chance. As much as I liked him, if we didn't establish a bond here and now, I had no doubt our chances for success would be ruined once I was back in Jackson. I barely made time for my own family. I couldn't see myself putting forth the effort for a man whom I'd known only a couple of days.

The drive to Jack's coffeehouse was quiet. But the silence wasn't strained. It was natural, expected. It was as if we both were caught up in our own thoughts. Once, we stopped at a red light. He clasped my hand and raised it to his lips. Such a sweet gesture. So smooth.

One part of me basked in the attention. The other half wondered how many women he'd charmed with so polished a move. *No!* I pushed the thought to the back of my mind. I'd made the decision to go with this feeling. I wasn't going to ruin it by letting negative thoughts seep in. I didn't want to know who he'd been with. He was with me now. In the here and now, that was all that mattered.

He held my hand. I squeezed back. I couldn't go so far as to kiss him but I could let him know what kind of effect he had on me.

Jack released my hand long enough to pull into a parking spot. It was even more crowded here than at the hospital. I glanced at Jack.

"Are you sure you want to go in there? It looks kinda crowded to me."

"It's a popular place, so it's always crowded. Don't worry about it, darlin'." He winked at me. "I'll get us a table."

"You must know somebody on the inside."

"I know a lot of somebodies," he admitted.

"I don't doubt it," I muttered under my breath. If he heard me, he didn't respond. Instead, he helped me out of the truck. His arm was wrapped securely, possessively around my waist as we walked up to the door.

From the moment we walked in, I could feel all eyes on us. I felt self-conscious at first, not unlike a bug under a magnifying glass. From the number of people who hailed him as soon as he walked through the door, I couldn't tell if it was because he was a sports celebrity or because he still frequented this place.

"Welcome back, Flash." A hostess greeted him with a kiss. She barely glanced at me. Why would she? Who pays attention to window dressing? That's how I felt. Like something to adorn his arm, like a watch or a cuff link.

"Hi, Andie. Got a table for me?"

"Always, sweet thing. Just give me a minute to clear out your regular spot. Next time, don't make yourself such a stranger." She disappeared through a maze of tables and booths.

"One of your old haunts?" I asked.

"Yeah, me and my boy, Mike, you remember him? The one who was on his honeymoon? We practically lived at this coffee shop while we were in school."

"I wasn't talking about the coffeehouse," I said, then winced. Did that come out of me, sounding like a jealous hag?

"Oh, you mean Andie? She's like a sister to me."

I rolled my eyes. I could grab any man here, plant a sloppy wet kiss on his lips, but that didn't make him my cousin.

Andie came back, crooked her finger at Jack, and led him to a table in the rear of the coffeehouse.

"Double mocha." She marked down Jack's order without asking. Then she raised her gaze to me. "What about you, ma'am? What can I get for you?"

"Iced cappuccino," I replied, surprised that she even noticed that I was there.

"Coming right up." Andie sounded perkier than the brew that she promised to deliver.

Jack held the chair out for me, kissing me on the cheek as he slid it under me.

"So," he said, as he took a seat across from me, "what shall we talk about?"

"What do you want to talk about?" I countered.

"You," he said simply, leaning onto the table.

I could feel my face growing hot under his direct glare. "Do you want to narrow the subject field a little? That's a pretty broad topic."

"Nope. I want to know everything about you, Shiri."

"That's impossible. Even I don't know everything there is to know about me."

"Okay," Jack relented. "Then let's start with something simple."

"Simple is good," I agreed, nodding enthusiastically.

"How's this for starters? Tell me how you feel about me."

I nearly choked, so unexpected was the question. Kinda early to start talking about feelings, though mine were running the gamut with this man. Why couldn't he ask me what my favorite color was or my favorite food? Why not start with something like where I grew up or the types of movies I liked. Any one of those would have been an appropriate first date question.

"What?" he asked, smiling smugly at my stunned expression. He knew that he'd rattled me. I guess that was his way of paying me back for playing it so cool at the airport.

"Simple?" I suggested, lifting an eyebrow at him.

"A man of simple needs and wants," he corrected. "Not simple of mind."

"What *do* you want?" I asked.

Now it was Jack's turn to raise an eyebrow. The heat in his eyes answered the question for me. The way his gaze swept over me caused my heart rate to quicken. My breath caught in my throat. I cleared it delicately and clarified my question by asking: "What do you want out of life? What happens when you've played your last game?"

"I'll be in my grave and hopefully heaven bound," he responded. "But seriously. I have other plans. Other ventures I'm working on. My sports center, for example."

He took a few minutes describing his business ventures to me. I listened intently, injecting questions to keep him talking. Anything to keep the focus off me. I think he knew what I was doing, but was willing to let me get away with it for now.

"And when I get too old to run those anymore," Jack continued, "I hope to settle into my old rocker, spend my golden retirement years on secluded, lakefront property somewhere. I'll spend my days fishing and watching my children, grandchildren, or even great-grandchildren grow up healthy, wealthy, and wise."

"I take it that means you want children?" I stated the obvious.

"Lots. Lots and lots and lots."

"You plan on having several wives then?" I teased. "One woman couldn't possibly have all of those babies."

"Maybe," he conceded, then took my hand across the table. "But won't it be fun trying, Shiri?"

"You weren't an only child, were you, Jack?"

"No. I have a younger sister, Joella."

"Does she live here?"

"Uh-uh. In Atlanta."

"And your folks?" I prompted.

"They live here in Birmingham. I'd like for you to meet them."

I tried to imagine Jack's father, an older version of himself. And what about his mother? What kind of woman was she to help raise such a man?

"What do they do?"

"Retired. My mother has a side business, selling jewelry that she designs over the Web. My father's retired from the state department."

"Do they—" I began, but Jack cut me off.

"Want to become grandparents. Of course they do."

"So, we're back to babies again, are we?"

"You have something against them, Shiri?"

"I come from a very large family, very close family. I would be a pariah if I said that I didn't want children."

"But how do you really feel about them, Shiri? I'm learning about you that what you say and how you feel don't necessarily go hand in hand."

By the intense way that he squeezed my hand, it seemed important to him that I answer yes. To be honest, I hadn't really thought about children of my own. I mean I assumed that one day I would get married and have kids. But that day wasn't here yet, so I hadn't dwelled on it.

"What makes you think that I wouldn't want kids?"

He shrugged. "Remember that kid at the airport?"

"Geoffrey? How can I forget?"

"He seemed to get on your nerves."

I started to laugh. "He was getting on my nerves, but only because he was after my bears."

I stroked Jack's hand, easing his concerns. "I love kids, Jack. Absolutely adore them. That's part of the fun of helping my folks plan our family reunion. I get to see all of my younger cousins again. That business about Geoffrey . . . well, that wasn't as much about kids as it was a certain kind of kid. My parents doted on us. But my brothers and I were raised very strictly. My parents didn't tolerate such ill behavior from us. And I won't tolerate it from my kids."

I think I'd answered that question to his satisfaction. I could feel the tension easing from his face.

"Anything else bothering you, Jack? Anything else you want to know?"

So we talked. And we talked . . .

So we talked. And we talked. And we talked. And we sipped. Then we talked some more. Sometimes over each other in our haste to get the words out. The floodgates had opened and the flow would not be stanched.

In a perfect world, we would have shared, in the three hours that we talked, a lifetime of memories. He, painting a picture of his world; me carefully outlining and censoring the details of mine.

I sat with my chin propped on my fist, watching his expression change with each glimpse he gave me into his life. His emotions bubbled beneath the surface. I imagined his entire body to be a percolator, constantly steaming, bubbling. To take in his aroma was to be uplifted, rejuvenated. I couldn't get enough of him.

And apparently, neither could the patrons of this coffeehouse. The longer we stayed in our corner, the greater the crowd grew. And though Jack did his best to keep the conversation focused on us, the more difficult the patrons made it for him to do so.

It started with one or two coming over for an autograph, a brief chat about the next game. Then three and four, groups of five, up to ten strong sometimes gathered around our table.

He got rid of them as expeditiously, yet politely, as he could. But with each interruption, it was harder and harder to get our conversational rhythm back. I was going to suggest that we leave, try again somewhere else, when suddenly someone shouted out: "Yo, Steeldog! You suck!"

Jack's eyebrows lifted. I could see a ripple of tension across his shoulders.

"You sure they aren't spiking the java?" I said lightly.

He shook his head. "No, I think he walked through the door loaded."

"You hear me, Steeldog? Couldn't hack it in the NFL so you make us pay jacked-up prices to watch you and the rest of you losers? What kind of crap is that?"

Jack visibly started, half raised from his chair.

"Hey," I said, touching his chin and turning his face back to me. "I'm over here."

"Sorry, darlin'," he muttered apologetically. "What was I saying?"

"You were telling me about the time you sneaked into your father's liquor cabinet."

"Oh, yeah." Jack chuckled, his expression turning sheepish. "Does the phrase 'sick as a dog' mean anything to you?"

"Yeah, I think every teenager has to have one of those days before he—or she—comes to her senses."

Speaking of senses, he played havoc with mine as we held hands across the table. As he drew lazy lines back and forth across my knuckles with his thumb, I felt the steady beat of his pulse through his fingertips. That's how I knew the loudmouth a couple of tables over affected him more than he wanted his expression to show. I felt the quickening of his pulse. When his back stiffened, it disrupted his easy caress, halted it.

"Hey, Steeldog! Catch this!"

A paper cup, with the lid still on, smashed against the wall between us. Lukewarm coffee splattered against my cheek and neck. It was more shock than pain that caused me to cry out and grab my face where the coffee hit.

"Son of a—" Jack stood up, nearly upsetting our own table with the abruptness of his move.

"Jack!" I held on to his hand, even as he started for the table across the room. "Where are you going?" I asked, lowering my voice. Hopefully, by keeping my voice neutral, matter-of-fact, I could defuse the situation.

"I'll be back in a minute," he said. His eyes were riveted to the table of hecklers.

"Oh, no, you won't," I contradicted. And I meant it. I knew enough football to read *blitz* in Jack's face. He was going to take them all on.

There were four of them at one table alone. I had to do something. If it got back to my grandmother that I was involved in a stupid brawl, she would ground me for the rest of my natural days. Lock me in my room and throw away the key. Grown woman or not, I would never hear the end of it.

"Take me home, Jack."

"Shiri," he said. There was anguish in his voice, anguish that I didn't want to recognize. The look in his eyes asked me not to stop him. He made a move toward the table, but stopped when I placed my hand against his chest. I didn't exactly push him, but I didn't let him move forward, either.

It must have looked strange to the curious onlookers, a five-foot-four munchkin in heels containing the fury of that six-foot-plus giant.

"I mean it, Jack." My voice had dropped to nearly a whisper.

I wasn't going to cause a scene. I wouldn't let him cause one, either. I picked up my purse and started for the door. He would figure out what I meant by my actions and would know that I meant business. I didn't have to nag him. I didn't have to say a single word. My stiff-backed, fast-paced march toward the door said it louder, more effectively than words ever could.

As I headed for the exit, I didn't look back. If he wanted to go after those morons, he did so knowing how I felt about it. I didn't turn back because I didn't want to see him if he did go to them. I was already ticked off because our date had been interrupted twice in one night by childish behavior. I didn't want to be disappointed, too.

When I reached the door I sensed, rather than heard, him behind me. Our eyes met in the reflection of the smoked glass. He put his hand on the door heavily. And for a moment, I thought he was going to put his fist through it. But at the last instant, his fingers splayed as he pushed against the door. It swung open, nearly slamming into a couple on their way in.

"Sorry," I murmured, skirting past them.

Jack ignored them, even when one of them greeted him with a "Good luck on the next game, Flash. Kick the spit out of Arkansas."

He didn't say a word as he unlocked the car door and helped me climb in. I didn't know what to say, either. How do you say, "Sorry I made you look like a weak-willed punk in front of your fans?"

Still, what could either of us say if he got his picture in the paper over a senseless fight? If he was worried about backing down, looking like a wuss in front of those loud-mouths, what would a gossipmongering news rag do to his image? By forcing him to walk out of there, I may have made him lose face in front of a crowd of thirty or so patrons. But thanks to me, I could have saved him the embarrassment of thousands. Hundreds of thousands. The entire circulation of the *Birmingham Post-Herald* and the *Birmingham News* combined.

Jack climbed into the truck, inserted the key into the ignition, and was out of the parking lot before he finally spoke to me. His movements were jerky, mechanical.

"Where are we going, Shiri?" Jack asked. His tone was clipped, precise, carefully modulated to dampen the irritation I knew he must have felt. I guess he thought that he was trying to be civil to spare my feelings. It didn't work. I knew that he was mad. He knew that he was mad. I think I would have felt better if he'd just been honest about it, instead of hiding behind that veneer of false civility. It made me feel worse to think that he couldn't be honest with me.

Where are we going? Nowhere fast, I thought glumly. All of the progress we'd made as we sat and talked was nullified in a single act of senseless aggression. *Hmmmph.* Just like football. It's no wonder I loathed the game so much.

I gave him directions to my parents' house.

TEN

"Take me home, Jack."

She might as well have said, "Take me to the moon," for all of the effort that it cost me to walk out of there. I couldn't leave for several reasons, only one of which was the desire to knock in the mouth the knucklehead who'd thrown that coffee at us.

Just as Shiri had not wanted to end our date at the emergency room, I didn't want it to end on that note, either. The look on her face when the coffee had splattered against her really got to me. She was angry, disgusted, and a little frightened. Not of the knuckleheads at the other table, but of me. Of my reaction. She'd taken one look at my expression and bolted for the door. I'd run her off.

She'd put up with a lot this evening. The constant interruptions. The overt flirting. Not from me. From my behavior, you'd never know that there were other women in the room. Where Shiri was concerned, I had tunnel vision. But that didn't stop other trains from trying to jump onto my tracks.

I don't know how she handled it and still managed to maintain her composure. Perhaps I'm jaded. I'd started taking all of that attention in stride. After all, football was the profession that I'd chosen. I'd known what I was getting into.

When I'd signed that contract, I knew that my performing for the crowd didn't always end at the last whistle. Sometimes when the game was over, especially after a win, we had to put on our best performance. Each and every one of us Steeldogs was a public-relations representative. We'd joined an exclusive club. We were charter members of the entertainment industry. It had its perks and its downsides.

Even with all of the talking Shiri and I had done, I hadn't had the opportunity to warn her about that particular hazard of the job.

Since we were at the beginning of the season, the press stayed all over us—keeping our images in the public eye. Good money was dished out to keep the excitement high, even to the point of creating rivalries and scandals. Grist for the rumor mill. If a fan became a little too enthusiastic, so much the better for the team's reputation. What that coffeehouse jerk failed to understand is that, underneath that jersey is a man—a man who was only going to let fanaticism go so far.

Maybe I was already too wound-up tonight. I'd skipped that second practice. Without that extra workout to release pressure and tension, what was I supposed to do? Adrenaline, testosterone, and caffeine—a dangerous combination. If it hadn't been for Shiri and her cooler head prevailing, knucklehead would have gotten a double-fisted dose of all three.

She knew it was in me. Must have seen it in my face. When she'd touched me once in the center of my chest, placed the flat of her palm against me so that she could feel the erratic pounding of my heart, something had drained out of me. Like a dampening rod in a nuclear facility, she had somehow absorbed my anger. Then, without a word, she'd left me. In doing so, she'd given me a choice. How I decided to act would tell her what kind of a man I was.

A man could talk all night long. He could reinvent himself with words, paint any picture that he wanted. But let a raw emotion like anger, or fear, or even love unexpectedly surface—that's when the true worth of a man came out.

Some people say that a woman can look at a man's shoes and judge his worth. Shiri had looked into my eyes. Whatever she saw there frightened her. It made her want to leave me standing there—all by myself.

As she'd left me, I'd taken a moment to collect my thoughts. I couldn't believe that just that quickly I'd lost her. But I had. Realization of her loss had swept over me and left me feeling conflicted, confused. I could have gone over to that table and pounded out my frustration and disappointment. I should have. After all, what did I have to lose? God knows that I wanted to. I wanted to show those knuckleheads that Steeldogs don't play. I wanted to show them that Jack Deneen was not a man to be trifled with. Jack Deneen was a man. Period.

Maybe that's what had changed my mind. The farther Shiri had walked away from me, the quicker the cloud of confusion had lifted. Jack Deneen was a man, all right. And nothing more. In a room filled with people, Jack Deneen was all alone.

More than I wanted to beat them down, I wanted my woman by my side. That's right. *Mine.* That's how I'd come to think of Shiri. I'm not sure when, or how, or even exactly why. I had no right to. During our conversation, there had been no grand declarations of love. Neither one of us had gotten on our knees or made other such sweeping gestures of devotion. I couldn't think of one good reason why I should make a claim to her. But I did.

So I'd left it all behind me. All of the anger, and the trash talk, and the macho bull posturing. I'd opened my wallet and carefully placed a few bills on the table. On my way out, I'd made a quick detour by their table. Hadn't said a word. Just walked by. It had taken every ounce of my self-discipline not to react, even as they continued to harass me.

"You suck, Steeldog!"

"Loser."

"Has-been."

"You mean never-was."

"You got that right."

"You bring that fine woman back here, boy. I'll give her some steel."

On the playing field, we talked a lot of trash. It's all a mind game, trying to get the opponent so rattled that they make a mistake. Everything was fair game—from making fat-mama cracks to offers of sexual services to opponents' wives. Everybody did it.

But the ones who really had the best mind games were the ones who didn't have to utter a sound. Just stood there. Just glared. If you could get your opponent to screw up with just a look, then you knew that you were at the top of your game.

The trouble was, we weren't on the playing field. Shiri wasn't my wife and she wasn't my mama. She didn't deserve having coffee thrown at her. So when I'd passed the table of knuckleheads without speaking, pinning them with a long, hard stare, I think it got my point across. I'd let them live— tonight.

I'd caught up to Shiri at the door. Her hesitation had been barely noticeable as she'd pushed on the handle to make her way outside. As I'd come up behind her, she hadn't seemed to acknowledge me. Yet our eyes had met in the dark glass. I'd watched as the tension drained from her face. Slowly, she'd closed her eyes as she let out a long, cathartic breath.

That had brought a fresh surge of anger in me. She'd been so worried that I'd start a fight. Did she see me as nothing more than a big, dumb jock whose only answer to being challenged was to start pounding? Maybe that had been my first reaction. She hadn't given me a chance to show her that I could be otherwise.

I'd opened the car door, helped her to settle into her seat. She'd said nothing, and neither had I. What could I have said? Sorry for standing up for myself? Sorry for trying to protect you? It hadn't seemed right. If I'd tried, my tongue would have stuck to the roof of my mouth. Apologizing for having a normal, typical male reaction would be like apologizing for breathing.

Still, as I'd watched her out of the corner of my eye, I'd had to say something. Anything was better than that smoldering, uncomfortable silence.

"Where are we going, Shiri?"

It wasn't a simple question. It was as close to asking "what about us?" as I could get without coming right out and saying it. Perhaps I was too subtle. I don't think she picked up on the hidden question within a question. Instead, she started going on and on about the different routes we could take to get to her parents' house, and the merits of taking one freeway over another.

I didn't want to hear that from her. If I really wanted to know how to get to her parents' house, I would have simply activated the Global Positioning System on the panel in front of me. The GPS could have gotten me wherever I wanted to go—without the slight tremor in its voice or the nervous wringing of hands.

We rode the remainder of the way to her parents' place in virtual silence. Except for an occasional clarification of direction—turn right here, turn left there—there was no noise. I didn't even turn on the radio or put in a CD. What is that old adage about misery loving company? I kept it quiet. I wanted her to experience every moment of agonizing silence along with me. Not because I wanted to hurt her. Heaven forbid! I would never intentionally hurt her.

What I wanted was for her to hurt for me, with me. I wanted to know if she was as broken by the untimely death of our budding romance as I was. If only I knew that she was feeling as desperate as I was feeling, then I would know that there was still a chance for us.

More than jealousy, or infidelity, or even the death of a partner, I believe that apathy is the greatest killer of love between a man and a woman. If she could bear the silence that had fallen between us, then perhaps she wasn't the woman for me. If the silence did not affect her as deeply as it did me, then there was no meeting of the minds. Without a meeting of the minds, there was no joining of our hearts. Chalk up this evening to just another wild time and call it quits.

As we drove, I divided my attention between the road and Shiri. The overhead streetlights alternated between illuminating her face and casting it in shadow. She stared straight ahead, with her hands clasped primly in her lap. As we approached her parents' house, she turned her face toward the passenger window.

That's when I saw it. She'd done it so quickly, it might have been a gesture to move aside a stray strand of hair. But I had been watching, hoping, for any sign. Any glimmer of hope on which I could focus.

The glimmer slid down her cheek. What I'd thought was a reflection of residual spring raindrops left on the windshield were tears. She'd been crying! I didn't know whether to laugh or cry myself.

If she felt this way, after barely a first date, then her feelings had to run as deeply as mine. I didn't have to guess whether I was alone in this feeling. Her silent suffering said it all.

Shiri cleared her throat and said softly, "We're coming up on my house now."

Shiri's parents lived in an older, well-established section of Birmingham—before planned communities had become all the rage and individuality had taken a backseat to conformity. Like Shiri, the house she'd grown up in made a statement. It was a curious mixture of old-fashioned Southern charm and modern-day conveniences.

The house was set back from the road several yards on a tree-lined hill facing the main road. An accent fence made of rocks and mortar, worn smooth with time and the elements, ran along the base of the hill. The same stones, ranging in hues from cream to deep russet, continued as part of a short flight of stairs and ended with a narrow path leading to the front door. The pathway was lit on either side by miniature, off-white lanterns giving off just enough light to guide.

The house itself was two stories tall, wooden, and painted the palest yellow with white trim along the windows. A large wraparound screened porch practically invited relaxation with porch swings on both sides of the deck. A single porch light cast a pale yellow glow that accented the front door, but didn't quite reach the farthest corners of the porch.

On the right side of the house, set back even farther from the main road, was a gazebo covered with purple flowers around the trellised wall and up the column supports.

I'd parked hugging the curb. Shiri's door opened just at the steps. As she walked up the path, her pace was considerably slower than when she had walked away from me at the coffeehouse. It could have been due to fatigue. It had been a long night. Wishful thinking made me hope that her pace was directly related to her reluctance to leave. She ambled with her hands clasped behind her, swinging the little purse by its strap.

I followed alongside her with my hands shoved deep into my pockets. As we walked, my elbow brushed hers once, maybe twice. To the casual observer, the contact might have been incidental. It wasn't. At least not on my part. I meant to touch her. I wanted a helluva lot more than just to rub elbows with this woman. But she'd shrouded herself in an air of impenetrable, personal space that I couldn't charge my way through.

She climbed the first step of the front porch, then the second. As she turned to face me, I could almost hear the mental gears grinding, turning. She was searching for a polite, socially acceptable method of telling me good night— and good-bye. Raising her eyes to the stars for inspiration, Shiri took a deep breath, shrugged, and said, "Well, at least it isn't raining anymore."

"No," I agreed amiably. "Looks like it's going to clear out quite nicely."

I suppose it was as safe as any conversation opener.

It didn't take long for her play-it-safe mood to change rapidly. I could see another emotion transform her face as irritation with herself set in. In our conversation, we'd gone well past the play-it-safe mode. Without preamble, Shiri stuck out her hand.

"Thank you for a lovely evening, Jack."

"A lovely evening?" I echoed without trying to hide the sarcasm in my tone.

She folded her arms and her expression changed again. Defensive this time. Good-byes didn't come easily to Shiri, and I wasn't cutting her any slack. If she was going to write me off, I didn't want mealymouthed platitudes. Give it to me straight. If she never wanted to see me again, then she was going to have to tell me. Right then, right there.

I wasn't going to leave until she told me where I stood. Or, if it came to that, where I could go.

"I had a good time," she confessed.

"But?" I pressed. "I definitely hear a 'but' tacked on somewhere at the end of that sentence."

"Are you putting words in my mouth?"

"No, ma'am. I'm not. I'm trying to draw them out."

"As much as I like you, Jack—and I do like you—I just don't think . . . that is . . . we can't . . . uh . . . we could never . . . the differences between you and I . . . you understand, don't you, Jack?"

Perfectly. But for the sake of one last shot at us, I pretended that I didn't.

"No. I don't. Why don't you break it down for me?"

She had a hard time bringing herself to tell me good-bye. Fine. I didn't want her to say it anyway. Though no one could argue that I hadn't given her every opportunity to say it. At the airport. At the restaurant. The hospital. During the long, silent drive to her house. She could have dismissed me at any time and avoided altogether the awkwardness of the after-the-disastrous-date-is-over drop at the front door.

Instead of a good-night kiss, she could have told me to kiss off, to go away. She could have urged me to forget that we'd ever met. Or, to temper that cruelty with kindness, she could have promised to stay in touch or asked that we always remain friends. She could have made her point any number of ways. But she hadn't. She'd stammered and faltered. And in that faltering, Shiri had given me the opening that I needed to try to change her mind.

ELEVEN

Mind over matter. Mental telepathy. Or some sort of sleight-of-hand parlor trick. It had to be. Otherwise, how could I at one instant be *this* close to giving Jack the brush-off, and in the next, be in his arms?

Not just holding him, or hugging him, but pressing myself against him as if he could absorb me into his skin. How did it happen? What did he do to me? Slip a mickey into my coffee? Or, did he wave a magic pendant in front of me to put me into a trance?

It wasn't supposed to end like this. I had my speech so carefully prepared. I was supposed to be kind, sympathetic, but firm in my resolve. I'd tell him what a good time I had, tell him what a sweet person I thought he was. I'd shake his hand, maybe give him a perfunctory peck on the cheek, then send him on his way. Simple, direct, all loose ends tied.

I held my hand out to him. A cordial, socially acceptable handshake of dismissal. He'd understand that, wouldn't he? Didn't all of his games begin and end that way? No matter how much he hated or respected the other team, didn't he always put aside his differences for a sportsmanlike ending?

But as I drew closer, my senses were suddenly over-whelmed.

"Shiri!"

He murmured my name and pressed his lips against my cheek. It wasn't the first time that he'd kissed me that night. He'd brushed butterfly kisses across my cheek, my hair. He'd even given my hand a very continental peck. But the passion in that single utterance after he kissed me on the front porch did more to excite me than all of the coy, flirta-tious, give-and-take conversation we'd shared during the night.

"Jack . . ."

I flung my arms around his neck, launched myself off the steps, and clung to him for dear life.

I should have been more discreet and thought how we must have looked to the neighbors. I should have worried about how that gossip would eventually reach my grand-mother's ears.

Even at three in the morning, I knew that *someone,* if not my own parents, would be watching. A strange, expensive car pulls into the neighborhood, parks in front of my parents' house—you'd better believe there would be talk among certain prominent circles in Birmingham.

Vestiges of those recriminations echoed in my ears like wind rustling through the poplar trees. Shiri Rowlan, the headstrong daughter of Doris and Sherman Rowlan, turned up her nose at perfectly good local schools to run off to God knows where, finally drags her fast tail home in the middle of the night with a strange man, and practically mauls him in plain sight. The hussy! What could she possibly be thinking?

He'd groaned my name and instantly, none of that mat-tered. None of those concerns bothered me when Jack held me, caressed me. He kissed my cheek, my jaw, my ear, my hair. I felt my spine melt away as his large hands splayed against my lower back, drawing me to him.

Kisses strayed to my eyelids, the tip of my nose. He caught my lower lip between his teeth, gently nipping, then moving along my jaw. All I could do was hold on as he literally carried me up the steps and pulled me into the shadows at the farthest corner of the porch.

Shielded by the flower-covered trellis connecting the porch with the gazebo, I used the false security of the shadows to push the bounds of propriety. Never, in ten thousand years, would I have imagined myself like this. Never, not even during my wildest, most rebellious teenaged days, would I ever have believed that I could be this desperate for a man's touch.

I'm absolutely certain that if my first sexual experience had been anything like this, I could have easily become known as the college campus skank. I would have done anything to seek out these sensations. Thank my lucky stars that my first time hadn't been anything like this.

A brief encounter behind the bleachers at my sophomore year's homecoming game had introduced me to the so-called mysteries of sex. Some mystery. The only mystery was my unexplainable impression that there had to be more to it than *that*. With hundreds of books, hundreds of thousands of movies (legal and illegal), billions of people populating this planet couldn't have been that wrong, could they?

That senior boy had seemed to get so much more out of it. The expression on his face, a contortion somewhere between pleasure and pain, had told me that he knew something, shared something that I didn't. For years after, I thought it was just me. Something had to be wrong with me if I didn't enjoy the act as much as he did. Maybe something was miswired in my brain, or misplumbed in my body not to share the sensations he'd experienced.

By my senior year I'd had a steady boyfriend and easy access to him any time I wanted. Plenty of opportunities to delve more into the mystery, to discover for myself what had been rumored to drive individuals stark raving mad if they didn't have enough of it. I'd gone stark raving mad, all right—every time he got himself off and walked out of my dorm room without so much as a peck on the cheek.

Once, he'd had the nerve to ask me whether or not I'd

come. Of course, I'd been able to truthfully respond. Come to my senses, that is. I'd dumped him. I did it kindly, with compassion, but kicked him to the curb just the same.

I'd had enough of that business. Maybe there was something more to sex. Maybe there wasn't. Until I could find out for sure, I hadn't had time to bother with it. I'd been a senior in the top two percent of my class. Finals had been coming up. I'd had a lucrative internship to lock down. I'd kept myself occupied to keep myself out of trouble.

That's exactly what Jack Deneen meant to my self-imposed dry spell—T-R-O-U-B-L-E.

As each of Jack's touches grew more insistent, I grew less fearful of discovery. I couldn't fault him for moving fast. I encouraged him. Not with words. I encouraged him with soft sighs as the mystery unfolded and with groans—greedy and guttural—as mystery turned to mastery.

Wordlessly, mindlessly I let him know in unambiguous terms how he affected me. When he found the right spot, and he did repeatedly, I rewarded him with more access. Heat from his palms warmed the backs of my thighs, slid upward past my thigh-high stockings, kneaded the contracting muscles of my bottom, bare and exposed by the thong Brenda had convinced me would help to make the lines of my dress lie smoother.

He pulled me closer, lifted me several inches, so that my feet dangled in midair. My back crushed morning glories on the wall as thick as carpet as he pressed against me. I felt him throbbing, lengthening, seeking me out.

As my knees separated, Jack settled between me, slowly, deliberately moving his hips in a rhythm that I was able to fall into naturally, as if we'd been dance partners for years. I gasped as his fingers probed warm, moist depths. Warmth ignited instantly to flame. I bit into his shoulder to keep from crying out.

At first, I might have been able to fool my parents into thinking my soft, mewling cries belonged to some kind of animal—a stray female cat in heat, perhaps. But what kind of cat calls out, "Now, Jack! Please!" in the middle of the night? Somehow, I had to keep myself together long enough to remember where I was.

"Back pocket," he growled, once again bringing to mind images of the untamed.

I didn't have to question what he meant. I knew.

I didn't know how much longer I could hold out. When I'd explored her, felt how she constricted around my fingers and imagined how she would feel with me fully inside her, I knew that it wouldn't be long . . . my ability to wait, that is.

Length, in other respects, wouldn't be a problem. I was a big man, in more than one sense of the word. I had no question whether I could satisfy her. It wasn't vanity. It wasn't an overinflated estimation of my sexual prowess.

I knew that I would because it's all that I wanted to do. All of my energy, all of my passion was focused on a single objective: to bring pleasure to Shiri Rowlan. I don't remember ever wanting a woman so much.

My deepest concern was whether or not I would hurt her. She'd seemed so small and tight. One finger, then two . . . I'd barely begun to explore before I felt early contractions— ever-widening ripples of pleasure making her tremble.

She'd called out my name and pressed her face into my shoulder in a futile effort to prolong the inevitable. You might as well have asked her to hold back an ocean tide.

"Back pocket."

I don't know who reached my wallet first, but it wound up in my hand. Shiri made up for her lack of quickness by aggressively tackling the buttons of my shirt. She managed to undo the first three before frustration and haste gripped her.

For someone so small, she surprised me with her strength. She yanked on either side of my shirt, sending several buttons flying into the thick St. Augustine grass. My own clothing became my worst enemy while I tried with one hand to hold her and with the other to undo the buckle of my belt and the clasp of my waistband. The sound of the zipper going down sounded more like a rip of fabric as I yanked it away from me. An apropos sound. Not unlike the rip of my sanity as anticipation of bringing pleasure to her bordered on the unbearable.

The humid, spring air was nothing compared to the heat pouring off my exposed skin. My head swam in delicious delirium as my heightened senses took it all in. The cloying smell of the flowers, the intermittent wind whistling through the trees.

"Let me," she offered, taking the foil packet out of my hand. Shiri carefully withdrew the condom and covered the tip of my penis with its lubricated coolness. Before fully sheathing me, she ran her hand up and down my taut skin. Her fingers closed around my girth, squeezing possessively until I cried out, "Enough, woman!"

I unfurled the condom as Shiri reached behind her and clung to the trellis. I grasped her hips, maybe a little too roughly. She gave a little gasp and bit her lip.

"Oh, no," she choked out, her face stricken.

"No?" I echoed. Not something I wanted to hear at this late stage of the game. "What's wrong?"

She lowered her head to my shoulder. Her voice was muffled as she said, "I have to go in now."

"What do you mean?"

"My mama . . . or maybe my dad . . ." She nodded in the direction of the front porch. "They've flashed the porch light."

"Flashed the porch light?" What was that, some kind of secret Rowlan family code?

"When I was a little girl, and stayed out a little past my curfew, the porch light coming on was my signal to come in," she explained.

"You . . . you've got to be kidding me."

"I'm not."

"Shiri, you're a grown woman." I smoothed my hands over her to emphasize my point.

"I know that I am. You know that I am. But to my family, I'll always be the Sweet Sherbet."

"Sweet Sherbet?" I wanted to laugh. Something told me that it wasn't a good time. The look on her face was deadly serious.

"A nickname my dad gave me. That's probably him flashing the lights on and off at me. I've got to."

"Pretend like you didn't see it." I moved to block her view of the porch. "See? Problem solved." I tried to pull her to me again, at least for another kiss. But she turned her head aside.

"Problem not solved. If I'm not in the house in five minutes, they'll turn the floodlights on us."

"And after that, what's next? The dogs?"

She then roughened her voice in a poor imitation of her father's. "As long as you're living under my roof, young lady, you'll obey my rules."

"You and your family are intentionally trying to drive me into the nuthouse, aren't you?"

"We don't have to try. It's a natural progression from prolonged exposure to us. I'm so sorry, Jack. I didn't mean for things to get this far . . . so fast."

"It's all right, Shiri." I mentally crossed my fingers behind my back at the little lie. It wasn't all right. I was hurting pretty bad. I'd live. I wouldn't like it. But I'd live.

"Promise me that you won't be mad at me."

"I'm not mad." Again, another half-truth. I could feel the punitive flames of hell licking at my toes. Lust and lies. There would be a seat at the right hand of Big Red himself for those two.

"Are you sure?" She looked askance at me, narrowing her eyes. She didn't believe me. I guess I wasn't a very convincing actor.

"I'm not mad," I said through clenched teeth. Flames rose higher, scorching my knees. At any moment, I was going to spontaneously combust.

"Yes, you are," she said, and planted a kiss on my nose. "You are mad."

"Okay, not really, really mad."

"I'm sorry, Jack. Are you still coming to the outing tomorrow?"

"I've got some things I need to take care of in the morning, but I'll be there."

"See you tomorrow, then. Good night, Jack."

I watched her turn toward the house. She looked back only once, waved, then hurried to the front door. Before she could get her key out of her purse, I heard the door creak open. She paused, speaking to whoever it was behind the door, then disappeared inside.

TWELVE

I hated to leave him like that, but what else could I do? Somewhere, in the great, unwritten parenting handbook, it has been decreed that parents will forever have that power over their children. I could be a hundred years old, blind, deaf, and toothless. It didn't matter.

Whenever that porch light went on, I'd better run toward it as if it were the light showing the way to heaven. I'd better hear my parents when they call my name loud enough to rival the final trumpet blast, and answer for my sins if they had to flash the porch light more than twice to get my attention.

Maybe that's why my brothers did so well in track and field. They must have unofficially broken several Olympic records trying to get home when the grapevine of neighborhood kids warned them that someone was flashing for the Rowlan kids.

As I sat and sipped my morning coffee, I contemplated the events of last night. Maybe things had turned out for the best. My mother turning on the porch light had saved me from what might have been a gross error in judgment. I had to admit, I hadn't been thinking very clearly.

I'd been acting on pure instinct. That was the trouble. Maybe I shouldn't trust my instincts when it came to Jack Deneen. He was so unlike anyone I'd ever met. I couldn't trust my usual defense mechanisms when it came to dealing with the opposite sex. What experience did I have? A few fumbling attempts in college?

And all of my dealings with the men on my job were strictly eight-to-five. I had no inclination to get to know them any deeper than the thickness of their three-piece suits.

Relatives, by default, weren't considered. I grew up with my brothers, learned by trial and error how to deal with them. Male cousins weren't much harder than brothers to figure out. But there, my experience ended.

You couldn't say that about Jack. He knew exactly what he was doing, and how well he was doing it. I had no doubt that given five more minutes, I would have firsthand knowledge of his skills.

"Oh, God," I groaned, pressing the heels of my hands into my eyes. This wasn't like me. This wasn't like me at all. How did things get so out of control so fast?

If anyone had told me that I would be getting it on with a virtual stranger, I would have sued him in civil court for slander. I just wasn't the spontaneous type. Just ask anybody. Shiri Rowlan was careful, calculating. The ultimate control freak. What had I gotten myself into? A better question to ask, why was I so quick to let him into me?

"Well, now. I didn't expect to see you up so early."

Mama leaned on the wall at the kitchen entrance, her arms folded, watching me. "Or didn't you go to bed last night?" Her tone was full of suggestion.

"I went to sleep. I didn't go to bed. . . ." The "with Jack" was left unspoken, but clearly implied. "Were you waiting up for me?"

She had barely said a word to me when she'd opened the door to let me in last night. But her sleep-filled gaze had taken in my disheveled appearance, my rumpled dress and matted hair. As I'd passed her, she'd reached out, plucked a crushed flower from the back of my hair, and set it on the foyer table.

"Of course I waited for you, Shiri. Just doing my job."

She moved casually over to the counter and poured herself a cup of coffee. Mama held the warm mug between her hands, staring over the rim before looking up at me. "Looks like I'm not the only one working overtime."

"And what's that supposed to mean?" My tone was more belligerent than I had a right to be.

Mama took the tone in stride. No one in the Rowlan household was ever their best before their first cup of coffee.

"Oh . . . nothing. But you'd better fix that scarf before your father comes down. It's cute, goes with the outfit, but clashes with that big purple hickey on your neck."

Unconsciously, I lifted my hand and adjusted the floral scarf knotted at my neck.

"So." She set the coffee mug down with a clink against the kitchen counter, then began to drag out pots and pans for breakfast. Her back was to me as she asked, "Do you want to tell me all about it?"

"There's not much to tell, Mama."

"I find that very hard to believe, Shiri."

She wasn't going to leave me alone until she had some sort of account of last night. I started slowly, gathering my thoughts and carefully choosing my words. "After we left the hospital, Jack and I went out for coffee."

"And?" she prompted.

"Cheesecake?" I suggested.

"More like beefcake," she muttered under her breath.

"I heard that!" I exclaimed, wagging a chastising finger at her.

Mama heaved a wistful sigh and bit her lip. "You have to admit, he is one very sexy man."

"Mama!"

"What?" Her expression was all innocence.

"But you're married to Daddy."

"Until death us do part," she said. "But I ain't dead yet, child. I've got eyes."

"It wasn't like that, Mama. We just talked."

"Talked?"

"Yes, Mama, we talked. You know, the lost art of conversation."

"You don't get a passion mark like that with just talk, Shiri. I may be old, but I'm not senile. I still have a vague memory of how it works between men and women."

She stood at the stove as she cracked eggs and dropped them into a sizzling pan with one hand. With the other, she stirred frozen orange juice concentrate in a Pyrex pitcher.

My eyes were glued hypnotically to the frozen lump as it dissolved, but my thoughts were elsewhere.

"Jack is a wonderful conversationalist," I said softly. "We talked about everything from politics to Puff Daddy."

"I hope you used protection, Shiri," Mama said bluntly.

"I didn't know there was protection against passion marks," I said flippantly.

She whirled around, waving a wooden spoon at me. "That isn't funny, Shiri."

"I know, Mama. I'm sorry. I didn't mean to smart off."

"We had this conversation when you were sixteen and again at eighteen."

"When you went with me to pick up a prescription for birth-control pills. I know, Mama. But the only thing I ever really used those pills for was to clear up my skin."

"Are you sure you don't need a refresher course? I'm serious, Shiri. You know how I feel about relations outside of marriage. We raised you up in church, hoping that you would follow the church's teachings . . . but . . . ." She paused and seemed to reconsider what she was going to say.

Was it something on my face that silenced her? An expression? I don't know if she could have accurately read my expression. Maybe because I wasn't exactly sure what I was feeling.

I was fearful of disappointing my mother, angry at myself for letting myself be so easily manipulated. At the same time, I was eager to see Jack again. I was secretly pleased that he was as aroused as I was; though my brothers would probably tell me that it didn't take much to get a man in the mood. I still wanted to believe that it was something about *me* that Jack wanted, not something that he could get from any old skank on the street.

"You're a grown woman. You do what you want to do. I just want you to be careful. They've got stuff floating out there these days that a penicillin cocktail can't cure. It kills."

"I'll be careful," I promised her. I didn't insult her by telling her that there was no need for care. I didn't promise her that I would abstain. How could I? I couldn't even promise myself.

"And next time, stay to the far side of the gazebo. There's a blind spot there where the porch light barely hits."

"How do you—" I began, then quickly closed my mouth with a click. I didn't want to know. The image of my parents in passion was more than this baby girl wanted to picture.

Mama then pulled up a chair beside me, folded her arms on top of the table, and whispered conspiratorially. "With those luscious lips, he's got to be one great kisser."

"He's all right," I said, cavalierly.

"Come on now, on a scale of one to ten, where does he fall?"

"You don't give up, do you?" I shook my head.

"If I was the giving-up kind, you and your brothers wouldn't have lived past puberty."

"What? What do you mean? We were such angelic children!"

"Hah!" Mama snorted in derision. "Just who gave you that impression?"

"Aunt Rosie. She said that we were wonderful kids. She told me that I was her favorite."

"She tells all the kids that. I was her favorite before you and your generation came on the scene. Besides, our aunt Rosie has a nasty habit of egging you kids on. I'm still not convinced that she wasn't the one who convinced Bailey to let you try his experimental hang glider."

"You remember that?" It seemed like ages ago. I couldn't

have been more than nine years old, maybe ten. That was a long time to hang on to a memory.

"You tell me how a mother is supposed to forget the sight of her daughter sailing overhead, dirty socks on your feet dangling in the air, screeching bloody murder as you crushed into old Mr. Lummus's crepe myrtle. The heartache of seeing your dusty socks was trauma enough. I'd just finished laundry. You could have at least changed."

"At least the hang glider sail was clean."

"Because you swiped it off my laundry line."

"How old was I?"

"Old enough to know better than to let some knot-headed boy convince you to do what you knew in your heart was risky."

"Old enough to know better," I echoed.

Apparently not. Not then, not now. I was still letting boys talk me into putting my legs up in the air. I should have stuck to hang gliding, I thought ruefully.

"I think you were just turning ten," Mama continued. "Headstrong and so bossy. I wouldn't be surprised if you ordered them to strap you in."

"I think I did," I said, staring up at the ceiling as if I could project those days up there. "Brenda and Essence told me not to do it. You know how much I hate being told what to do. I like doing the telling."

"And you did it often. All three of you girls took turns, being the little general. When the three of you played together, it was hard to tell you apart by tone alone."

"Speaking of bosses," I said, turning my ear to the direction of my parents' room above our heads. I could hear water rattling in the pipes. "Sounds like Daddy is up."

I think my mother took exception to my crowning my father the boss of the house, especially since my father's favorite words to my mom were *yes, dear.*

She sorta huffed and pushed back from the table to check on the Canadian ham sizzling in redeye gravy in that cast-iron skillet on top of the stove. She turned down the flame so that it no longer licked the sides, but burned with a pale blue glow on the underside of the pan.

It wasn't as if my father was henpecked or whipped. He wasn't. My father was a strong man, a quiet man—deeply committed to his family. He just knew that things went a lot smoother when they did things my mother's way. If I was bossy and controlling, I came by it honestly.

I should have been more honest with Shiri and told her how her abrupt shutting-down had affected me.

As I sat out on the back patio, mulling over my breakfast of cranberry walnut muffins and sliced fruit in light cream, I thought about what my little untruths might have done to the foundation of this fledgling relationship.

When Shiri had left me last night, she'd known that I wasn't being truthful. The way she'd kept insisting that I shouldn't be mad let me know that she had an inkling of how I felt. It was only an inkling, however. There was no way she could know the full extent of my emotions. Hell, I didn't even know. I didn't want to dwell too deeply on them last night. It was much better for my sanity if I concentrated on other matters.

I'd left her, driven around the city for a while, letting the necessity of focused thinking to navigate the Saturday-night streets of Birmingham occupy my attention. I'd driven until the needle indicating the level of gas in my tank had sunk dangerously close to empty.

In the calmer light of day, I can honestly say that I wasn't really mad at her. That is, I'd thought about it and come to the conclusion that she wasn't deliberately being a tease. Her responses were too open, too unrestricted to be practiced.

In those heated moments, she'd wanted me just as much as I'd wanted to have her. It must have taken just as much effort for her to emotionally withdraw as it had taken for me to physically withdraw.

Was I mad? That wasn't exactly the right word. It didn't fully sum up the cauldron of emotions boiling barely beneath the surface. Disappointed, yes. Frustrated, somewhat. Aroused? Definitely. The combination of all three had put the scowl on my face that she'd translated to anger.

They say that discretion is the better part of valor. Loosely translated, rather than make a foolish mistake and force her to accept my passion, I'd backed off, letting the cooler head on my shoulders prevail.

Some of my teammates would have encouraged me to "go for it." To "get it while it was hot." Others would have advised me against letting a woman know right from the get-go how to get to me. But the ones whose advice I trusted, the ones who would have recognized that I'm looking for something more than a quick lay, would have held up my friend Mike as the perfect example.

He'd made it very clear early on how Barb turned him on. She didn't have to read the heated thoughts burning in his head. Every touch, every whispered offer, every heated glance he tossed her way melted down her token resistance. In the end, she would only let him go so far. Mike had left it up to Barb to decide just how far he would go.

They went, all right. All the way down the aisle.

As I toyed with the idea of calling Shiri to apologize, I decided against it. She'd backed off last night, put some distance between us. In doing so, she'd put something in my mind. It was my turn now. It was my turn to give her something to think about. Would she think about me?

THIRTEEN

"Whose idea was this anyway?" I grumbled.

"I believe it was your grandmother's," Mama reminded me. "There, I think that's all of it."

She compared the items crammed into the trunk of her compact car to the items on her list. Coolers filled with ice, canvas chairs, first-aid kits, poles, tie-downs, and a blue-and-white striped awning that could have rivaled Barnum & Bailey's best tent. How in the world did she get all of that in there?

"Are you sure that's all? I don't think we've hit critical mass yet. There's still a centimeter of space remaining in the far left corner of the trunk."

"Good. You can put your sense of humor in there. That ought to fill that tiny space right up," Mama replied as she slammed the trunk shut. Or rather, she bounced on it a couple of times until she thought that she heard the lock catch.

"Do you have the directions to the recreation center, Shiri?"

"Uh-huh." I nodded. "They're in my purse in the trunk."

Mama looked at me with laser-beam eyes, charring me on the spot.

"Okay, okay. It was just a joke. I put a copy in the glove compartment," I relented, waving my hands to ward off the evil in her gaze.

"And what about Jack? Is he going to be able to make it?"

"He promised that he would try."

"That really was sweet of him to donate some of his personal items and to volunteer his time for our family fundraiser."

"Volunteer? He told me that Granddad practically held him hostage and forced him to submit."

"That's Daddy for you. He never was one to let an opportunity pass."

"He could have at least waited until Jack came out of the bathroom before pouncing on him."

"I think Jack handled him like a gentleman," Mama said.

"He probably thinks that we're a family of nutcases."

"And he'd be right." Mama opened the car door and tapped on the horn. "Sherman! Sherman, let's go. Time to go!"

Actually, it was more than a tap. More like a *boooooooommmmmp! bomp-bomp! bomp-bomp-bomp!*

Loud enough so I could see a couple of our neighbors poking their heads out of doors or peeling back window curtains to look, then shaking their heads in silent disapproval.

"Do you want me to go up and get him, Mama?" Anything to stop her from leaning on the horn again.

"No, he'll be out in a minute. She leaned on the horn again. This time, if it was even possible, more obnoxiously. "He can't stand it when I do that."

"He's not the only one," I remarked.

Daddy flung the door open, working his lips at Mama. I couldn't read the words, but I understood the gist. As he approached the car, he said, "You know I hate it when you do that, Doris Jean."

"What?" Mama said innocently, raising her eyebrows. "Oh, you mean this?"

She reached her arm inside the car door again.

"Don't do that again unless you want to draw back a nub."

"You're the boss," she said, casting a glance at me. "Let's get this show on the road."

"We have plenty of time, Doris."

"I'm sure Mama's already there, wondering where we are and how she could have raised such inconsiderate children to keep her waiting."

"I just got off the phone with George. That's what took me so long to get out here. They're just setting out themselves."

"Then let's hurry up and get there before they do, Sherm."

It was a constant battle between them. Mama hated to be late. She would rather arrive at her destination twenty-four hours early than arrive one or two minutes late.

Daddy, on the other hand, hated to be rushed. I think it had something to do with being a roofing contractor. He learned in the early days of his business that if he rushed a job, even at the client's insistence, it usually meant that he wound up with mistakes—mistakes for which he had to eat the costs.

"I'll drive," Daddy offered. He adjusted the seat to accommodate his longer legs. Mama pulled back the seat to let me climb in. Then she took the front seat, rummaging through the glove compartment for the instructions to the recreation center.

He cranked up the engine. " 'Bout time for a tune-up, Doris Jean."

I turned my head, listening for what he was sure he heard. I couldn't tell a thing. I glanced over at Mama. She shrugged and said, "I'll take it in tomorrow morning first thing."

The car had started right away. By the way he'd cocked his head and frowned, I expected to be leaving a trail of clunking car parts down the road.

"No, I'll take care of it. How long has this oil light been on?"

"Is the oil light on?" Mama sounded surprised as she peered over my father's shoulder at the dashboard.

Again, my father's lips moved, but no sound came out of his mouth. It was like watching a ventriloquist's dummy without the ventriloquist to provide the sound.

"You all right back there, Sweet Sherbet?" Daddy called out to me.

The floor was covered with extra bags of ice so I'd swung my legs around and bent my knees. My feet rested on the armrest of the opposite door.

"Just fine, Daddy."

"Good. Now, duck your head down while I back out."

He rested his right arm along the headrest behind my mother while his left hand made tiny adjustments of the steering wheel to back out of our drive.

"You sure you can see, Sherm?" Mama also craned her neck to help keep watch.

"Yes, dear," he replied automatically.

"Watch out for that kid on the bike, Daddy," I pitched in.

"Will you let me do this? I've been driving since long before you were born, little girl."

"Yeah, but it's a lot easier using three-sixty vision when you're sitting on top of a horse, Daddy," I said sweetly.

"Oh, you want to crack on your old man? You hear that, Doris Jean? That's your daughter. Do you want to say something to her about that smart mouth?"

"Shame on you, Shiri. You know perfectly well that your father didn't get his driving practice on a horse," Mama said. She paused dramatically for effect, then said, "Everybody knows that the Model T's provided perfectly good viewing distances way back then."

"Oh, ho! It's going to be like that, then? I knew I should have ridden with Bailey and Sean. Let me slow down to about forty so you two can jump out."

"Daddy, you wouldn't put us out."

"Say I won't, when I will."

"We love you, Daddy!" I sang out, leaned forward, and kissed him right in the center of his bald spot.

"I love you, too, Sweet Sherbet." He reached behind his head and patted my cheek. "Say, what time is that beau of yours coming to the outing?"

"Beau? Daddy, no one says beau anymore."

"Your father does," Mama said.

"What do you call him, then?" Daddy asked.

"He's just a friend, Daddy."

"A friend, huh?"

"Uh-huh."

"A real friend would have gotten you home sooner than three o'clock in the morning, Shiri."

I glanced at Mama. She cleared her throat delicately and touched her neck. I didn't have to guess that she was talking about my hickey.

"He said that he had some things to take care of this morning, but he would be there as soon as he could."

"He'll probably be there waiting for us when we get there," Mama predicted.

I had my doubts. After the way I'd left him high and dry, I didn't think he'd be in too much of a hurry to see me again.

"How do you know?" I asked.

She smiled back at me; her eyes were warm and kind. "Call it mother's intuition."

I've got a bad feeling about this.

I'd heard that line in a movie once. The hero had ventured out, far away from home (in a galaxy far, far, far away, I think) on a foolish quest to rescue the damsel in distress. As the hero and his band of loyal followers willingly went into what he knew had to be a trap, he mustered his courage and proceeded, despite the overwhelming odds.

That's how I felt as I pulled up next to the pavilion where Shiri's family had gathered. Completely overwhelmed. I was walking openly, willingly into a trap. A very cleverly disguised trap, but a trap all the same. They were going to suck me in. Me. Jack Deneen, Lone Wolf, was about to willingly volunteer to become part of the pack.

I wasn't fooled by the pleasant surroundings. A huge awning was decorated with balloons, and streamers fluttered in the strong, spring breeze. Music blared from four-foot-high speakers. Hordes of running, screaming children playing freeze tag darted around the pavilion. Even the table laden with every artery-clogging entrée I could think of shouted at me to beware.

I stood by my SUV for a minute, taking it all in. There were more relatives here today than there had been at the anniversary dinner the night before. I thought I recognized a few faces, but few of the names came to mind. Maybe it just seemed like more of them, now that they were all spread out—not restrained by the confines of the restaurant.

"Yo! Booger picker!"

The thirteen-year-old who'd nearly busted a gut laughing at Brittany's predicament last night shouted at me from across the field. What was that kid's name? Baal? No, that wasn't it, as much as I'd like to believe that he was the spawn of Satan. His name was Jamaal. That was it.

His arm heaved forward and launched a football at me. He had amazing distance. One of these days, he was going to make some college football coach proud. If only he could have done something about that aim. The ball arched high over everyone's heads, then came plummeting down again. Its target: an invisible bull's-eye in the middle of my windshield.

Instinct made me reach out. The ball slapped against my outstretched palm. I didn't give myself time to think or bobble the ball. I squeezed my fingers, palming the pigskin, not unlike a basketball player palms a basketball. I snapped my arm against my chest and counted myself lucky that the sun wasn't in my eyes.

I tossed the ball back to him. "Here you go, little man."

A spontaneous round of applause broke out. Playing to

the crowd, I gave a mock bow. "Thank you. Thank you very much." Elvis couldn't have said it better himself.

"Can anyone tell me where Shiri Rowlan is?" I called out to the nearest relative.

"Shiri? I think she's under the big tent, setting up for the auction."

"Thanks."

I slung my bag filled with two signed jerseys, a football, and a stack of fresh-off-the-press program booklets over my shoulder. I shook a few more hands, then headed for the tent.

As I approached it, I saw Shiri on the far side. Her back was to me—which was all right with me. I was rather enjoying the view.

She reached up high above her head, trying to catch a runaway stack of paper plates sent airborne by the huge fan circulating under the tent. She wore a pair of lime-green, hip-hugger shorts that clung to the curves of her round bottom so closely, it made me jealous of the material. Along with many of her relatives, she wore a purple T-shirt bearing the words JOHNSON FAMILY REUNION in script and circling a silhouette of a large oak tree. Her flair for making a fashion statement made her stand out from the rest of the crowd. A silk, floral scarf that picked up the color of her shirt, shorts, and the highlights in her hair added the perfect touch to her outfit.

Someone tapped her on the shoulder—her cousin Brenda, I think it was—and pointed her out to me.

"Hey!" Shiri called out, waving to me. She pushed a handmade, crocheted quilt into Brenda's hands, sidestepped a baby stroller pushed suddenly into her path by a child barely walking herself, and batted at a balloon that had whipped free from its streamer.

"You made it," she said breathlessly.

Secretly, I wished that it was the sight of me that had caused the flush in her cheeks and not the virtual obstacle course she'd just traversed to make it to my side.

"I said I would," I reminded her.

"I know," she said, looking up at me. And in doing so, the scarf around her neck shifted a bit. Fashion and function. I resisted the urge to trace the purplish passion mark peeking out from the bottom of her scarf.

"Did I do that?" I whispered. My hand involuntary reached up to adjust the scarf.

"No, I was attacked by leeches," she retorted, then softened her tone. "But that's all right. It's making everyone curious about me. Thanks for coming out, Jack. I know this is a busy time of year for you, with your first game of the season coming up and all of your practices and stuff."

Anything for you, Shiri, I wanted to tell her, but not under the watchful gaze of her relatives. I knew that she was being especially cordial, and equally as cool, for their sake.

I followed suit, keeping my hands firmly in plain sight. "Not a problem, really. I'm glad I could help."

We stood for several seconds without speaking, letting our expressions tell each other what we were too cautious to say out loud. When the silence grew long enough to attract attention, I cleared my throat and coughed delicately to remind her that we were about as unobserved as bugs under a magnifying glass.

"So." She drew out the word as she tucked her hands into her back pockets. "What did you bring?"

"Oh, a few things. Some T-shirts, a few program booklets. Stuff like that."

"Cool! Come on, you can lay them out over here."

I followed her to the auction table. The handmade, crocheted comforter was one of several retail-quality craft items that would be auctioned off to help raise money for Shiri's family reunion.

"Wow." I whistled under my breath. Impressive. The craftsmanship of the collection of rag dolls, lace doilies, and pottery made me believe that there was plenty of creative energy and talent within Shiri's family. A lot of time, effort, and love had gone into the making of those items.

For a moment, I felt uncomfortable. All I'd done was grab some things out of my closet, collect a few printer overruns, then scrawl my signature. In comparison to the devotion her family members had put into these craft items, where was the value in what I'd done?

I felt a little better when I saw a food processor, still in its original packing, among all of the handmade items. As I continued down the table, a collection of hunting knives caught my eye. I lifted one of the blades, pulled it from its sheath, and admired its workmanship. Sunlight glinted off the blade as I moved it back and forth in the air.

"Who are you supposed to be, Jim Bowie?" Shiri teased.

"Say, how can a brother get in on this action?" I asked.

"It's an auction," she said slowly, as if pointing out the obvious. "Did you bring your wallet?"

I couldn't help teasing her in turn for that Jim Bowie crack. So I patted my back pocket. My meaning was perfectly clear. It had the effect I wanted. Shiri colored quite nicely, then lowered her eyes.

"Do you take credit cards?" I asked.

"What do you think this is? Macy's? All transactions are cash or check only. And we'll need two forms of identification for all checks over ten dollars."

"Boy, you Johnsons are tough."

"We have to be. We have a lot of expenses if we want to make the next reunion a success. We're raising money to cover reunion costs, set up a college scholarship, and leave enough money left over for the next reunion committee to have some seed money to start off with." She ticked off the items on each finger as if she were noting a grocery list. "We take our family reunions very seriously. So, if I seem a little avaricious, don't take it personally. It's only business." She patted my cheek, à la Al Pacino in any number of his gangster movies.

Patting my cheek was the only physical contact that Shiri would allow me while we were gathered in front of her relatives today—a considerable change in her behavior since the party. She'd been very willing for me to demonstrate my affection for her then.

In fact, she'd seemed to welcome my less-than-casual

touches throughout dinner. It had been as if she wore me on her arm like a charm, a prize to be displayed before all of her gawking relatives.

The mood certainly had changed. Now, she would barely allow me within a foot of her invisible boundary of personal space. It was too dangerous to go any further, like holding hands or a casual, friendly hug. Anything more would reignite the passion she'd doused when she'd left me cooling in the shadows of her parents' gazebo.

"You hungry?" she asked.

She must have read my mind. But it wasn't food that I wanted. My soul needed sustenance. I needed to take her in. All of her. I wondered if there was a way that I could convey those feelings to her without sending her running to the safety and security of her parents.

"Sure."

"We've got tons of food over here. Enough to feed a small nation."

"Did you cook any of it?"

"I'm on the fund-raising committee," she said.

"That means no," I translated. "Can you cook?"

"When I have to."

"And when is that?"

"When my credit card is maxed out, I've run out of checks, and it's after hours for the restaurants that deliver," she said without one iota of shame.

"Pitiful." I shook my head and *tsked-tsked*. "I guess this means that a brother could starve to death waiting on a home-cooked meal from you, then."

"A brother had better learn how to dial for Domino's Pizza," Shiri replied. She stopped and surveyed the spread laid out on the row of tables. "Or make frequent trips to my grandmother's house. You'll always have plenty to eat there."

The way she said it gave me a small ray of hope. I'd always have plenty to eat there. *Always.* She expected me to be there. She wanted me there. She wanted me. Maybe I was reaching, searching for a secret coded message in the

seemingly innocent conversation. Let me stretch. I needed
the exercise anyway.

She started at one end of the first food table and picked up
a foam plate and plastic utensils prewrapped in a decorative
napkin.

"Try some of this." She ladled a more-than-generous
portion of potato salad onto my plate. From the weight of
the salad as it hit my plate, I had a feeling that it was going
to sit just as heavy at the bottom of my stomach. This wasn't
a pureed or reconstituted mashed-potato-flake-made salad.
This was the real deal. Huge chunks of potatoes, egg, onion,
and pimento were held together with real mayonnaise, mus-
tard, and a secret ingredient. On the recipe card in front of
the dish, it actually stated, *Secret ingredient to be taken to
my grave.*

"My Aunt Pam's recipe," Shiri noted. "Personally, I
think she went a little heavy on the pimento. It's still very,
very good."

"Sounds like you've sampled some of the wares."

"Not some—all. I personally sampled every last dish on
this table. It was a tough job; but I take my duties as chairman
of the fund-raising committee very seriously."

"What has the fund-raising committee to do with food-
tasting?"

"Somebody has to make sure that the food is delectable,
or, at the very least, edible. All of these recipes will go into
a booklet that we'll sell at the family reunion. If the food's
no good, folks will remember that and won't buy the recipe
book next time. There goes our revenue."

She ushered me further down the line. "Now, here is a
grilled chicken dish that will make the old Colonel himself
jealous. I think this is my uncle Andre's recipe. Tender,
juicy. Careful when you pick it up. The meat just falls off
the bone."

By the time we'd reached the end of the first table, my
plate was nearly buckling under the weight.

"There's no way I'm going to eat all of this at one sitting,
Shiri," I warned her.

"Pace yourself," she said. "We haven't passed the dessert table yet."

She handed me a huge Dixie cup filled with mixed punch of indeterminate flavor. It was purple, as if that could be a flavor. As we searched for a seat, I took a sip. Whoa! It was sweet enough to send me into a diabetic coma. Even the pulp from sliced lemons, oranges, and limes floating in the liquid couldn't disguise the pound of sugar that had probably gone into the concoction.

"You may want to cut this," I suggested, swallowing hard to get the taste down.

"More ice, Bren!" she called out to her cousin and pointed to the huge yellow-and-red cooler. Making the punch was a carefully coordinated production. Someone stood on top of a bench, alternately pouring sugar and ice into the cooler. Another person mixed with a long, metal spoon, while a third set cups of punch out on the table for people to grab as needed.

Shiri grabbed a cup of ice and shook a little into my cup. Some of the liquid spilled over my hand and soaked the slices of homemade potato bread Shiri had dropped, with a flourish, onto my plate, saying, "My grandma always said, eat more bread. It'll fill you up. I think that was her way of making food stretch for all of us."

We had just found a seat on the outskirts of the pavilion when Shiri's grandfather stood up at a makeshift podium.

"All right, everybody, quiet down. May I have your attention, please?"

He banged a wooden spoon until it cracked. One piece flew off into the air. Yet the conversation continued around him until Mrs. Johnson stood up with a microphone.

She tapped it. "Is this thing on? Is this thing on?"

A squeal of feedback and a burst of static from the speakers got everyone's attention.

Mr. Johnson knelt down to adjust the speakers' volume control.

"Oh, goodness. That's better," Mrs. Johnson said, pressing her finger to her ear. "I want to thank everyone for coming out here today. It's so good to see so many new faces. How are you doing, sweetheart?''

She waved and blew a kiss to a young mother with a cooing, waving child in her lap.

''George and I also want to thank you for all of the lovely presents last night.''

''I don't know what we've done to deserve it, but the Lord has certainly blessed our family.'' Mr. Johnson also clasped his hand around the microphone and leaned to speak into it. ''Let's take a moment now to join hands, bow our heads, while we thank Him for what he's brought to this family and what, I know, He'll continue to bring us through.''

Shiri reached out and took my hand in hers without hesitation. She looked over her shoulder and took the hand of another relative.

The prayer lasted only a moment, but I could tell the relatives were starting to get restless. Many had come a long way to be here today and didn't relish the trip back. It was time to cram as much fun into the time remaining. They wanted to start the party. They wanted to get the auction going.

I originally had my eye on that collection of carving knives and was determined not to be outbid. But a four-foot woman with eyes of cold steel stared me down. Once the bidding started, she called my bluff.

''Sold! Come on up here, Annie Mae, and get your Ginsu knives.''

When she ran up to collect her merchandise, she practically gloated and stuck her tongue out at me in passing.

''Be nice, Auntie.'' Shiri laughed. ''Nobody likes a sore winner.''

The auction went on for about an hour. Merchandise, money, and mayhem all exchanged hands. There was so much going on around me, I couldn't keep track of it all. Shiri did what she could to keep me informed. But she had her own responsibilities, helping this fund-raiser run smoothly.

"And now," Mr. Johnson said dramatically. "The moment we've all been waiting for . . . Somebody give me a drumroll, please."

Tables rattled as Shiri's relatives pounded on their tablestops and stomped their feet to give the effect he wanted.

"I want to welcome a special guest here today. Let's give a handclap of praise to one of Birmingham's finest—Jack The Flash Deneen! Come on up here, son."

I pointed to myself and mouthed, "Me?"

"Yes, you," Mr. Johnson insisted. "Don't be shy. Come on up here; let us see your goods."

Someone from the crowd whistled. It think it was Shiri. When I looked back over my shoulder, she was standing at the rear of the tent with her thumb and middle finger poised above her lips.

As I approached the podium, I started to reach behind Mr. Johnson. My intention was to start the auction of my items with a T-shirt. But Shiri's grandfather spun me around to face the crowd and patted my shoulder with wide, exaggerated motions. "Fine, fine, young man. All right, all of you unmarried ladies out there, who's going to start the bidding?"

Did I misunderstand him? Had I heard him correctly? It sounded like . . . no! I couldn't have heard what I thought I heard. It sounded as if he was going to put me on the auction block.

Panicked, I looked over at Shiri. Her eyes had grown to the size of saucers. Her hands were clamped over her mouth— whether in shock or to stifle her laughter, I couldn't be sure.

"Did you know about this?" I mouthed to her.

She shook her head, lifting her hands in innocent protest, but she was laughing openly now, holding her stomach and hanging on to her cousin for support. If this was some sort of practical joke, I wasn't getting it. I wasn't getting it because *I was it.*

I turned to Mr. Johnson, reaching for the microphone. "Wait. I think there's been a mistake. I'm not—"

"Getting any younger," Mr. Johnson glibly ad-libbed as

he jerked the microphone out of my grasp. "I need a bid, folks. What's it going to be for this Steeldog?"

"Ten dollars!" a cry rose up from the corner of the room.

"Ten dollars? Oh, please, don't insult our guest. Ten bucks wouldn't buy you his sweat socks. I know you can do better than that."

"Twenty dollars," came the counterbid. It was Shiri's cousin Essence enthusiastically waving two bills in the air.

"Twenty? Now you're hurting *my* feelings. I'm not doing my job as a preacher if I can't sell you on one of God's wonders of the world!"

He slapped me soundly on the back again. "But twenty's the bid. Who'll give me twenty-five? Twenty-five, anyone?"

"Twenty-five dollars and fifty cents!" Shiri stood up and tossed a couple of quarters to Essence.

"You're not helping me," I called out to Shiri. She smiled sweetly and shrugged.

"Thirty dollars!" Another offer on the table.

"Forty-five."

"Fifty!"

The bids flew back and forth across the room like volleys of ammunition.

"Hold on a minute, now. Let me make this official. The bid is fifty. Fifty. Fifty. Fifty. Do I hear sixty? Sixty? No? What about fifty-five?" Mr. Johnson's voice was rapid, staccato, hypnotic in its rhythm.

"Fifty-one dollars and seventy cents."

"Chump change," Mr. Johnson scoffed. "Lift up your arm, boy."

He grabbed my elbow. "These ladies obviously don't appreciate a real he-man when they see one. Why don't you flex a little for the ladies?"

There was no getting out of it. I was up there. I was for sale. If I didn't want to go down for an embarrassing fifty-one dollars and some change, I'd better do something to sweeten the pot.

Without giving myself time to talk myself out of it, I reached for the hem of my shirt and pulled it over my head.

The cry that went up in response brought a grin to Mr. Johnson's face. "One hundred dollars!"

"Now, that's what I'm talking about, son." He congratulated me on my quick thinking. "For one hundred dollars, you can have the shirt," he said, tossing it toward the woman who'd made the last bid.

She reached up to snatch it out of the air, but was elbowed by the woman with the Ginsu knives.

"One hundred. One hundred. Can I get a one-fifty? Lawdy, somebody give me one hundred and fifty dollars for this man."

"One hundred fifty."

"Two hundred!"

"Two twenty-five."

"Two hundred and fifty dollars."

"You people are nickel-and-diming me to death. Come on, now. This man is a local celebrity. I bet if he said he could wrangle a date with Denzel that you'd get off the dollar."

"Ooh, Denzel! Make it three hundred dollars!"

The bidding went on for several more minutes between a group at Shiri's table and another group of women across the room—all ranging in age from teen to twilight years.

By the time Mr. Johnson banged his makeshift gavel and yelled, "Sold!" my bidding price had practically doubled the amount they'd gotten for the previously auctioned items.

"Come up here and claim your prize."

I looked questioningly at Mr. Johnson. Just what was it exactly they were supposed to get? Not one word was spoken of T-shirts, program booklets, or autographed footballs. As far as getting them a date with Denzel Washington, I'd probably have better luck getting one with George Washington.

I made a mental note to visit Mr. Johnson's church. He must be quite a persuasive pastor. If he devoted as much passion to selling his congregation on the benefits of heavenly treasure as he did to convincing this crowd to part with their money for momentary, earthly pleasure, I imagined that his entire flock would be heaven-bound.

"Claim their prize? And just what would that be, Mr. Johnson?" I asked. What had he planned on delivering for his enthusiastic auctioning abilities?

"Just give each of the gals a hug and a smooch on the cheek," he muttered out of the corner of his mouth.

I looked over at Shiri, but Mr. Johnson grabbed my chin and turned my attention back to the women rushing up to the podium.

"Don't worry about Shiri, son. It's all for a good cause. She'll understand."

Understanding was one thing, since it was for a good cause and all. But liking was a different matter altogether. Things were still too new between Shiri and me to assume that her fledgling feelings could withstand competition. Even worse, competition from her relatives.

I know that I'd be concerned if a group of men surrounded her, ogled her—expected her to give something up to each of them. As well-intentioned as Mr. Johnson was, I wasn't going to risk alienating Shiri. Not even for the sake of the almighty dollar.

As the first young lady stepped up to me, I reached for a T-shirt and cordially shook her hand.

FOURTEEN

"Stop that!" Mama slapped my hand away as I reached to pinch off one of the apple crumb cakes that she'd left cooling on the baking rack. "Those are for the meeting."

"I can't help it, Mama. They smell *soooo* good."

With my elbows on the counter, I stuck my face over the pan of pastries. The light steam rose, swirled around my face, and tickled my nostrils. Those pastries had my name all over them.

I cupped my hand to my ear. "What did you say, little pastry? You say that you're all alone? I'll save you. I've got a special home for you right in the middle of my stomach. Plenty of room for you." My fingers reached for a golden, sticky-sweet corner.

"Don't even think about it," Mama warned. Her back was turned to me, so it was a mystery how she knew what I was doing. One day, I was going to pull her hair back, search for the eyes in the back of her head, and poke them out Three Stooges style. You'd think that after all of these years, those eyes in the back of her head would need bifocals. But not today. They were as sharp as ever.

"But, Mama. They're calling my name. You always told me that it was rude not to answer when someone called."

"Unless your name is 'extra unwanted pounds,' you'd better stop snacking between meals, Shiri. Here, this should hold you until Karen and Pamela get here." She tossed me a granny smith apple.

"It's not the same," I grumbled as I peeled off the produce sticker and rinsed the apple at the kitchen sink before biting into it.

"Maybe not. But it's better for you."

"Let me think about that. Sweet, golden, crumbly buttered coffee cake on one hand. Hard, crunchy, pesticide-covered apple on the other hand. Pound-adding. Poisonous. Poisonous. Pound-adding."

I moved my hands up and down as if weighing the options. "I'm sorry, Mama, but the cake is the definitive winner. The scales don't lie."

"Speaking of scales, what are yours tipping at these days?" Mama raised an eyebrow at me.

"One thirty-five," I said promptly. "But I don't believe them. They lie. They lie. They lie like a rug."

"Shiri," Mama began, then paused as if carefully considering her words. "Baby, I'm not trying to pick on you or hurt your feelings. You're a beautiful, intelligent, successful young woman."

"Oh, I bet you say that to all of your daughters," I teased, since I was her only daughter.

"And it's not about size. If you're a size sixteen, then be a size sixteen. But be a healthy, sensible size sixteen. Do you understand what I'm trying to say to you?"

"I get it, Mama. See?" I took another bite, exaggerating my chewing. Chomp, chomp, chomp. Gulp. Down it went.

"Not that I'm trying to run your life. I'm just making a suggestion. When you get to work, take some fruits and nuts with you."

"As if I don't have enough of those around me at work already," I replied, deliberately making a funny face to make her smile.

She went on with hardly a break. I guess I needed to work on my comedic timing.

"Uh. Yeah. Well, keep the kind that you can eat in a bowl on your desk. The next time you feel like making a trip to the snack machine, reach for an apple instead."

"If I don't make snack-food runs, how else am I going to get my exercise?"

"With all of that extra fiber in your system, trust me, you'll have plenty of opportunities to make a run."

"Great. That's all I need for a great reputation at work is to stink up the ladies' rest room every day."

"Twice a day if you're eating right," Mama quipped.

I sighed and leaned on the counter again. "When are they supposed to be here?"

"Soon."

I waited a full minute before asking, "Are they here yet?"

"No."

Another minute ticked by. "Are they here yet?"

"No, Shiri."

This time, less than a minute before asking, "Are they here yet?"

Laughing as hard as I was at her expression, I barely missed the wooden spoon she swung at my head.

I ducked, but she swung again.

"Girl, are you trying to work on my last nerve?"

"I've got a lot of time to make up for," I said. "Being away so much, I don't get these rare opportunities to remind you why you and Daddy worked so hard to get me through school and out of the house." I planted a wet, sloppy kiss on her cheek.

Mama made a grand display of wiping it off with a dishtowel.

"You were just here last weekend for your grandparents' anniversary. If I'd known you'd come back so soon, we would have worked triple jobs to get you into a school further away from home."

"You know you miss me, Mama," I said, wrapping my

arms around her ample waist, rocking back and forth until she squawked.

"Of course I miss you. That's why I asked you to help with the reunion planning. If me and your father couldn't get you to come back on your own, maybe the power of the whole family behind us could get you to come back. So, why don't you make sure that everything is set up in the family room before Karen and Pammie get here?"

"Are you trying to get rid of me?" I asked in mock hurt.

"Now, whatever gave you that idea?" she asked as she shoved me toward the door.

"If you wanted to get rid of me, all you had to do was to start talking about the weather." I raised my eyebrows at her, à la Groucho Marx. I wanted her to know that I wasn't fooled by their little tête-à-tête in the restaurant bathroom with Aunt Karen, Aunt Pam, and Grandma Lela.

Mama opened her mouth as if to protest. She knew better than to try to deny it since it was obvious that I was on to her. She didn't get the chance to. The doorbell rang, saving her from trying to deny that they'd been talking about us cousins.

"Are they here yet?" I asked, barely managing to keep a straight face.

"No. It's Ed McMahon with my Publishers Clearing House multimillion-dollar check. Of course it's them."

"It sure took them long enough. It isn't as if you ladies don't all live within a stone's throw of Grandma Lela's."

As I headed for the door, I asked, "Did you ever think about moving out of Birmingham, Mama?"

"What for?" she asked, trailing behind me. "Everything I needed, ever wanted is right here."

Shrugging, I tried to make her understand. "I don't know. Travel, see the world, find out what life's like outside the city limits. You and Aunt Karen and Aunt Pam were raised here. I'm sure you've seen everything there is to see. When you were old enough to be on your own, why didn't you move away like me, Bren, and Essence?"

"When our wandering foot gets to itchin', we pick up

and go," Mama said defensively. "Me and your aunts and
sometimes your grandparents get in the car and drive until
the itch is satisfied."

"There's so much more out there," I protested. "Places
you can't get to in a day or a weekend drive."

"Yes, there's more out there," Mama echoed. "And
they're standing on the front porch waiting to be let in.
Don't keep your aunts waiting, Shiri. Besides, didn't you
ever see that movie *The Wizard of Oz?*"

"Ooh. I'm telling Aunt Karen and Aunt Pam that you've
called them wicked witches!" I said, deliberately misunder-
standing her.

"I did not! You stop playing around and open that door."

I flung the door open and welcomed my aunts' warm
greeting with open arms and kisses of affection. Brenda
stood behind them, grinning at me and waving one of Jack's
autographed T-shirts in my face. I reached for it, but she
held it high out of my reach.

"Where's Essence?" I asked, trying to hide the disappointment in my voice. I was hoping to see her before taking
off again for Jackson.

"She couldn't make it for this meeting," Brenda told me.
"She said that she'd try to be here for the next one. She
didn't say much, you know how Essence is, but I think Miss
Sadie's not doing well."

"Oh, I'm sorry to hear that," I murmured.

"Come on in, ladies," Mama said, ushering Brenda and
my aunts inside. "Let's not put Essence's business out in
the street. Shiri, make sure that you call Essence and see if
she needs anything, or if there's anything we can do to help
out."

"Yes, Mama. But you know how she is. So independent.
Miss Carry-the-world-on-her-shoulders."

"Just like her mother," Aunt Karen remarked. "She'd
work herself to death before accepting charity."

"It's a crying shame that she had to work herself sick,"
Aunt Pam added. "She wouldn't have to work so hard if
Essence's no-good father would lift a finger to help."

"How do you know he's no good?" Brenda asked, breaking the cardinal rule of interrupting their conversation. You never did that. Not only was it considered rude, but you didn't find out any good gossip that way.

"Had to be a no-good, trifling son of a so-and-so," Aunt Pam went on. "Otherwise, he'd be there to help out."

"If help comes from you and Brenda, it won't be so hard for her to accept," Mama said, quickly changing the subject.

"Come on in, ladies," Mama said. "We're meeting in the family room."

Aunt Pam sniffed the air. "Doris Jean, I know that isn't your world-famous, pound-adding, make-you-want-to-reach-around-and-slap-your-mama apple crumb cake I smell baking in there."

"It sure is." Mama laughed "You'd better be glad that you showed up when you did, Pammie. Shiri was just about to eat it all."

"Not all," I contradicted. "Just most of it."

"Go into the family room. I'll be back in a minute with cake and coffee."

"Need some help in the kitchen, Aunt Doris?" Brenda called out.

"Suck-up," I muttered out of the corner of my mouth. She smirked at me as she took a seat on the divan.

"No, I've got it, honey. But thank you for offering."

Mama returned, setting down a silver platter with a carafe of coffee and the "good china"—plates and cups, silver server, cream, and sugar bowls.

"Why don't you give me that coffee cake recipe, Doris?" Aunt Karen asked, reaching for the wedge-shaped dessert server.

"I thought I gave you the recipe already."

"You must have left out an ingredient or instruction or something. It didn't come out quite right," Aunt Karen complained.

"Tell the truth and shame the devil, Karen. It came out like a brick. I broke a cap biting into it," Aunt Pam insisted.

"Sat in the dentist's office for thirty minutes in agony while I waited to be treated."

Mama glared at Aunt Pam. "Be nice, Pammie. Not in front of the girls."

"Oh, don't mind us," Brenda said, scooting to the edge of her seat and leaning forward into the conversation. "This is just getting good."

"You certainly are getting mean in your old age, Pammie," Karen said, pouring herself a cup of aromatic coffee.

"I am not getting mean. Doris was always the mean one. It wouldn't surprise me if she made a switch in the recipe on purpose to keep the secret. Something like two cups of plaster instead of flour. Yes, that would be just like her."

"I was not the mean one," Mama protested, stirring cream into her coffee and taking a sip.

"Yes, you were. You were the mean one. I was the gifted one. Pam was the smart one," Aunt Karen insisted.

"I thought I was the gifted one." Aunt Pam sounded wounded.

"You're both wrong. I was the smart one *and* the gifted one," Mama corrected them all.

"Nuh-uh," Aunt Pam said adamantly. "I was. And I was Aunt Rosie's favorite, too. She told me so."

I bit into my cake to keep from laughing out loud. Aunt Rosie had a pretty good scam working. As long as we were all her favorites, we would all bend over backward trying to please her.

"Are we ready to start?" Mama asked. "Let's join hands and bow our heads. Karen, would you lead us in prayer?"

I clasped hands with Brenda on one side and Aunt Pam on the other. We all had our heads bowed dutifully, but not before I sneaked a peek at everyone's solemn expressions. All kidding was aside now. As soon as the last echoes faded from the "amen" in unison, I knew the banter would return—the rapid-fire jabs and sibling one-upmanship. If ever I'd wondered where I'd gotten my acerbic tongue, the doubts were erased in the presence of my aunts. My wit had been carefully honed by these three Johnson sisters.

But for now, there was no sarcasm, no silliness. Giving thanks was serious business. And this sprawling family had much to be thankful for. We had all gone our separate ways—some paths keeping us closer to home than others. But one thing was certain. My aunts and uncles had done their share to make certain that my path was always a secure one.

As I grew older and ventured out on my own, I experimented. I tested. I tried their collective patience. But when I fell, someone was always there to help set me on my feet again. Sometimes with a gentle nudge in the right direction; sometimes with a figurative kick to the seat of the pants to get me going.

As Aunt Karen continued to pray, punctuated with a fervent "yes, Lord," or "help us, Lord," from Mama and Aunt Pam, I felt a shiver run through me. Brenda squeezed my hand. She must have felt it, too. She turned her head toward me and smiled. I could have sworn that there were tears in her eyes.

I wouldn't be surprised. A lump that had nothing to do with the apple crumb cake formed in my throat as well. Something about my aunt's voice brought to mind a flood of memories. And I wondered . . . how many times had my family prayed that same prayer of guidance over us?

Late at night, when we were all tucked safely in our beds or going about our day-to-day business, how many times had their prayers gone up to cover us? How many disasters had we averted due to their diligence?

The love that spanned generations was evident in my aunt's plea for continued strength and guidance. I used to wonder where it all came from—the patience, the wisdom, the humor it took to raise us.

This third generation of Johnson children certainly did our best to try to use it all up. If we'd truly known that their strength was divinely derived, I don't think we would have tried so hard to irk them. Backed by legions of warrior angels, our mothers and fathers, aunts and uncles, cousins and extended family kept us on the straight and narrow—

sometimes dragging us kicking and screaming, but inching along just the same.

"Amen," I echoed at the close of Aunt Karen's prayer.

"Shiri." Mama's voice was oddly subdued and a little trembly. "Read back the minutes from the last meeting."

I nodded, because I didn't trust my own voice yet. Placed my portable computer on my lap.

"Okay, let me see. Old business meeting notes. We settled on how many committees we're going to create to help with the planning. Seven committees in all including budget and finance, correspondence, family history, food, programs, reunion site hospitality, and transportation."

"You missed one," Mama noted. "Remember, Uncle Curtis suggested we create a first-aid committee."

"I might have know that Scrape-a-day would suggest something like that," Aunt Pam said, reaching for another slice of coffeecake.

"Scrape-a-day?" Brenda and I questioned in unison.

"That's what we used to call your uncle Curtis from the time he was about seven years old. He couldn't get through the day without falling down, bumping into something, or otherwise injuring himself."

"Okay, adding first-aid committee to the list." My fingers flew over the keyboard. "We also roughed out a budget and mailed out reunion questionnaire surveys."

"I've already started to receive some responses back." Aunt Karen pulled out an expanding file folder. "Out of three hundred surveys that we sent out, we've gotten sixty or so back. Looks like our folks are showing a preference for Orlando over Nashville."

"Sixty responses back already. That's not bad. Up from last year. Remember how we had to beg and plead to get those surveys back?" Mama reminded them.

"Almost everyone is up on e-mail now," Brenda said. "When we put pictures from our last reunion out on that Web page that Uncle Andre created, that generated a lot of excitement."

"I'll send out another e-mail in a week or so to remind

everyone to get those surveys back so we can really make some headway in the planning." Aunt Pam made a note to herself and I added that information to the action items section of the meeting notes.

"Last but certainly not least of old business, Aunt Pam, Aunt Karen, and Mama opened the checking account at First National so we can start to deposit funds. We can add $2,163.14 raised at the auction last week."

That drew a round of applause from all of us.

"Thanks to a certain Mr. Deneen," Brenda said, holding up the shirt she'd bought. "That was very nice of him to volunteer his . . . uh . . . services."

"Yes. Yes, it was," I said stiffly.

"I hope you thanked the nice man for his effort, Shiri," Aunt Pam teased. "Because of him, we've got a good chunk of seed money to start this reunion planning off right. You know how our folks hate for us to beg for money. Now, we don't have to beg as long or for as much."

I cleared my throat delicately. "If I run into him again, I'll be sure to pass along your sentiments."

"If?" Brenda picked up on my uncertainty. "What do you mean, if?"

"If means if. As in maybe. As in I don't know."

"You're joking, right, Shiri? You must have plans to see him again." Brenda grabbed my hand and squeezed.

"Why are you making such a big deal out of this? I didn't have plans to meet him the first time. Or the second time. That was all your doing," I said, pinning each aunt with a stare. "You are the ones who set me up."

"Are you complaining?" Aunt Karen wanted to know. "Because if you are, I know a couple of your cousins who'd jump at the chance at being set up with such a fine figure of a man."

"She's not complaining," Brenda said, throwing the T-shirt at me. "She's just mad because she didn't think of the idea herself."

"Stop teasing Shiri." Mama came to my defense. "She has a lot on her mind these days, without us meddling."

"Meddling?" Aunt Karen and Aunt Pam protested. They looked at her as if she'd turned traitor.

"*Humph.* Noboby mentioned meddling when a certain someone introduced that sweet little girl from the Botanical Society to Papa's brother's wife's youngest cousin. I won't mention any names." Aunt Pam pursed her lips and stared directly at Mama.

"Her name was Linda," Mama said coolly. "Did you know that she's already expecting? They say it's going to be twins."

"I should have known. I've been dreaming about schools of fish lately," Aunt Karen insisted.

I covered my eyes with my hands. My family. Had to love 'em.

That's how it went for the entire meeting—the back-and-forth teasing. And somehow, in the midst of it all, we moved the family reunion planning just a little bit further along.

By the end of the meeting, I was exhausted. My typing fingers had blisters on top of blisters. When I remarked on that to Brenda, she huffed, then rolled her eyes at me. I recognized that look. She wasn't teasing anymore. There was something on her mind.

"What?" I mouthed to her, shrugging.

"Nothing," she replied in a tone that I knew meant anything but that. Something in her voice caught my mother's attention. She looked questioningly at us.

"Let me take care of these for you, Aunt Doris," Brenda said quickly and gathered up the dessert dishes.

"Thank you, sweetie," Mama said. She glanced over at me, not-so-subtly tilting her head to indicate that I should follow Brenda. I gathered the coffee carafe and cups.

"All right, Bren," I challenged as soon as we were out of hearing. "What's up?"

"I told you. Nothing's the matter."

"I don't believe you."

She whirled around to face me. Her mouth was a tight line. "And I don't believe you, Shiri!"

"What did I do?" I exclaimed. My mind raced back over

the events of the meeting, trying to figure out what I could have said or done to make her angry with me. I know that I'd grabbed the last piece of crumb cake, but she'd insisted that I take it.

"Nothing," she repeated.

"I swear, Bren, if you say that one more time, you're gonna be wearing the last of this coffee," I warned.

She shook her head, her face an odd mixture of humor and disapproval. Carefully, she set the dishes into the sink. I moved next to her, wrapping my arm around her shoulder.

"No, don't try to make up with me," she said, hitching her shoulder to move me aside. "I'm mad at you."

"Why?"

"Because of what you're doing to Jack."

"And that is?" I prompted.

Brenda formed her lips to say "nothing" but changed her mind. "What did he do to make you want to blow him off?"

Now it was my turn to say the favorite word for the afternoon. "Nothing," I murmured.

Brenda stifled a giggle. "Then what you're doing doesn't make any sense. You should count your blessings, girl. Without even trying, you've managed to find a man like Jack. A man any girl would kill for. Why are you passing up on a perfectly good man?"

"Of course you would say that. You've only seen what you've wanted to see. You've only seen him at his best—charming, handsome, and generous."

"Have you seen him any other way?" Brenda asked. "Has he ever been anything but the perfect gentleman to you?"

"No . . ." I admitted slowly.

"So, what's the problem?"

She had a point. The longer that I thought about it, the more I realized that's all he'd ever shown me, as well. He wanted me, was giving me his best. And until he showed me otherwise, I should take it. Take a chance.

"I should call him," I murmured.

"You've got that right," Brenda urged. She reached for the wall phone and extended the receiver to me. "What's the number? I'll dial it myself before you chicken out." Her finger was poised over the buttons.

"He's probably not home," I said, making up an excuse.

"Then leave a message. I'll bet you he'll call back."

"I can't call him. What if Mama or the aunts walk in?"

"I'll keep watch on the door. You're running out of excuses, Shiri. Keep jacking around and you'll lose that man. No pun intended."

"All right, all right." I gave in.

So, even though I had misgivings I called him—with Brenda standing right there, staring me dead in my mouth.

I kept it vague, loose, giving him an out if he wanted one. When he'd told me that he couldn't meet this weekend, I had the sinking fear that maybe Brenda was right. Maybe I'd played it too cool and lost my opportunity.

Then again, maybe not.

He had other commitments this weekend that he couldn't get out of. But he'd sounded so pleased that I'd called.

"What about next weekend, Shiri?"

"Can't," I said. "I won't be in town then. Work stuff. You know how it is."

I was spending an awful lot of time and money flying home every other weekend to help my family plan this reunion. I suppose I could have handled it over the phone to try to save a few pennies. But this was an opportunity that wouldn't come my way again for a while. Next year, someone else would be picked to serve on the reunion committee.

Though this opportunity was costing me. My work was starting to suffer, not to mention my bank account—even though reunion funds took care of half the tab for my travel expenses. One of the perks of being the chairperson of the fund-raising committee.

I'd used my share of reunion funds, but I was also spending a lot of time helping to generate funds, too—organizing family fund-raisers, soliciting donations from private companies, stuff like that. If I wanted to hit my own company up, I'd better show my face around there. I hadn't spent the extra time in the office like I needed in order to stay ahead of the pack.

"What about the week after that?" Brenda suggested excitedly, not ready to give up on us just yet. I clamped my hand over the phone, but Jack had heard her and started laughing.

"Is that Brenda?" he asked.

"Yes," I admitted. "She's here."

"I'll tell you what, Shiri. I've got a game in a couple of weeks. I can get you some tickets. As many as you want for you and your family. We can hook up after the game. How does that sound?"

"Works for me," I told him. A stadium full of screaming fans wasn't exactly what I had in mind; but if that was the best that he could do on short notice, I wouldn't turn it down. Besides, a lot could happen in a couple of weeks. Maybe something else would come up before then. We could still meet and I wouldn't have to go to the game.

"All right. See you in a couple of weeks."

"Bye, Jack."

"And, Shiri?"

"Yeah?"

"I'm glad you called."

"So am I, Jack. So am I."

An awkward silence filled the line, as if he wasn't quite ready to hang up; but I could hear my folks stirring, their voices growing louder.

"Bye," I said quickly. Then hung up the phone. "Happy now?" I addressed Brenda.

She squeezed me tight. "Now that's the Shiri that I know and love! And it's not about my being happy. Not this time. This is about your love and your happiness!"

FIFTEEN

I hated football. I absolutely despised it. It was idiotic and barbaric. I couldn't find a single, socially redeeming quality whatsoever in the game.

So when I found myself, two weeks later, sitting five rows back from the fifty-yard line, screaming my head off, I could only justify my behavior by conceding that I must be certifiably insane.

And each time I leaped to my feet, threw my hands in the air, and shouted, "Whoooaaa!" along with the other enthusiastic participants of the "wave," I imagined that I could feel my little gray brain cells dying off—one by one.

"Look, Bailey, there he is!" I grabbed on to my brother's arm and pointed excitedly down on the field at Jack. "See him? That's Jack!"

"Yeah, yeah. We all see him, Bailey yawned as if bored and brushed my hand off. He then turned to the complete stranger sitting behind us and said, "Everybody, look. My sister, Shiri, has finally found a man. Everybody, look here!" he pointed with both index fingers, shouting loudly and drawing enough attention to make me want to sink down beneath the seats.

"Stop that!" I said, punching his arm as hard as I could.

"Ow! What did you do that for?"

"See what you did? You made me miss the snap. Look, he's going out for a pass! Go, Jack! Go! Whoooo! Way to go, Flash!"

I grabbed Bailey's arm, just below the elbow, and squeezed with both hands. He didn't notice the viselike grip on his arm. He was too busy trying to avoid my stomping on his feet as I jumped up and down.

"He's going all the way!" Bailey predicted as Jack broke free from one tackle, pivoted, then reversed directions to barely sidestep another tackle. In his effort to get away, he nearly collided with this own teammate. The third time proved not to be the charm as what I could only describe as King Kong in a football jersey launched himself at Jack. He wrapped his massive arms around Jack's waist and slung him, back first, to the ground.

"Leave him alone, you big turkey!" I shouted.

"Turkey?" Bailey made fun of my choice of insults.

"It's the first thing that popped into my head." I shrugged. I turned back to the game. "Oh, now, that's not fair! Look at them piling on my baby for no good reason. Why won't the referee throw in a penalty flag? That hit was obviously a late hit!"

"Shiri, let the boys play," Bailey complained. "Nothing makes a game drag on longer than officials who want to stop the game every two minutes."

"They didn't have to sit on his head like that," I complained.

"Didn't Flash tell you, Shiri? Jack's a player who uses his head."

"You are *so* not funny."

"Don't worry about him, baby sister. Jack isn't going to let anyone mess with that pretty face of his. He has to have something to fall back on when he's too old to play anymore."

Fourth quarter and only inches to go if they wanted to make a first down. Only three minutes left in the game. The score had been frozen since the third quarter at thirty-nine to thirty-eight, in favor of the visiting team—the Arkansas Twisters.

Would the Steeldogs play it safe and go for the first down? Or would they risk losing possession for the sake of scoring to go for the win? If I hadn't just had them done, I would have bit my nails.

"Go for it!" I shouted, wondering why they were taking so long in the huddle. What was there to decide? They wanted to win, didn't they? Go for the score.

"Go for it!" I shouted again, and to my surprise, the crowd around me picked up the chant, waving their pennants in time with the chant. "Go for it! Go for it!"

I knew if Jack had anything to say about it, there wouldn't be any debate. A tie, in his book, was just as good as a loss. A tie was just as bad as admitting that some other team was *just* as good as the Steeldogs. Or, if they tied with a third-rate, sorry team, a tie told their fans that the Steeldogs weren't doing their jobs. They weren't giving their fans their money's worth.

"Ohhh! Tell me when it's over, Bailey. I can't watch!" I exclaimed, burrowing my head in his shoulder. However, I made sure that I left one eye uncovered just in case I found the resolve to take a quick peek.

I felt so ridiculous, holding my breath, crossing my fingers, and sending up prayers for a game against which I had become a one-woman crusader. I couldn't help it. That was my man down there. It had taken a while to come to grips with that fact. Besides, who could resist? He looked so hot in that butt-hugging uniform.

"They're going for it," Bailey said. "Jack's split out. My guess is that he'll run a post right up the middle."

"The Twisters' coverage has been weak there the whole game," I agreed. "But to play it safe, they'd better send someone across the field to draw some of that attention away from Jack if he's going to be the go-to guy."

"Look at you, Coach Rowlan." Bailey nodded in admiration of my play-calling ability. How quickly he'd forgotten.

Daddy and I used to sit and scream plays at the television as soon as we got home from Sunday service.

"If they'd just kicked that field goal when I told them to, instead of that weak quarterback sneak, we would have this game in the bag."

"What is this 'we' stuff all of a sudden? I thought you hated football."

"Yeah, I hated it so much, I got us tickets for the next three home games. Are you complaining about my fanlike dedication, big brother?"

Bailey turned an invisible key to seal his lips and tossed the key over his shoulder. His silence was short-lived. He let out a shout as Jack crossed into the end zone with the football tucked snugly in his arms.

"Did you see that? That's my baby!" I screeched and blew him a kiss. Could he see me? I couldn't be sure. It wasn't as if I didn't stand out. Correction—I would have stood out if I'd been walking down the middle of the street dressed as I was. I wore a Steeldog T-shirt—not the printed one, the classy embroidered one. A cap was barely jammed down over my recently done hair. Ouch! What a feat that had been pulling my braids through the rear opening of the cap. I wondered if he could see me if I waved the giant, foam number-one finger.

When the clock ticked down to seconds and another win for the home team, like everyone else, I broke out into the celebration song.

It was only the first home game of the season, with thirteen more games scheduled. Yet the mood was undeniably jubilant. Over fourteen thousand fans had crowded into Legion Field. We were all singing with one voice—one loud, off-key, offbeat voice. That was okay. It was the thought that counted.

As the players filed off the field, the celebration song changed.

All of us waved good-bye to the defeated team. The chant echoed up to the rafters. Everyone was all hyped now, with two away-game wins and one home-game win under the team's belt. I wondered whether this enthusiasm would last the entire season. We fans could be so fickle.

"Come on," I said, edging past my brother.

"Where are we going?"

"Down there." I pointed to the row of seats directly above the players' exit. I didn't wait to see if Bailey would follow. I wanted to tell Jack congratulations. I wanted him to know how proud I was of him, before he got preoccupied with postgame wrap-up.

When I looked over my shoulder to locate Bailey, I made a small noise of disgust. He wasn't paying attention to me at all. He was too busy trying to get a phone number from a pretty little spirit leader of the Steeldog Show Steelers.

Moving against the flow of traffic, I made my way to the player exit just in time to see Jack pull off his helmet and swipe his hand across his forehead.

"Jack!" I called out to him, waving my arms in the air. But I was competing with a hundred or so other stragglers. They were all calling out to the players as if they were as intimately acquainted as I was with Jack.

Perhaps, in their minds, they were. That was all part of being a fan. When you followed their careers, celebrated their victories or mourned over their defeats, memorized their player statistics before they did, studied the game so that you could offer advice to make them better players, it brought you close to them—or as close as security would allow you to get.

I placed my thumb and middle finger to my lips, whistling shrilly. That had to get his attention. It was a sound I knew he'd recognize. He'd heard it the day my grandfather almost sold him off to several of my cousins.

Jack's head snapped up, scanning the crowd until he zeroed in on me. When his face lit up in recognition, I blew him a kiss in answer to his wave. He held up both hands and opened and closed them twice rapidly. Twenty minutes. Give him twenty minutes and he'd be ready to go.

I nodded and gave him the thumbs-up sign. It was all prearranged. Underneath my T-shirt, I wore my going-out clothes. All I had to do was pull off my tennis shoes and socks. I'd stuffed my dress shoes into my large, leather shoulder bag. When Bailey came up to me, I was sitting in a seat, sliding on my shoes and fluffing my hair.

"Well?" I asked, knowing full well from his expression that he hadn't had much success with asking one of the Show Steelers out for a date.

"Those girls are tough." He grinned at me. "Won't give a brother no play."

"Maybe," I suggested sweetly as only a baby sister could, "it's because your game is weak."

"Good game, man. Good game."

I shook the hands of my opponents, hugged those who had been friends and former teammates from previous jobs. It had been a close game, a hard-fought one, with both sides scratching and clawing for every inch, every point.

I hadn't been sure if we would be able to pull this one out. It sure felt good to win. But what felt even better was seeing Shiri's face. Knowing that she was there pulling for me, cheering for me, made every blow worth it.

Speaking of blows, I think I took a hard one in the ribs. Each breath felt a little like sucking chili peppers into my lungs. I knew that I was going to be feeling the effects of this one for a while. At least, until the next game, when I would be psyched up with so much adrenaline that I wouldn't feel the first few hits.

Adrenaline could only take you so far, however. The rest was training, conditioning, and willpower. I would keep going out there, game after game, hit after hit, until by the end of the season I was a walking mass of sprains, bruises, and pulls.

How I loved this game!

I welcomed every tackle. The harder they hit me, the more I enjoyed it. Sounds masochistic, but nothing could be further from the truth. I didn't want to be hit for pain's sake. I wanted to be chased down for what it meant to the mind-set of the opposing team.

The fact that I was a target let me know that I was doing my job. If the opposing team's players didn't fear what I could do to run up the score, they wouldn't bother with me. If I was a candy-ass, not worth their effort, I could run fake routes by them all day long and never get a scratch.

Let me nurse my wounds. Each ache, each twinge, each minute soaking in a tub of Epsom salts or icing down a limb brought us that much closer to the championship. By next game, I'd be out there again—goading them to bring it on.

"Say, Flash. Is that your latest?" The big, offensive lineman whose block made it possible for me to get into the end zone slapped me on the back of my head to get my attention.

"What's the matter with you, Flash? You got wax in your ears? Look up there."

I looked up and saw Shiri waving frantically at me. I grinned and waved back.

She put her fingers between her teeth and whistled shrilly again—long and loud. So that's where that noise had come from. I'd heard it before, just as the game ended, but hadn't paid it too much attention. I suppose I was still in game mode, completely focused, drowing out any noise that didn't help me make my plays.

Now that the football game was over, my thoughts turned elsewhere. To her. As far as my heart was concerned, Shiri was now the only game in town.

"What do you mean latest? That's my last, my only. Hopefully sooner rather than later, my baby's mama."

"Damn, Flash. You serious?"

"As a heart attack."

"You sure you didn't take another shot to the head on that last play? Since when?"

I shrugged. "Since Mike rode off into the sunset with his one and only. It's got me thinking."

"Yeah, right. Thinking with the wrong head. What did Mike say to you to convince you to let your brain make decisions about women? Do you realize what you're passing up if you go one-on-one?''

He waved and grinned at a couple of ladies leaning so far over the safety rail, I was sure security would be scraping them up with a spatula before long. When they caught Big Dog and me looking, they leaned even farther—giving us unrestricted views of their bountiful cleavage.

"Been there. Done that. That stuff gets old, man. Either that or I did. The older I get, the more I realize that it doesn't make any sense to pass up something . . . someone . . . you know is right.''

"What did she whip on you? Some kind of Southern black voodoo magic?''

"I don't know. Whatever it is, it's working pretty strong.'' I held up my hands, indicating how long I expected to be in the showers.

"Why don't you bring her by the crib tonight? I'd like to meet the woman who took Jack Deneen down.''

"Why? So you can try to take her away from me? No, thanks. I'll keep Shiri to myself until I've had a chance to warn her about you dogs.''

Big Dog chuckled. "Nothing's going to happen to your friend, Flash. I'm having a little afterparty to celebrate our humiliation of the Twisters.''

"Did I hear you invite some of their players to the party, too?''

"Yeah. So? What about it?''

"That's like fraternizing with the enemy.''

"Fraternizing? Who's fraternizing? I'm just getting my party on. Are you coming by or not?''

"I don't know. Shiri's only in town for the weekend. I don't want to waste a minute of it jacking around with you clowns.''

"Are you sure?''

"That you're clowns? Absolutely positive.'' I laughed.

Big Dog shook his head and *tsk*ed at me. "Crying shame. Lost your manhood and your sense of humor at the same time. That girl's got you totally whipped.''

Big Dog snapped his wrist—his rendition of cracking a whip.

"We might stop by later," I conceded. It did no good to earn the grudging respect of your opponents, yet have your own teammates ridiculing you. We might go, if only for just an hour to show our faces.

"You know the party won't get good and started until after midnight. You've got enough time to handle your business." He took another look a Shiri and made a small sound of appreciation. "Or get your business handled. She's a tiny thing, Flash. Don't hurt her."

It was something more than a gathering of closest friends and just shy of an orgy. Jack inched along, maneuvering his truck past the line of illegally parked cars to get a parking spot that was secluded, yet close enough to the road to not get blocked in.

"Is it like this all of the time?" I mused, watching a steady flow of people moving in and out of the house and all about the grounds.

"What do you mean?"

"So many people. Does your friend—what's his name?"

"Big Dog," Jack supplied.

"Oh, yes. How could I forget?" My tone was pure sarcasm. "Does Big Dog know all of these people?"

"Not by name. But I'm sure if you ask him, he'll say that there was something familiar about the faces."

I looked over at Jack. It was on the tip of my tongue to ask whether he'd ever thrown a party in which he only "remembered the faces." I didn't want to ask. I thought it sounded tacky, suspicious, and jealous. Things had moved incredibly fast for us. Too fast for me to think I could exercise any claim of ownership.

"And what sort of parties do you put on?"

The words came out anyway. So much for being tactful and discreet.

"The private kind," he said, lifting my hand to his lips.

"The kind where I not only remember the faces, but cherish them."

I smiled despite myself. Even if he had thrown a wild party or two in his lifetime, for the moment his answer mollified me. It wasn't only his words that soothed my anxious spirit. When he'd held me in his arms tonight, I'd felt nothing less than cherished.

As he eased into a parking spot and shut off the engine, I took a deep breath. I wasn't sure if I was ready for this— to be thrust into the limelight as Jack's latest conquest. I didn't want anyone who might have known Jack's other girlfriends to compare me with them.

I'm no slouch, but I'm realistic about my body. If I could, I'd trim a few inches off of my thighs and slap them up on my breasts. If I was doing the sculpting, I'd make myself a little taller, a little sleeker—at least enough so I wouldn't look like a munchkin walking in on Jack's arm.

He saw me hesitate. He'd already opened the car door and was climbing out, and I hadn't taken off my seat belt yet.

"Are you all right, Shiri?"

"Of course. What makes you ask?" I opened my purse and put on a show of searching for my lipstick to justify my hesitation. I don't think he was convinced.

"We don't have to go, if you don't want to," he offered.

"Don't be silly. You drove all of this way. Of course we're going in."

"Are you sure? Say the word and we're out of here."

"I dare you to try to back out of that parking spot after all of the maneuvering you did to get here." I smiled at him. "Just give me a minute to fix my face." A quick flick of my wrist to take the shine off my nose and forehead. Pucker. Swipe. *Voila!* Instant luscious lips. I was as gorgeous as I was going to be; so I unbuckled my seat belt and climbed out.

The path to the front door was marked by white lights running along both sides. As we approached the door, someone stumbled outside, leaned against the Roman-style pillar, and proceeded to be violently ill in the pink azalea bushes.

Jack looked down at me and said sympathetically, "We won't stay long. I just want you meet some of the guys."

"That isn't one of them, is it?" I asked hopefully.

Jack took a few steps back, lowered his head to try to get a good look at the face, then shook his head. "No . . . no, I don't think so."

"Oh, good!" I said with exaggerated relief to show him that I had a sense of humor.

He placed his arm around my waist as we walked up the stairs. Jack rang the doorbell as we entered, only as a matter of courtesy. The door was wide open. I doubted if anyone would have heard the bell over the music anyway.

A live band was playing somewhere near the rear of the house, but speakers had been set up in every room to carry the sounds where the strength of the lead singer could not.

"Keys, please." A young woman dressed in what looked to me like a bikini made of mint-green dental floss held up a huge, wooden salad bowl in outstretched hands.

Jack fished his keys out of his pants pocket and dropped them into the bowl.

"Thanks, Flash." She eyed him for a moment—too long of a moment to make me comfortable—and disappeared into the crowd.

"I take it that when we're ready to leave, we'll have to hunt her down to get the keys back."

"Uh-huh," he said distractedly, looking over the heads of the partygoers as if he was searching for someone. He didn't appear to notice the key keeper. But I wasn't taking any chances.

"I'll tell you what," I suggested. "When it's time to go, you let *me* hunt her down."

Something in my tone must have caught his attention. He looked at me as if he was actually pleased that I was the teeniest bit jealous.

"Come on. Let's see if we can find the big man himself.

The sooner we show our faces, make introductions, the sooner we can get out of here.''

We left the foyer, past the formal dining room, back through the kitchen, and finally outside where someone said they might have seen Big Dog. The house, in square footage, wasn't that large. But it was packed with more people per square inch than I'm sure the fire marshal would consider acceptable. I could almost see the sign on the door being torn down and trampled: MAXIMUM OCCUPANCY NOT TO EXCEED 200.

There was maximum partying going on here. There were people everywhere, in groups of twos, threes, and more, all trying to hold conversations over the sound of other conversations and the ever-present thump of the music. There was a definite lack of chairs. Some had found seats on countertops. Others leaned on stair railings or sat on tables. I don't think anyone minded the bumper-to-bumper bodies. Nobody but Jack and me.

He lead the way, his tall frame parting a way through the crowd like Moses and the Red Sea.

"Hey, Flash. Glad you could make it, dog.''

Dog. It was the universal greeting of all the men here tonight—whether they were on the Steeldogs' roster or not.

"Big Dog.'' Jack greeted his friend with some sort of complicated, soul-brother handshake that I'd sometimes seen my brothers give when they met up with their friends.

"And I see you brought some class to my little soiree.''

Big Dog looked me up and down like a pit bull eyeing a cut of prime rib. He smiled at me with a mouth full of gold-capped teeth. The top row spelled out *Big*. The bottom row spelled out—you guessed it—*Dog*.

He was a big man, not as tall as Jack, but with a tree-trunk neck, wide shoulders, and squat, muscular legs. If I were the man he'd blocked trying to make room for Jack's run into the end zone, I would have stayed down until the team trainer came to check on me, too. There was no way I would have tried to get up and risked having him hit me again.

I was having a hard time imagining how something so big, that looked so unwieldy, could move so fast. I must have stared a little too long, a little too hard. It was Jack's turn to call up the green-eyed jealousy monster. He tightened his arm around me and said with an edge in his voice, "If you could spell soiree, Big Dog, then I'd believe you could hold one."

"Why don't you introduce me to your new friend, Flash?" Big Dog suggested.

"Big Dog, this is Shiri Rowlan. Shiri, this is my boy Dolan Cantrell. But everyone calls him—"

"Let me guess," I interrupted. "Big Dog?"

"In the flesh," he said.

And plenty of it, I thought. I lowered my eyes. Staring too long might send out the wrong signals. I didn't want to give Dolan Cantrell any ammunition for locker-room teasing. Boys would be boys. And the first thing boys did together in the locker room was talk about girls. I wasn't going to give Dolan Cantrell anything he could use to strain his relationship with Jack.

"Thanks for inviting us to your soiree, Mr. Cantrell," I said, putting extra emphasis on the *us.* I wanted to let him know that Jack and I were a couple. We were together. Make no mistakes about it.

Holding out my hand to him, I hoped that he wouldn't try to greet me with that soul-brother handshake as he'd used to greet Jack. It was too complicated for me, never the same shake twice.

"You're always welcome in this dog's house," he replied and leaned in as he took my hand. "With or without Flash."

I pulled away, without responding to his comment. That is, I didn't respond verbally. Instead, I moved closer to Jack, practically sealing my hip to his.

Big Dog stepped back. "Make yourselves at home. There's plenty to eat. Whatever you want to drink; if I don't have it we'll send for it. My castle is Sue's castle."

He'd slaughtered the phrase, but we got the gist of it. So

did everyone else. The way his house was being used, you'd think that the guests paid the mortgage there.

"Are you hungry?" Jack asked.

"You mean fight that crowd to get to the snack table?" I asked, raising my eyebrows. "You're a braver man than I thought."

"It did look swamped," he agreed.

"There probably isn't anything left worth fighting the crowd for anyway," I suggested—the very model of sour grapes.

"Probably right. Maybe some leftover cold cuts."

"Or mixed nuts with only those nasty Brazil nuts left."

"I hate those things," he said amiably.

"Yeah, me, too. Nothing short of a pile driver can crack them."

It was stupid, boring, party small talk and we knew it. But we were here and here we had to stay until we'd made a decent showing. We stood, pressed against a far wall for a moment, each of us in our own way trying to determine when would be a good time to make our exit. I didn't want to be here. Judging from Jack's expression, he really didn't want to be, either. He was there because his teammate had asked him to come.

"So," he said loudly. He had to. The music had been cranked up another notch.

"Yes?"

"Do you want to dance?"

"A chance for what?" I shouted back.

"No . . . dance!" he corrected, pointing to an area by the pool where the patio furniture had been cleared.

Because of the type of music that was being played, there wasn't as much dancing going on as there was stomping, flailing, and pumping it up—that stupid lift-your-palms, raise-the-roof motion. Geez, I'll be glad when that fad dies. It was almost as annoying as the dog-pound *whoop* that Arsenio Hall had made popular on this talk show.

I shook my head and shouted, "Maybe the next song."

He nodded in agreement. But the next song wasn't much better. Or the next. Or the next.

Was I getting old, or was this music really bad? I remember when people went to parties to dance. Even if we didn't hold each other, we at least looked at each other. With the antics going on in front of the band's stage, you didn't even have to look at your partner.

The woman could stand there and gyrate while the man stood by and ogled. Occasionally, to remind the woman that he was still around, if she was really lucky, the man would slap her rear as a mark of ownership.

Moo! A cowboy applying a burning brand to a heifer did so with more finesse.

Jack leaned against the wall, one arm around my shoulder. His free hand clasped the neck of a long-necked beer, which he sipped very, very slowly. In the twenty minutes that we stood there and people watched, I don't think he went through a third of it. Still, I kept an eye on his intake. With the other eye I kept a lookout for that string-bikini-clad babe to make sure she didn't come over and jiggle her ample set of . . . keys at him.

The band finally took a break, leaving enough dead air that I could hear my ears ringing. I shook my head briskly before speaking.

"Good group. They should go far."

"You mean like to Antarctica? That wouldn't be far enough for me."

I grinned at him. "Come on now. You have to admit that the lead singer . . . what was his name?"

"Baby Z," Jack supplied. "He only said, 'Baby Z in the house,' about umpteen times."

"I couldn't tell what he was saying. He had his mouth too close to the mike . . . all of that spittle and static made it difficult to understand. But you have to give him credit for his energy and enthusiasm."

"I wonder how many college credits he has," Jack mused. "I'm sure a more learned man wouldn't have tried to make *stupid* rhyme with *looptid*. Is *looptid* an actual word?"

His ability to make me laugh reminded me why I'd fallen so quickly and completely for him. I didn't get a chance to respond. The music started up again. Not the band, a jukebox. I guess faced with the pressure of actually having to speak to someone, the collective partygoers had decided that it wasn't worth the effort.

The jukebox contained a slightly different repertoire of songs. I believe someone referred to them as "old school." The first song that blared out was an old George Clinton song. An oldie, but goodie. "Atomic Dog," "Dog Catcher," whatever you called it, most everyone recognized the opening riffs.

Oh, what did they have to do that for? That one song managed to get more folks out there on the floor dancing than the entire repertoire of Baby Z and his gangsta rap trio.

Jack looked at me. I looked at him. The next thing I knew, we were out there, too. He had to go. Playing that song was the pied piper's call. Any Steeldog who wouldn't get out there and dance to George Clinton had better not show up to the next practice without a good excuse—broken spine, alien abduction, demonic possession. Stuff like that.

It had been a while since I'd been dancing. Not since my freshman year in college when I'd made it my solemn duty to try to hit every frat and keg party now that I was away from home—and legal.

I wasn't even sure if I was making all the right moves. But it really didn't matter if we were doing the latest moves. It was all about the music, all about the mood. It was all about sharing the memory of where you were and who you were with the first time you'd danced to that song.

"Atomic Dog" faded easily into the expanded version of the "Electric Slide." Now, instead of everyone dancing in pockets of three, four, or ten, we were in lines, moving up, moving back. Clapping in unison, laughing and getting one another back on track if someone missed a step. If they turned left when they should have moved back, cha-cha'ed when they should have slid, no one judged; they just got out of the way and kept dancing.

When someone turned off the jukebox to announce the band's return, the crowd actually booed. You couldn't dance to them. You could grind close enough to expect paternity suits nine months later, but you couldn't dance now.

Baby Z tried to take the mike to get his trio started for the next set; but the crowd wasn't having any of that.

"This could get ugly," Jack mused. But he didn't look as if he was ready to go just yet. I think he was just getting into the party mood.

A choice of music was made when someone identified only as Bone Crusher pushed Baby Z off the stage.

I gasped, held my breath. "Did you see that? He can't do that, can he?"

"He just did," Jack said matter-of-factly.

"Someone should call 911."

"The time to call was when Baby Z took that stage. That so-called music was killing me." Jack stopped me as I put my cell phone up to my ear. "Save the minutes. He's not hurt."

I craned my neck to see. Baby Z had landed into a field of outstretched arms and was carried, hands over head, around the pool area and somewhere out of sight. The remaining duo of Baby Z's group didn't want to be pushed. They took a running jump and launched themselves into the cheering crowd.

With the live band easily dispatched, the jukebox started up again.

Bone Crusher snatched the mike, and in a burst of static announced, "And now, I want to slow it down for all of the lovers in the house tonight."

The mood shifted as the jukebox suddenly crooned some of the most well-known, old-school love songs ever collected.

Jack didn't even have to ask, just opened his arms to me. He folded them, cocooning me. By this point, we were both a little sweaty. But he smelled so good. I pressed my face to his chest, not minding the warm dampness. It was like being enveloped in a towel fresh out of the dryer, but not one hundred percent dry.

As the music played on, I felt a fresh longing rise up inside me. Jack had done a pretty thorough job of taking care of my needs—enough to see me through to next month when I got back into town again, I'd thought. Evidently not. Through no fault of his own. I was the needy one. Definitely time to make an exit.

Jack was feeling it, too. He pressed me closer to him, his arousal evident as he throbbed against my pelvis.

"Let's get out of here," he whispered harshly against my cheek.

"I'm with you," I agreed. "But I've got to make a stop first in the ladies' room." I stood up on tiptoe and kissed his cheek.

"Don't get lost," he said, squeezing me in the small of my back.

"I won't."

When I left him, he was talking to a group of fans who'd taken advantage of my absence. As long as I was by his side, and he was obviously interested in no one but me, we were left mostly in peace—except for an occasional fan who swooped by, fast enough to get a steely look from Jack for the interruption.

The first bathroom that I tried downstairs had a line that snaked all the way around to the den. The bathroom in the downstairs master bedroom was also in great demand.

I jostled my way up the stairs to a guest bedroom and adjoining bathroom. The anteroom had his-and-her sinks and enough track lighting to illuminate a small airstrip. It made the perfect congregating place for female guests to re-apply their makeup and tighten up that hair. Nothing like a good, dancing sweat to loosen up those bonded weaves. Bottles of hair bond passed back and forth almost as much as unopened foil packages of condoms. I would have passed this room up, too, and taken my chances on the long drive back, but the door leading to the commode was ajar.

"Are you next in line?" I asked the girl standing closest to the door.

"Nuh-uh. You gon' ahead."

"Thanks."

As soon as I shut the door behind me, I heard a burst of laughter that the door couldn't muffle. Something told me that they were laughing at me. It wasn't something. Someone. A group of someones. As I listened to the conversation that followed, I realized that I was the topic of conversation. They'd raised their voices deliberately so I could hear them. Three distinct voices.

"Was that . . . ?"

"It sho' was."

"I know that wasn't that *ho* all over J.D.?"

My jaw dropped. Who were they calling a *ho?* Which one of them was it? If my panty hose hadn't already been down around my ankles, I would have stepped out and made some very serious corrections to their perceptions.

"Damitra, girl, wasn't J.D. supposed to be your man? What's he doing pushin' up on her like that?"

"I don't know . . . but I know one thang, I know he'd better not be doing her in the same bed that he and I did it."

"I told you that you shouldn't have given it up to him so fast."

"What did you expect me to do? You know the man's attention span ain't nuthin' but that long." I heard her fingers snap. "He stays as horny as a dog. Whenever he wants some, he wants it right then, right there. If I'd said no, he would have been out sniffing around somebody else that much sooner."

"Don't worry 'bout it, Damitra. He'll get tired of banging that cow. You wait and see. As soon as she drops her panties, he'll drop her. Kick her to the curb like trash."

"That's right. Don't even worry about it. Don't even think somebody like her could take your man."

"I wish she would try. I'm gonna bust up that heifer's action right now."

I strained, but I couldn't hear how she was going to do it. Their voices faded. Either they'd gotten tired of shouting through the door, or they'd moved on.

Though tears of white-hot anger scorched my cheeks, I told myself that it didn't matter. Whoever that Damitra was, she was just jealous. She was jealous of the fact that she wasn't woman enough to hold on to Jack. She'd called me a heifer. A cow. So what if I had a little extra going on? That only meant that I was woman enough for both of us.

I told myself that she was just one woman. Only one. But what if there were others? How many others? How many times would I have to listen to variations of this conversation? How many times would I have to compare myself against the women in Jack's life and tell myself that there was nothing wrong with me? It was all them. Sooner or later, however, would the stacks of *them* grow insurmountable?

Just listening to this once was more than enough for me. I didn't think I could stand any more like Damitra, out there, ready to clue me in on Jack's past.

As I sat with my cheeks propped on my fists, my elbows resting on my knees, I wondered how I was going to get through the rest of the evening without letting Jack know that my feelings had been hurt. I wondered if I had the courage to continue to nurture the relationship even though I had doubts.

Mostly, I wondered which one of those heifers had used the last of the bathroom tissue and left without replacing the roll.

SIXTEEN

I didn't want to go, but Mama insisted as only mothers could. *Insisted* was just a nice way of saying *threatened.* As I sat in the den with my feet propped on the table, the remote to the satellite dish permanently attached to one hand while my other hand burrowed into a bowl of heavily buttered popcorn, she said in crisp, unarguable tones, "Get up, Shiri."

I looked up at her. I wasn't as if I had a choice. She'd positioned herself directly in front of the television. Her arms were folded resolutely across her chest. I bit my tongue to keep the smarty-pants remark from popping out of my mouth. If we'd been kids and that had been one of my brothers standing in front of the television, he would have definitely gotten a remark about "asses not made of glass."

Instead, I said respectfully, "Ma'am?"

"Get up off the couch. You're coming with me."

"Where are you going?"

"Not me—we. We're going to the botanical gardens. I'm on the schedule to volunteer today, and I want you to go along with me."

It was on the tip of my tongue to ask her where on the

schedule I was, but I didn't. If I didn't want my tongue to be pulled from my head, I'd better keep it civil.

My shoulders slumped farther into the couch cushions. It was bad enough that I was giving up my weekends to help with the family reunion planning. I didn't complain because all I had to do was take meeting minutes, hardly enough work to break a sweat. I'd cracked a nail or two as I typed on my computer keyboard, but nothing that a quick trip to the manicurist couldn't fix.

That wouldn't be the case if I went volunteering with Mama today. I'd seen what they made some volunteers do. Imagine willingly putting yourself in the position of weeding, pruning, and tilling. It wasn't for me. Not on a Saturday afternoon.

"Do I have to?" I felt all of twelve years old, whining to my mama. I just wasn't in the mood.

"Yes, you have to. Come on. You might enjoy it."

"Digging, weeding, and pruning. Yes, Mama, that ranks very high on my list of things I'd rather be doing on a Saturday afternoon. It ranks right up there with getting a root canal without the benefit of anesthesia or having bamboo shoots poked under my fingernails."

"No bamboo shoots under your fingernails today, Shiri. If you're in the greenhouse, you'll be wearing gloves."

"You don't know what a comfort that is to me," I muttered.

Mama reached behind her and switched off the television. *Ah-ha!* I had the remote control. All I had to do was angle the infrared beam around and behind her just so and . . .

The television came on again. The western I had been halfheartedly watching cut back on at the loudest possible moment—with the hero firing a hail of bullets at the bad guys. As hard as it was imagining Mario Van Peebles as a rough-and-rugged, heart-of-gold desperado, I kept my eyes glued to the television. As long as I was watching, I didn't have to think. As long as I wasn't thinking, I didn't have to remember. Remembering led to feelings of loss and regret.

That's what all of the television-watching was really about—avoiding those feelings.

It had been four weeks since I'd said good night to Jack. Good night had really been good-bye, because I hadn't called him before I'd gone back to Jackson. I hadn't returned his call when he'd left a message with my parents. I'd screened all of my calls through my answering machine at my apartment.

It didn't take him long to figure out that I wasn't going to return his calls. Not quite two weeks, almost ten days, and his calls had stopped coming. I didn't know whether to be relieved or angry that he didn't try harder. It was my game; but he wasn't playing by the rules. A man who'd obviously been around as much as he had should have a pretty good grasp of the rules. He just wasn't playing by them.

To keep from feeling the pain, I filled my head with pulp fiction. With over three hundred channels brought conveniently into my parents' home via satellite, it was easy to lose myself in melodrama rather than believe I'd lost a perfectly good man. No, not lost. Thrown away.

"Turn that thing off or I'll take out the batteries and hide the remote," Mama threatened.

"When I grow up and have kids of my own, I'm going to let them watch television until their brains rot out," I announced.

"I should live so long."

"To see your grandkids?"

"For you to grow up," Mama retorted. "Now, go upstairs and change into something a little less comfortable."

"What's wrong with what I have on?" I teased, pulling at my T-shirt.

"I'm not going to be seen with you in those jeans. Look at them. Cut up nine ways 'til Sunday. More holey than righteous, is what they are."

"These aren't holes, Mama. They're a specially designed ventilation system."

"Ventilation system? Now that's just plain nasty. I

wouldn't go around telling people that you need a ventilation system around your behind, Shiri.''

"Mama!'' I tried to sound shocked, but I couldn't. I was laughing too hard.

"You brought it up,'' she reminded me. "Now, for the last time, go upstairs and change. Why don't you put on that pretty sundress that your grandmother bought for you?''

"The one with the huge sunflower print?'' I said with a neutral face. Sure. Why not? I shrugged fatalistically. "I don't want anyone to accuse me of not getting into the spirit of the botanical gardens. I have a better idea. Why don't you stick me in a flowerpot and let me wave to the guests as they tour the facility?''

"You're wasting time. I don't care how you stick your lip out. You're going. And you're going to enjoy it.''

"I will? How do you know?''

"Call it mother's intuition.''

"Do you get mother brownie points for saying that?'' I asked. But I trudged toward the stairs anyway.

"Hurry up, Shiri. The gift shop opens at ten. I want to pick up a few things before we have to check in.''

It was only eight in the morning, but as I told you before, Doris Jean Rowlan hates to be late.

"I'll be down in a minute, Mama,'' I promised. "I just want to jump in the shower.''

"Shiri, we don't have time for that.''

"Do you want me to show up on time and funky or five minutes late and smelling like a rose?''

"Use the body wash in the guest bathroom,'' she suggested.

"I thought so,'' I muttered.

It didn't take as much time to get ready as I'd thought. Once I was finally up off the couch and moving around, I could convince my body that it wasn't a weekend, laze-about kind of day but a midweek, oh-my-God-I'm-late-for-work kind of day. I cut corners from my usual morning routine wherever I could.

As the water ran in the shower, gradually warming, I

slathered on facial cream and added a dollop of toothpaste to my toothbrush. I brushed my teeth in the shower, spinning around three times to let the water splash all over my body. Spat down the drain, opened my mouth to rinse, and swiped off the facial cleaner at the same time.

You have to be careful to time the spitting and rinsing. Coordination is crucial. If you don't rinse your face well enough before you open your mouth to wash the toothpaste away, you wind up with a mouth full of facial cleanser. And if you don't rinse your mouth well enough, you could wind up having your face tartar-controlled with minty-fresh toothpaste.

I stepped out without completely drying off and smeared cocoa butter all over to seal in the moisture. Extra lotion to my elbows, knees, and heels—notorious trouble spots of dryness on my body.

I'd just stepped into my underwear when I heard my mama's distinct call.

Boommmp! Bomp-bomp.

She was already outside, tapping on the horn with her trademark impatience.

"All right. All right. I'm coming!" I could let myself sound as irritated as I wanted to. With the sound of the bathroom exhaust fan whirring, I knew that there was no way she could hear me. Then again, there were times when I thought she couldn't possibly hear me and she busted me anyway.

I shimmied into my dress and reached behind me for the zipper. The dress was sleeveless, with a scooped neck and full, flowing, A-line skirt that fell an inch above my knees. I twisted my hair off my head into a loose ponytail, swiped honey-glaze lipstick across my lips, and I was ready to go. All I needed was to slide my feet into my white leather mules and I was ready to go.

Stubbornness. Nothing but pure bullheadedness kept me from picking up the phone and calling Shiri. I'd already tried that, and she'd made it very clear that she didn't want to have anything to do with me. Fine. If that's the way she wanted it. But the least she could have done was told me to my face—not hid behind the formidable wall of her relatives.

I don't even know what I could have done to make her shut me down so hard. One minute we'd been at Big Dog's, enjoying the music, enjoying each other, the next—nothing.

"Take me home, Jack."

Just like that. No warning, no preamble, just "take me home." It wasn't even the kind of "take me home" that led me to believe that she wanted to leave to restart that private party of our own. That's where I'd thought we were heading once I'd started to slow-dance with her. I could tell by the way that she moved with me, and against me, that she'd been feeling the mood as much as I had. Her body, supple and suggestive, had molded perfectly against mine. When she'd pulled away from me, I'd had to do some creative standing to keep everyone else at the party from knowing what I'd been thinking.

Shiri had only been gone for five minutes. Maybe ten. Something must have happened in that time. But she wouldn't tell me. Wouldn't talk to me. She'd ridden home in silence, with her arms folded across her chest, her face turned toward the window.

"Shiri, what's the matter?"

"Nothing."

I *hated* that "nothing" crap. Why did women do that to me? Don't sit there and tell me nothing when it's obvious that isn't the case.

"Nothing" doesn't put that scowl on your face that broadcasts to the world that I've screwed up—though for the life of me, I can't figure out how.

"Nothing" doesn't make you pull away when I reach out to take your hand.

"Nothing" doesn't make you slam the door and jerk your head aside when I try to kiss you good night.

"Nothing" hurts.

As I stood in front of the mirror, preparing to shave, my hand started to tremble. At first, I believe it shook with suppressed anger. No one wanted to be blown off, to be cast away without an explanation, no matter how brief the acquaintance. I'd thought she was feeling me as much as I was into her. Could I have been so wrong? Could my instincts have been so off?

As my hand continued to shake, so violently that I had to clench my wrist to stabilize it, I had an inkling that my tremors were something more than mere emotion. I sat on the end of the porcelain, claw-foot tub, collecting my thoughts and massaging my hand as the trembling subsided and numbness set in.

I pressed hard into my palms with my thumb, sliding it up and down the center for several moments until I realized that I couldn't feel my thumb working. I only knew that I pressed one hand into the other because I saw it happening with my own eyes. I heard the soft hiss of skin against skin. But I didn't feel it.

Five minutes passed. Maybe ten. I'm not sure how long I sat there, trying to get feeling back into my hand. I sat there long enough until I felt my rear starting to numb, too. But that was no mystery. Sitting on the small lip of the tub as it dug into my behind, no wonder at all that it started to numb.

I got up when I heard the cell phone sitting in its charger start to ring.

"Yeah," I answered, my voice surly, uncooperative. Whoever this was, I didn't feel like being bothered.

"And a blessed good morning to you, too, Mr. Deneen."

It only took a second to recognize the voice and the phone number. The caller ID indicated that the call came from the same phone that called me to invite me to Mrs. Johnson's anniversary dinner. The voice was distinctly Mrs. Johnson's. Strong, stern, and unmistakable.

"Mrs. Johnson?"

Why in the world would she be calling me now? Something had to be wrong. Something had happened to Shiri.

That's why she hadn't returned any of my calls! That had to be it!

But the casual question that followed crushed my hopes that something serious had made her turn away from me like that.

"How are you, Mr. Deneen?"

"How am I?" I echoed like an idiot. How did she think I was? She didn't seem like the woman who'd appreciate sarcasm . . . that is, she wouldn't appreciate it directed at her. There was no problem with her dishing it out. Still, she struck me as a woman who did nothing casually. She'd called for a reason. If I wanted to find out what it was, I had to keep her talking. I kept my tone as neutral as possible.

"I can't complain." That is, I wasn't going to. She knew that I was hurting; otherwise why would she call? That didn't mean I had to behave like a punk and let her know how deeply that wisp of a woman had dug into me.

"And how are you, ma'am?"

"A touch of arthritis but, if the Lord is willing, I suppose I'll make it."

"I'm sorry to hear you aren't feeling well," I responded. Inside, I felt like screaming. What was the point of this conversation? If she wanted to exchange information about injuries, I could go on, pain-for-pain, until she threw up the white flag.

"Mama, give me that phone!" I heard someone in the background call out.

"Let me do this!" Mrs. Johnson's voice was muffled, as if she'd placed her hand over the phone.

"Let me talk to him before you scare him off."

"I'm not going to scare him off. Let me handle this, please, Pammie!"

Moments later, Mrs. Johnson was back on the phone. Not a trace of her earlier annoyance was evident in her tone.

"Aren't you wondering why I called, Mr. Deneen?" she asked pleasantly.

"Of course I am. I was trying to be polite and wait for you to offer an explanation."

"You're running out of time! They'll be leaving soon, Mama!'' Shiri's aunt Pam said loudly. She must have been standing very close to Mrs. Johnson, directing her words into the mouthpiece.

"All right. All right, Pammie. I couldn't think of a single, reasonable way to be subtle, Mr. Deneen, so I'll just come right out and say it—''

"You need to get your lovesick behind over to the botanical gardens today. This very afternoon.'' Aunt Pam's order came out loud and clear over the phone.

"And why is that?'' I asked, not sure which one I was talking to now.

"Why are you asking me so many questions when you could be talking to Shiri?''

Shiri! She was in town and hadn't called me. Instead, I was talking to her relatives.

"I don't think that's a very good idea,'' I hedged. She didn't want to see me. If she did, she would have called me instead. I wasn't going to go chasing after her.

"That's the problem with you young people. You think when you should be acting and run off half-cocked when you should be firing your brain cells instead. Are you going to tell me that you don't want to see my granddaughter again, Mr. Deneen?''

"Of course I do, but—''

"But nothing. She'll be at the botanical gardens all day today working at the Gate House gift shop. It closes at four, so you have plenty of time to figure out why you were so foolish in the first place as to let a wonderful girl like Shiri slip away from you.''

"Yes, ma'am,'' I said dutifully. "Closes at four. I'll be there.''

But I had a split second of indecision. What if Shiri and I managed to patch things up? What if we eventually married? What if we ever argued and she ran to her relatives for support? I could see that no matter what the case, I would always be the villain. They would always take her side over mine, her word over mine. Even knowing that, I still wanted to be with her.

"I've also taken the liberty of making dinner reservations for you at the Café de France for six-thirty."

"I don't know what to say," I admitted.

"That's why I've called you so early in the morning, Mr. Deneen. I've given you plenty of time to study up on ways to impress a woman—assuming, of course, that after flexing your muscles, you've exhausted your repertoire of ways to attract them."

"Flexing is a good start, though, Flash," Aunt Pam interjected. "Don't stop doing that."

Good ol' Aunt Pam. At least someone was on my side.

"Another piece of advice, Mr. Deneen," Shiri's grandmother continued. "When you go calling on Shiri at the botanical gardens, don't bring flowers. Your gesture might go unnoticed in light of where you are."

"I'll try to be more creative." This time, my own sarcastic bent slipped out.

"Something about one carat in a marquise cut shows a hell of a lot of creativity, Flash!" Aunt Pam suggested.

"Don't be crude, Pam," Mrs. Johnson chastised.

"Just trying to help the man, Mama."

"Good-bye, Mr. Deneen."

"Good-bye, Mrs. Johnson. And thank you. Both of you."

SEVENTEEN

"Thank you and come again," I said pleasantly as the last of the gift-shop stragglers collected their purchases. But under my breath I muttered as they passed through the door, "Get out and stay out."

It was well after three o'clock. They'd come into the shop twenty minutes ago—just browsing. I knew what that meant. That was just a code word for killing time without intentions of buying.

Even though I'd followed them around the shop, making gift suggestions to hurry them along, nothing had seemed to work. I don't think they'd taken too kindly to me breathing down their necks. One woman had actually stopped, turned, and stared at me until I'd moved aside with a solicitous "Let me know if I can help you find anything."

After that, I'd stayed behind the counter. But I'd made it obvious that I was watching them. Sometimes, a carefully timed glare could give the appearance of stalking a customer without physically invading their space. Aunt Rosie had taught me that little trick from her restaurant business.

When the place was packed and she had stragglers at a table who just wouldn't leave, all she had to do was position a server just within hearing distance of the table conversation. It didn't take long for them to get the message. Even if the conversation was innocent, no one liked to feel like they were being eavesdropped on. They settled their tabs and got out—sometimes leaving a generous tip if they thought that their server was being especially attentive.

By four o'clock, Mama had returned from her meeting with the other members of the botanical gardens' President's Circle. She paused in the doorway, taking note of how many patrons remained, then mouthed to me, *I'll be right back.*

"Wait!" I waved to get her attention, but she ducked out again before I could catch her.

I blew out a frustrated breath, but turned a winning smile to one of the customers who'd made it up to the counter with a stack of glossy postcards.

"Long day?" The elderly gentleman made casual conversation as I slipped the postcards into a plastic sack.

"You might say that."

"Don't worry, sweetheart. As you get older, your days will get shorter. They'll whiz by and before you know it, you'll be dead."

And to think that I'd come out here to the botanical gardens to take my mind off my troubles.

"Yes, sir," I said politely.

He leaned closer, peering at the temporary name tag pinned to my dress. "Shiri," he said, trying out my name. "That's a very unusual name. Do you know what it means?"

I shook my head.

"It means *song.*"

"Oh, how . . . interesting," I said flatly, handing him the bag and the receipt.

"Do you sing?" he wanted to know.

"Not even in the shower." I laughed.

"With a name like that, you were meant to bring music to someone's life."

"What a sweet thing to say." My voice softened. Maybe he was a flirty old man, but he'd reminded me of something—something that my wallowing in self-pity had made me forget.

People came to the botanical gardens to surround themselves with natural beauty. I had dampened that spirit with my sour attitude. Even though it was already closing time, I resolved to do better and make waiting on the last few customers a more pleasant experience.

By 4:30, Mama had returned. And so had my sour mood. So much for pleasant experiences. The last customer had argued over the price of a planter, comparing the sticker price to the price that I'd scanned when I'd rung it up at the register.

She hadn't known that my old eagle eyes had seen her peeling the price tag off the planter and switching it with another, less expensive item. She'd actually argued with me! She must have thought *volunteer* was a code word for cheap, incompetent help. Not this flower girl. I wasn't going to embarrass my mother by letting the register come up short.

Mama greeted me with a kiss on the cheek.

"How was your day, sweetheart?"

"If you'd asked me twenty minutes ago, I'd say on a scale of one to ten, that it was off the charts."

"That good?" Mama said hopefully.

"Nope. That bad. It was so bad, it never even made it to number one on the scale."

"Come on now, Shiri. It wasn't that bad, was it?"

"I've got dirt under my fingernails, a rash from handling some fuzzy plant that I've never seen before in my life, blisters on my feet, dust in my eyes, and bugs in my hair. And that was just in the first twenty minutes of my volunteering. You knew I didn't want to come, Mama. Why did you make me?"

"I thought it would help you take your mind off of your troubles. Give you something to think about other than yourself for a change," she said in that motherly, concerned yet disapproving way to let me know that I'd been selfish.

Slowly, I shook my head. She just didn't understand. I wasn't me that I'd been so preoccupied with lately. It was

Jack Deneen. I couldn't stop thinking about him. I missed him so much.

And the more I missed him, the madder I got. Why couldn't I stop thinking about him? How could a man I barely knew figure so heavily in my emotional well-being? I must have been crazy. Certifiably insane. Or hopelessly, desperately in love.

I don't know which sucked worse—thinking that I was crazy or being in love. At least there was medication for crazy. A double dose of Prozac would get me off this emotional roller-coaster ride, I was sure. But what about love? There was no magic potion for that. No little green pill or shot in the behind. I had these feelings and I was stuck with them.

"Can we go now?" I insisted. I felt another crying fit coming on, and I didn't want her to be a witness.

"In a minute. I want to make sure that the shop is properly closed."

"What's there to check? Close and lock the door and it's done," I said testily.

"Did you check the back storeroom? Make sure that everything was prepared for tomorrow's opener? It's every volunteer's responsibility to keep things tidy for the next, you know."

I blew out a huffy breath. "All right, all right. I'll check the back storeroom."

For her sake, I made a grand show of rearranging a few stock items. Spools of decorative ribbon, extra bags, receipt paper for the cash register. By the time Mama was satisfied that I'd done my volunteering duty, it was five o'clock. I noticed that even though she was so concerned with the gift shop passing some sort of volunteer-readiness test, she did little to help me. She watched over me and kept just as close an eye on the clock. If I'd been in my right mind, I'd have been suspicious. As it was, I was just tired. Ready to get back to the house, climb on the couch, and prepare for another marathon of mindless television.

"Time to call it quits," I announced.

"Almost," she agreed.

"Mama, what are we still doing here?"

"I told you. To get your mind off of your troubles."

"And exactly how was I supposed to accomplish that?" I blew up at her. "How was I going to feel better watching these way too happy couples parading up and down the gardens in front of me? You tell me how I was supposed to feel!"

I was a little too loud, a little too strident. But I needed to say it. It felt good to say it. After weeks of avoiding how I was feeling, it felt good to dig into the wound, to stir up all the emotional pus and purge it from my body.

"You tell me," Mama said, seemingly unaffected by my outburst. "You haven't said much to me these past few weeks about your feelings."

Her extreme calmness deflated me. I sank back against a counter. "I guess I haven't been much fun to be around lately."

"No, you haven't. You've been moody, grouchy, sometimes openly nasty to your father and me."

"Why'd you put up with it for so long? You wouldn't have let me talk to you that way when I was a kid."

"You aren't a kid anymore, Shiri. You'll always be my baby girl. But you're a grown woman now. I tried to give you the space that you needed to work things out."

"I haven't done a very good job of it. Maybe I'm not as grown as I thought, Mama. I run into my first life-size problem and the first thing I do is run home to my mama."

"It's what you're supposed to do. It's what I'm here for. I want to help you, Shiri. That's all I ever wanted to do."

"Mama, I don't know what to do!" My voice cracked as tears welled in my eyes and spilled down my cheeks. "I feel so stupid."

"You are not stupid!" Mama said sharply. "I don't ever want to hear you say that again, Shiri Annise Rowlan."

"All right, all right. I'm not stupid. But you have to admit that I've done some pretty flaky things lately."

"Now that you can own up to them. Come here, Sweet Sherbet," she said. "Come tell Mama all about it."

She held her arms out to me, rocking me as if I were a small child. I didn't mind. For the moment, I didn't *want* to be a grown woman. I wanted my mama to make it all better.

I laughed softly. Mama had been right. Since breaking it off with Jack, I had talked at her, around her, and about her. I'd done everything to keep from talking to her. Maybe because she had the uncanny ability to cut through the bull and help me see the truth. I was ready to hear it now. I wanted to see it.

"I messed things up," I admitted, "between Jack and me. He was offering me a chance at something special, and I totally screwed it up, Mama. I threw it back in his face like it meant nothing."

Mama shook her head, her expression sympathetic. "Why'd you do that?"

"Because I was stup—that is, I stooped to the level of some brainless, no-account hoochies."

"That's a bit harsh, Shiri. I taught you better than that."

"Trust me, Mama. I'm holding back and being kind. I can't believe I let them run me off like that. I can't believe that I let them ruin my good thing."

"So, what are you going to do about it?"

"I don't know." I shrugged helplessly.

"Yes, you do," Mama insisted. "You know what you have to do."

"I can't go running back to him."

"That's foolish pride talking. There's nothing wrong with your legs. What's stopping you?"

"It's too late for me. He's probably found someone else by now."

"Not if what you felt for each other was as special as you say it was."

"I feel like it was, but now I don't know. It all happened so fast. I don't know whether or not to trust my feelings, my instincts."

"Do you trust mine?"

"That's a silly question. Of course I do."

"Then trust me, it's not too late. Do you care for him, Shiri?"

Without hesitation, I said, "Yes." A reluctant smile tugged at the corners of my lips. "Though the Lord only knows why. All I know is that when I'm with him, it all seems so right. Then again, maybe I'm just wishing that it's right. Maybe it isn't really. How do I know that I haven't tricked myself into thinking that it is when it really isn't?"

"Shiri, I know you well enough to know that you don't make decisions lightly. You plan, you strategize, you agonize."

"Agonize is right. I think I've had root canals less painful than this, Mama."

"Do you remember when you were a senior in high school?"

"Vaguely," I said dryly. "Like it was oh-so-many years ago."

"You sat at the kitchen table, stacks of college brochures and applications spread out in front of you. You pored over each one. We prayed over each one. And when the time came, you picked the one that was right for you. When you graduated and had several job offers to select from, what did you do?"

"Nearly pulled my hair out by the roots trying to decide which offer to accept."

"But you picked one. When you did, you told me, 'This one feels right, Mama.' You debated as much as you could with your head and settled on the one that felt best in your heart. This is no different. Do what feels right in your heart and let the Lord take care of the rest."

"But we've only known each other for a little while."

"Stop looking for ways to kill your joy, Shiri! What does love matter if it happens in one day or one year? Adam and Eve had less time than that."

"Yeah, and look how they turned out—consorting with serpents and murderers."

"Jack Deneen doesn't strike me as that kind of man."

"He consorts with worse. Football players." I gave a mock shudder to show her that I still had my sense of humor.

"It's going to be all right, Shiri," Mama promised.

"Let me guess. A mother's instinct?"

"You've got it."

"Not yet I don't," I returned as I planted a kiss on her cheek. " 'Cause like Grandma Lela says, I'm a good girl."

I hugged my mother tightly, squeezing her to let her know how grateful I was for her counsel. "You know that I love you, don't you?"

"Of course."

"You're my *favorite* mommy," I complimented her.

"I'm your only mommy." Her tone was wry, but appreciative.

"That makes it even better."

"Since I'm your favorite . . ." My mother's voice turned too casual to be natural. "Would you do me a favor?"

"A favor? What kind of favor?" My sneaky-mother-trick radar detector went way up like those antennae from *My Favorite Martian.*

"A small one."

"There are no such things as small favors."

"Do it for me."

"Okay. What do you need?"

"There's one more customer I want you to take care of out there."

"A customer?" I blinked, not quite sure I heard her correctly. "Out there. I thought the shop was closed."

All of this time, I'd been snotting and crying all over her shoulder and there was someone outside.

"It *is* closed," she said. "But I opened it up again as a special favor. Please, Shiri. If you trust me, do this for me."

They'd told me that it couldn't be done. But I wasn't going to listen. Experience had taught me that with the proper motivation, you could accomplish whatever you wanted.

Waving around a platinum credit card seemed to be the proper motivation at the time. So, I whipped mine out, laid it on the glass counter in front of the nice sales assistant, and told her exactly what I wanted, how I wanted it, and by when.

"That doesn't give me very much time, sir," she insisted. I think she added the "sir" after she saw the platinum credit card.

"So, why waste a moment of it talking about why it can't be done?" I said silkily. At least, I hoped that my expression was cordial. It was all I could do to keep it that way. Inside, I rather felt like I'd been tied up in cords. My stomach was tight. My heart felt squeezed. And my fingers tingled as if constantly jolted with electricity.

If this had been any other moment, I would have checked myself into the nearest hospital with a self-diagnosis of cardiac arrest. My malady wasn't unusual. Millions had suffered through and survived. This wasn't exactly my first time afflicted. But I hoped that it would be my last. I was suffering from terminal "nose-wide-openness." The Big L. Love. I was a goner and proud of it.

"Five-foot-four, did you say?" The sales assistant peered at me over the rim of her glasses and double-checked her notes. I'd talked so fast, in a hurry to get my words out, that I wasn't sure if she'd gotten all of my specifications.

"At least." I held up my hand to indicate the height. "With braids. Must have braids."

"A bear with braids. Very unusual."

"So is the woman it's for," I replied.

"And a football jersey," she verified.

"Not just any jersey, this one." I tossed one of mine onto the case. "And this hat."

"Oh, the Birmingham Steeldogs," she said excitedly. "You must be quite a devoted fan."

"Yeah, something like that." Of the game. Sure, it was my job. A fan of Shiri's? Definitely. A fan by choice, not by profession.

"Can you do it? If not, I'll have to take my business

somewhere else.'' I reached for the credit card, but she whisked it out of my grasp.

"No, sir.'' She read the name and her smile grew bigger. "No, sir, Mr. Deneen. We'll get it done for you. You can count on us.''

"I certainly hope so.''

I checked my watch. A few more stops to make before my next crucial appointment. I could not be late. I would not be. Especially not after Mrs. Johnson's urging. Her admonition alone was enough to make me break speed laws. But she was not alone. It seemed as if several of the Johnson clan had suddenly had a change of heart. Instead of shielding Shiri from me, they guided me to her. If Mrs. Johnson's call could make me blow past speed traps, it was Mrs. Rowlan's encouraging message that made me want to break the sound barrier.

She'd called me, not long after I'd hung up the phone with Mrs. Johnson. The conversation had been short and sweet, direct—sorta like all of the Johnson women.

Out of all the things she could have said to me, out of all the questions she could have asked, she asked only one. Did I or didn't I? That's all she wanted to know. Did I or didn't I?

The question might have been cryptic. I could have chosen to interpret it any way I wanted to. But as the mother of her only daughter, there was only one question she could be concerned about. Did I or didn't I what?

Love Shiri, of course. Did I or didn't I want her? Need her? Yes. A thousand times yes. Ask me a thousand times and I'd answer the same. Of course I did.

When she'd asked me, I'd answered: I do.

"Good,'' she'd replied. And I could hear the smile in her voice. "Now all we have to do is get you two to the altar so that you can say those two words to her in person.''

"How are we going to do that? I can't even get her to agree to go to a movie with me anymore, Mrs. Rowlan. She won't answer my calls and I have no earthly reason why not.''

"Something must have scared her off."

"If she was frightened, she didn't tell me why."

"No, she wouldn't. Shiri doesn't like appearing weak or vulnerable."

"Yes, I can see that."

I remembered the day that I'd first laid eyes on Shiri Rowlan. I'd watched her struggling with those ridiculous bears, fighting with her contact lenses, holding back her fear of flying. She was not only going to face her fears, she was going to stare them down. Beat them into submission. Everything about her said strength. She was a fighter when she believed she had something—someone—worth fighting for.

I am that someone. I was the one for her.

All I had to do was convince her. To do that, I had to get her attention. To get her attention, I had to get past whatever it was—or whoever it was—that had convinced her I wasn't.

I checked my watch again—3:45. Not much time left. Not if I was going to make the schedule that Shiri's relatives had laid out for me. By four o'clock, I'd gotten the call from the eager-to-please sales assistant. Everything was there, ready for me, waiting to be picked up.

Five o'clock, on the dot, I was at the botanical gardens gift shop after closing, waiting to be let in. What a conspicuous sight I must have made. A grown man pulling a little red wagon loaded with balloons and two monstrous bears. I didn't care how it looked.

Not really.

Okay, maybe just a little bit. I did care how I looked. Someone from the milling crowd recognized me, called my name. As I looked up, he snapped my photograph.

Something told me that I could expect to see my picture prominently displayed in the *Birmingham News* with some ridiculous headline—LOCAL FOOTBALL HERO BEARS ALL. Or some other such silliness.

I paced in front of the gift shop, dragging my wagon behind me and rehearsing what I'd say once I was face-to-face with Shiri again. I tried several different approaches, each one sounding cornier than the last. I don't know why I was having so much trouble coming up with the right words. I'd only been thinking about this since the moment I'd sat next to her on the plane.

As the plane had started to dip, then climb into the clouds past the storm, I'd gotten past the flight attendant with an urgent plea that my wife needed me. A ruse. That's how I'd meant it originally. Something to say to get her to leave me alone so I could sit next to Shiri.

I think my declaration was more along the lines of a prophecy. I'd spoken the words without hesitation, as if they could be true. Without fully understanding why at the time, I'd wanted them to be true. For the first time in my life, I'd met someone whom I'd considered that way.

Now, as I contemplated what I could say to make it come true, I thought that I couldn't trust this to mere words. I might screw them up, say the wrong thing to set her off again.

Maybe I'd let the bears speak for me. Not that they were talking bears. All the platinum cards in the world couldn't find me talking bears in that short amount of time. But the symbol of what they represented said it better than any fine words I could have managed.

Two bears, dressed like Shiri and me, sat in a wagon draped with streamers in my team's colors—a nice addition. I hadn't asked for that. That was something the sales representative had added. She'd certainly earned her commission this afternoon. But with the final touch—the one that I had asked for, had insisted on—she'd followed my instructions to the letter.

The bears were bound, hand in hand, by a single gold chain. Dangling from the chain was a ring. And it was as Aunt Pam had suggested. One carat. Marquise cut. Simple. But effective.

Mrs. Johnson had said to be creative. There hadn't been time. So I'd shamelessly borrowed from Shiri's act of love. I knew what Shiri had meant when she'd given the bears to her grandparents for their anniversary. In her own way, she'd meant to honor their years of loyalty and devotion to each other.

We had no such history. Not yet, we didn't. But I hoped that she would understand what I meant by offering these bears to her. Here was to our history—a history yet to be. Here was to memories I hoped to create, love and laughter I hoped to share, generations that I hoped to beget.

When Mrs. Rowlan unlocked the gift-shop door and beckoned to me with a single finger pressed to her lips, I complied, though not without some trepidation. She wasn't exactly sticking to the plan. She was supposed to give me a sign— an indication of how receptive Shiri would be toward me and my offering.

I felt like a pagan, waiting on trembling knees to see if my offering would be acceptable. If Mrs. Rowlan came out of the back room and gave me the thumbs-up sign, I knew that everything was copacetic. We could proceed with my hastily conceived but well-intentioned plan. But if she came out and made a slashing motion across her throat, I knew I'd better slink out of there, with my bears tucked between my legs.

"Well?" I whispered harshly as I maneuvered the wagon out of the line of sight. When Shiri came out, I didn't want her distracted by the rolling toy circus I'd dragged behind me. I wanted me to be the first sight she saw. I wanted to be the one to bring the light to her eyes, not the ring.

"How did it go?"

She smiled softly and said, "I'm going to go and get a cup of coffee at the café. When I come back, you tell *me* how it went."

I shook my head in confusion; but she stood on tiptoe and kissed me on the cheek. "No matter what happens, Jack Deneen, you're a good man."

"That doesn't exactly fill me with confidence, Mrs. Rowlan."

"Trust me on this one," she insisted. She turned her head over her shoulder and called out, "Shiri, can you come out here please? We need your help."

Before she left me, she said, "The ball is in your hands, Steeldog. Don't fumble it."

"Now, that kind of talk I can understand."

As Shiri came out of the back storeroom, I watched her facial expression rapidly change from surprise to suspicion. She'd obviously been set up—again! Just as quickly, she lowered her eyes, an admission of shame.

No matter what had happened between us, I didn't deserve to be dumped like that. Not without an explanation. Not without a chance to defend myself, to set things right again. *If I could.*

Maybe whatever I'd done to her was indefensible. Maybe there was no fixing it. Call it selfishness or stubborn male pride, but I thought I deserved a chance to understand why she'd gone.

She glanced at the retreating figure of her mother. Her mouth twisted as she rolled her eyes. "Traitor," she whispered.

She'd been set up and abandoned. No family to hide behind. She had to face me now.

"Hi," she said simply, lifting her hand and letting it fall again to her side.

"Hi," I returned, giving a mock salute.

Not exactly the most sparkling conversation. But it was the first time I'd heard her voice in weeks. I'd take it.

"You . . . uh . . . you look . . . that is, you're looking well." I gestured awkwardly at her dress.

"Thanks. It was a present from my grandmother." She flounced the material, fanning it out to expose the full, floral pattern.

"A special occasion?"

"Uh . . . no . . . just because . . . I think she thought the bright colors would cheer me up."

"Did they?" I asked, taking a step closer.

Shiri bit her lip, shaking her head. Her eyes glittered.

"No," she whispered. "Lately, I've been inconsolable." Then, she gave a small laugh. "Intolerable, actually."

"Do you want to talk about it? I'm a good listener."

"I'm . . . I'm not sure what to say."

"You can . . . start off by saying how much you missed me," I suggested, moving closer to her.

Shiri balled up her fists and put her hands on her hips, but she didn't back away. "Putting words in my mouth, Steeldog?"

"No, ma'am," I insisted. "Just trying to draw them out."

She nodded her approval. "I did."

"Did what?" I wanted to hear her say it. I had to see it in her face, watch the emotion in her eyes.

"Miss you," she stressed. Then, as if floodgates had been opened, she started talking so quickly that the words tumbled over each other. "I wanted to call you. Wanted to do it a thousand times. But every time I did, I kept hearing their voices in my head, laughing at me, reminding me of all of the things I wasn't and all the things you needed and I was so sure that you and I could never work because of the type of person that you are and the—"

"Whoa!" I said sharply. "Time out!" If I'd had a whistle, I would have blown it. I'm sure her running monologue broke some kind of record for speed and incomprehensibility. "You've been hearing voices?" I repeated.

"Not crazy-in-the-head voices," she elaborated. Then, she reached up to smooth my cheek. "But I admit, a girl would have to be crazy before walking out on you like I did."

"Shiri, just tell me what's wrong. I'll make it right. I promise. I'll fix it."

"You can't fix me, Jack," she insisted. "It's not you, it's me. The problem is all with me."

"There's nothing wrong with you. You're perfect."

"No, I'm not!" she vehemently denied.

"You're perfect for me, then. Try to argue with that."

"Give me enough time. I can argue with anything," she said somberly.

"I'll give you all the time you need," I insisted. "Just don't make me spend it alone. I want . . . I want to spend it with you."

"I couldn't believe that you would," she confessed. "When those girls at Big Dog's party—"

"What girls?" I reached out, grabbed her by the shoulders, and squeezed. Not hard. Just enough to let her know that I wasn't going to let her slip away from me so easily this time.

"I don't know. Some girls." She shrugged. "I heard them talking about you. And me."

"What did they say?"

"I can't remember exactly. It doesn't matter now."

"Yes, it does, Shiri. If they could do this to us, if they have that kind of influence over you, I want to know. I want to know who's been messing with your head."

"It's not so much what they said but what they represented, Jack. Don't you understand?"

"No. I don't. And if it makes you want to leave me, then, to be perfectly honest, I'm not sure that I want to."

"I understand now that they were just being vicious and jealous. They were angry because I was with you. And who was I? A nobody. I wasn't some famous actress or model or glamour queen. I was just me. Walking in on your arm in all of my big-hipped, full-lipped, small-breasted glory."

I stood back from her, amazed that this was the image she had of herself. Is that what she thought I saw in her? How could I make her see? How could I make her understand?

Maybe it was her physical features that had originally caught my eye at the airport—the color of her hair, that cute upturned nose, not to mention that sweet, sculpted behind!

But it took more than that to make me want to give her a second look. It was more than physical attraction that stopped me from looking at all of the other pretty women. Her poise, her coolness, even her wry understated sense of humor kept my head turned in her direction.

I'm not saying that I would never look at another woman. That was impossible, unreasonable to ask. A man was always going to look. Any man with eyes in his head was going to appreciate the pleasant proportions of a well-built woman.

But a man who spent all of this time, his energy *just* looking was going to be a man looking alone. I'd had enough of that. The whole point of looking at something—for something—was to find. I'd found it in Shiri.

Here was a woman I could look at. And when I was done looking, I could talk to her. Unlike so many others who were long on looks and short on everything else, she was quick-witted and knowledgeable, up on current events, and down with her family roots. Funny and introspective. Caustic and committed.

I'd learned from our date at the coffeehouse that she could not only hold a conversation, she could keep me rapt during the span of it. Even through the constant interruptions, she'd kept me coming back to her, wanting to soak in every word, every statement.

She had the uncanny ability of stating her opinions as gospel, and casting shadows on what I'd always taken to be factual. Her views on child-rearing would make educators cringe. Her passionate stance against the death penalty and war made pacifists seem like slackers.

And after all the talking was done, when there was nothing left to be said, here was a woman I wanted to love. She'd take and she'd give. I'd give and she'd return. Why would I keep looking at others when I'd found it all?

"Come here, Shiri." I held out my hand to her and walked her over to the doors marked for the rest rooms.

I considered which door for a moment. Years of habit and conditioning immediately made me swing toward the one marked for men. But Shiri hesitated, so I instead pushed on the door marked for women. A better choice anyway. It had what I needed to get my point across.

With my hands still on her shoulders, I guided her toward the full-length mirror.

"Tell me what you see," with my cheek pressed against hers, I whispered in her ear.

I knew that she was carefully considering her answer, because she took what seemed like ages to me to speak. Finally, simply, she whispered back, "I see us."

"That's right. Nobody else here but us. Just you and me."

"Nobody here but us chickens," she remarked.

"Are you afraid of me, Shiri?"

She shook her head. "I'm afraid of what I've done to you. I'm so sorry, jack. I never meant to hurt you. You know that, don't you?"

I kissed tenderly her on the cheek. "Even when we aren't standing in the bathroom in front of a mirror, Shiri, when I'm with you all I see is us. All I want is for us to be together. I thought that's what you wanted, too. But then you ran. And now I'm not so sure. So I want to know. I have to know. Do you want me?"

When she didn't pull away, I kissed her again on the jaw, then lower on the neck and again on the shoulder.

Shiri moaned softly, tilting her head away to give me more access as I brushed aside her hair. I slid my arms down her arms and rested them lightly at her waist before pulling her back against me.

The thin fabric of her dress didn't leave much to my imagination. I felt the warm press of her bottom against my thighs as she settled back against me.

"Tell me that you want me, Shiri," I insisted, massaging her outer thighs.

"You know that I do." Her voice was husky, thick with emotion.

"I want to hear you say it!"

Shiri threw her head back against my chest as my hands slid under her dress, seeking the scrap of fabric that restricted my access. She tried to speak; but her words were unintelligible—mewling sounds of pleasure as my palms found her heated core, resting there while she pulsed against me.

I probed, making her bite her lip against the exquisite torture.

Warmth. Wetness. Willingness.

She reached behind her head, clinging to handfuls of my shirt, as I took my hands away long enough to search for my wallet.

"Just you and me," I echoed. "That's all I ever see,

Shiri. I don't care what anyone has told you, I don't care what you've heard. When I'm with you, that's all there is. Just you and me.''

"You and me," she repeated, as she spun around to face me.

"I mean it, Shiri. I want you in my life."

"I'm here, Jack. I'm not going anywhere."

"Yes, you are," I contradicted.

She looked at me, puzzled.

"I'll explain later," I promised as I reached for the rear zipper of her dress, hardly paying the pretty fabric any mind as it slid to a silent heap on the floor. I stood for several moments, memorizing every line, every curve.

"I love you, Shiri Rowlan. I want to make love to you."

Shiri stepped away from the dress and led me by the hand to the lip of a small, porcelain counter. "No porch light to stop us now," she teased as I grasped her hips and lifted her onto the counter.

Without taking her eyes from my face, she guided me toward her, inside her.

As I shifted, settling between her knees, I insisted, "You and me, Shiri. Me and you."

My carefully timed thrusts emphasized my commitment to that soulful, sensuous mantra. She cried out in wondrous rapture as passion claimed her. Tremors made her shudder. Heaving. Clinging. Gasping for precious air. Even as her body signaled the culmination of release, I didn't stop. I couldn't, even if I'd wanted to.

I had not spoken to her in weeks. Had not touched her like this for even longer. Even though propriety and fear of discovery should have cooled me, our surroundings had just the opposite effect. Knowing that any moment someone could walk in, see us, and know that I'd claimed her for my own aroused me to greater passion. Our sighs mingled in the air around us, echoed, and bounced off the walls. The sultry sounds were magnified, as if the small confines of this room could not contain the maelstrom.

Our reflection in the mirror was my ultimate undoing—

two bodies, coiled, connected, wanting, writhing. Like fluid from a sacred gourd, I spilled my offering into her.

And as I rested, spent both physically and emotionally, against her shoulder, I lamented that for now, for safety's sake, the full expression of my love remained sheathed— trapped within the confines of latex.

I bode my time, anxious for the moment when I could come to her, inside her, with a precious offering of life.

"Jack?" Shiri whispered, nestled comfortably in my arms.

"Uh-huh?"

"Can I ask a favor?"

"Anything, Shiri."

"Can I get off this countertop now? It's cold and biting into my behind."

"Lucky counter," I replied, pinching her on her rear end. She gave a mock punch to my arm. "You are so bad!"

"Actually, I've been a very, very good boy." I backed away. "You wait right here and I'll show you."

"Where are you going?"

"Not far. I promise." I kissed the tip of her nose. "Never again."

"But—" she protested.

"Wait right there. I'll be right back. In fact, cover your eyes and count to . . . oh, thirty should do it."

"Cover my eyes?" she repeated.

I grasped her wrist and raised her hand to her face. "Cover your eyes," I insisted. "And soon you'll see a big surprise."

"I don't like surprises," she warned me.

"Then you're going to absolutely despise this one," I assured her as I ducked out of the bathroom, then hurried around the counter to where the bears were still waiting.

Out of the corner of my eye, I thought I saw Mrs. Rowlan milling around at the front of the store. She peeked in, shielded her face against the glass, then raised her shoulders in silent question.

Grinning, I gave her the thumbs-up sign. She reached for the door, about to unlock it, but I shook my head.

"No. Not yet." Holding up one hand, I indicated to give me five more minutes alone with Shiri. On second thought, another hand went up. I considered taking off my shoes and wiggling my toes, but that would have been greedy.

She nodded in understanding and pointed toward the garden. Ten more minutes.

Carefully, I maneuvered the bears out from behind the counter and tugged the wagon toward the rest room. Okay, so it wasn't the most romantic place in the world to propose to a woman. But it was private, secluded, and smelled pine-forest fresh. A man couldn't ask for more than that.

As I approached the bathroom, I heard water running, so I tapped on the door before going in.

"Shiri?"

"Just a minute," she called out. Then, "Okay. You can come in now."

"Do you still have your eyes closed?"

"Oh, I forgot. Okay. They're closed again now."

Slowly, I opened the door just a crack before poking my head in the door. "Shiri?"

"I'm not peeking," she promised.

I opened the door a little wider, pulled the bears inside, then maneuvered until I was directly behind her. I wrapped my arms around her waist and squeezed once, before putting my hands on top of hers.

"Umm," she hummed. "Is this my surprise? I like."

"This is only part of it. You can look now," I murmured, pulling her hands down.

She turned her face aside, to stare curiously at me. But I indicated with my eyebrows where she should turn her attention.

"I don't believe it!" she exclaimed. "Look at them. They are so cute! Braids! Jack, where'd you get a bear with braids?"

"They look kinda cute, sitting there together, don't you think?"

"Absolutely adorable! I love them. Wait until Grandma Lela sees these. She collects bears, you know."

"Well, she's not getting her hands on these. Look a little closer. I think she'll be more interested in what the bears are bearing."

"Bears are bearing?" she echoed, stepping a little closer. I guess the streamers and the ribbons and the huge bows were a bit much. She didn't even notice the ring.

Shiri walked closer to the wagon, then bent down with her hands resting on her knees. Her finger traced along the chain wrapped around the bears' wrists.

"Kinda kinky there, big fella. I didn't know you were into bear bondage." She looked back at me and grinned.

"A little-known secret from the darker side of my personality. Look closer."

When I heard the sharp intake of her breath, that's when I knew she'd found it. She made a little sound—something between a sigh and a strangled cough—and staggered back.

"Jack?" Her voice was barely above a whisper. "What is this?"

"What does it look like?"

"Looks like a hell of a lot of money. I would have accepted a simple kiss-and-make-up teddy bear. Not even giant-sized."

"Not this time, darlin'. Make no mistakes about it. If I have to tie you up with golden cords, I want you by my side, Shiri. I love you and I want to marry you."

Again, the small, shocked gurgle. "Marry me . . . as in proposals and weddings and girls in ugly satin dresses?"

"The whole nine yards."

I unhooked the chain and dropped the ring into my palm.

"I . . . I don't know what to say." She shook her head uncomprehendingly.

"Woman, after all the hoops I jumped through to get here, you'd better say yes." I took her hand and slid the ring on her finger. It looked so right there.

Shiri just stared at it, biting her lip.

"Well?" I prompted. "Are you going to stand there or are you going to say something?"

"This is . . . this is . . . this is certainly something, Jack."

"Not quite what I had in mind. Then again, I shouldn't complain. Your grandmother had wanted me to do this over a romantic, candlelight dinner. Do you want me to drop to one knee? Would that make it seem more like a proper proposal?"

"No one gets down on one knee anymore," she informed me. "Besides, you don't want me to run and tell all of your friends that I brought the great Jack 'The Flash' Deneen to his knees."

"Go ahead. Tell all of my friends. Some of them gave me some pretty interesting suggestions on what I could do down here on my knees."

"*Interesting.* That's just a polite word for *raunchy,* isn't it?"

"Marry me and find out."

She looked up toward the ceiling, appearing to give my offer some great thought. "I'll do it on one condition."

"And what's that?"

"That if that heifer Damitra and any of her friends take one step near the wedding ceremony, you won't try to stop me while I pull her hair out by the roots."

"Damitra?" How in the world did she find out about that ancient history . . . unless . . . oh, yeah, Big Dog's party. If she'd been there, she wouldn't have taken too kindly to seeing me with Shiri. Tough. After four years, she should have been over it by now. Moved on.

"Stop you? I'll help find her real roots, if that'll make you happy."

"In that case, the answer is yes. Yes, Jack Deneen. I'll marry you. If that's what you want."

"Yes, that's what I want." I held my arms out to her, encircling her, promising myself that there was no way I'd ever let her out of my arms or out of my heart again.

EIGHTEEN

"Come to Papa. That's it. Bring it on home."

I took off from the scrimmage line knowing that the ball was coming to me. Passing plays were the only ones we'd used with any kind of success against this tough Baton Rouge team. Having the home-field advantage and crowd behind them to pump them up, they'd practically run over our offensive line, sacking our quarterback and making him eat artificial turf more times than he could count.

Handoffs in the backfield were stopped cold. Our running game was a joke. With a quarter left to play and us down by a couple of touchdowns, speed was our best offensive maneuver against these human steamrollers.

If I could burn their defensive end off the line, get past him, and avoid their roaming safety, the ball—and the score—was as good as mine.

The snap count was short and irregular. Its cadence was meant to keep the opposing team off guard, maybe even draw them off sides. At this stage of the game, we weren't proud. Anything that got us closer to the goal line worked for us.

The center snapped the ball to the quarterback, who faked

a handoff, pivoted, and instead heaved a long bomb down the right side. I sprinted. Nothing fancy. My instruction from Coach Brodie: Just catch the damn ball. It was an old-fashioned, all-out footrace between me and the Baton Rouge Blaze defender who was following only two or three steps behind me.

The game had gone back and forth forever. Fatigue sucked the strength from my legs. But I could already feel the telltale tingle in my fingertips. A subtle reminder of my hands' desire for the ball. A quick glance over my shoulder. A few steps. A few steps more. The ball arced high overhead, then began its downward spiral.

With the goal line only yards away, I could almost taste victory. Not of the entire game. There was still a quarter to go before that was decided. The taste of victory was the taste of the moment. Sweet and swift, tantalizing and transitory. Moments was like this, I knew in my head that this was just a game. But it was also moments like this, when every cell in my body surged with energy, that I was thankful that this was *my* game. I was on top here. I was in my element.

Out of the corner of my eye, I saw the Baton Rouge defensive end reaching for the ball. The other hand stretched out—reaching for my shoulder, too. He wasn't supposed to do that. No contact ten yards past the line of scrimmage.

Yeah, right.

I dared any player worth his salary to try to play the game keeping his hands to himself. It would be like a professional hockey player playing with the stick firmly bonded to the ice. What fan didn't go to a hockey game hoping for a high-stick penalty? Or attend a baseball game, waiting for the pitcher to throw heat past an unsuspecting batter's head to keep him from crowding the plate? Baseball, hot dogs, and a bench-clearing brawl. If a sporting event was the civilized combat arena, aggression was our arsenal.

When the defensive end reached out to me, I had a decision to make. Catching the ball was the ultimate goal. But I had some other considerations to make. Did I kick my run into overdrive, risk overshooting the ball to mess with that player's mind? All night long this sucker had been talking trash, either in my face at the line of scrimmage or trailing me just close enough to trip me up if I didn't give it my best effort each time out.

All night long I'd been listening to variations of how old and slow I was getting. After this forty-yard dash, if I could pull away from him, that would show him who was getting old. That he would prove that he didn't have the speed to catch up to me. Maybe make him doubt his own abilities the next time we went out. Or, at the worst, get him just as tired as I was.

Or did I slow it down and make him crowd into me, possibly drawing a pass interference call?

As the ball came plummeting to the turf, my moment of indecision cost me a few spare inches. If I was going to catch that ball, I was going to have to lean for it, maybe dive for it. As it came over my right shoulder, I heard it whistle past my head. Hands outstretched, I had it. It was mine.

And then, suddenly, it wasn't.

Something happened. I'm not quite sure what. One minute, I was reaching for the ball. The next, pain exploded in my chest as artificial turf reached up and smacked me hard.

Some women say there is no pain like childbirth. I agree. I can also attest that there is no pain like thousands of tiny, artificial fibers, reaching out to rip the flesh from your body—hair by hair.

My curse of frustration was smothered as the defender landed abruptly on top of me. Our legs intertwined for a moment so I kicked out, trying to roll free. I don't think he liked that little move. In fact, I know he didn't. If he did, he wouldn't have cursed me as a certain male anatomy-sucking offspring of a female dog.

His epithet didn't bother me any. Let him get mad. He should have been watching where he was going. I was more concerned with how the referees would call this last play—fumble, pass interference, or down by incidental contact. It would be a difficult call to make. The line judge had trailed us, five, maybe ten yards back. From that distance, I knew that he could see the defender reaching out to grab me. But I'm not sure if the defender ever really got a firm hand on me, enough to make the referees believe that he was more interested in taking me down than catching the ball.

There were several flags on the field. That told me that several of the refs had seen the infraction and had made a judgment call. I stood by the sidelines, examining what amounted to some pretty nasty burns on my elbows and shins as the judges conferred.

A decision finally made, the head referee jogged to the center of the field, turned on his microphone, and announced to the crowd the call of pass interference against the Baton Rouge Blaze defensive end. This being an away game, that decision didn't sit too well with the home crowd.

As I said before, I didn't give a flip. Actually, I must have flipped pretty well. In addition to scraping off several layers of skin, I'd wrenched something in my back as well. I'd hurt it badly enough to have to ask to sit out the next play. Coach Wood agreed, giving me a strange look. He knew that it wasn't like me. I never asked to sit out. When I came, I came to play, every game, one hundred percent. All the time. But not today. Not this game.

I sat by for two more plays, until the last moments of the fifteen-minute-long quarter ticked away. Watching in helpless anxiety, I sat with an ice pack pressed against my back to settle the spasms. Each time I tried to stand, my back tightened, forcing me to the bench once again.

By the time the game was over, I was limping off the field as dejectedly as our defeated Steeldogs. I wasn't looking forward to the bus ride home. Knowing that I wanted to do something to help the team, but couldn't, added to my frustration.

We all listened to the aftergame pep talk from the coaching staff with half an ear, half a mind. The other half of our attention was still on the game. Each of us went over every play, wondering what we could have done to prevent the loss. By the time I hit the showers, dejection surrounded me as effectively as the steam.

I'd had sprains before. Cramps were a longtime acquaintance—even the occasional spasm. But something about this time didn't feel right. I made an offhand remark to that effect to Billy, the team's trainer.

"I could talk to the doc for you," he offered as he helped me onto the massage table. "See about getting you a prescription for some muscle relaxants. Maybe you've been pushing yourself too hard, Flash. Between pulling double duty as a receiver and defensive back, managing your business ventures, and taking care of the new lady in your life, I don't see why you aren't a bundle of quivering nerves."

To emphasize that point, he dug his fist into a corded section in my back. It felt as if he'd found his way to the center of a burning brick lodged there.

"Thanks for the massage, Billy," I said, grunting as he pounded at the spot. "But I'll pass on the muscle relaxants. You know I don't like pills. They make me woo-woo in the head."

"Coach Wood's going to go woo-woo if you drop another pass, Flash."

"Didn't you know, Billy? I didn't drop that pass. I was interfered with." I turned my head to grin at him. "That's what the refs said, anyway."

Billy grasped my head with both hands and gave a quick twist, starting a chain reaction of muscle contractions and releases down my neck, across my back—contractions that I could feel all the way to the balls of my feet.

"Interference, my left eye. You got lucky. That boy hardly laid a hand on you," Billy scoffed.

"That 'hardly' made the difference between a wasted down and moving us to within range of the goal line," I reminded Billy.

"Fat lotta good it did. We still didn't score."

"Rub it in, why don't you?" I complained.

Billy could massage away the ache in my back. He couldn't take away the pain of disappointment in my heart.

It was the next to the last game of the season. If we won the last one, we'd tie for third place, and still had a decent chance at the ArenaCup championship. Billy must have noted something in my expression.

"Pluck up, Flash. If you take that woe-is-me attitude back to your lady, you won't score at home, either."

"Anybody ever tell you that you've got a dirty mind, Billy?"

"Dirty of mind. Pure of heart." He winked at me.

"That's not just any woman you're talking about. Shiri's going to be my wife." I grinned in remembrance. Mrs. Johnson had said to be creative. What I'd lost in original thought, I'd made up for in enthusiastic delivery.

"Yeah, I heard you'd gotten engaged. Heard all about it. The bears, the ring. Saw that goofy picture in the papers. Congratulations, Flash. Now you and Mike will be harder to tell apart than ever. Both of you with the smell of p-whip all over you."

He tossed me a small tube of topical rub to ease my aches. "If you won't take the muscle relaxants, try some of this."

"Geez, Billy, I can't use this. This stuff stinks. Shiri won't be able to get within ten feet of me."

"That's the whole idea. If you're not gettin' any, maybe you can channel some of that frustration into our play-off game."

"You must want me to kill somebody," I insisted. "That's what'll happen if you try to keep me from Shiri for that long."

"She must really have your nose wide open."

"And that's the way I like it, too," I said, shrugging into my clothes. "Thanks." I held up the tube.

Billy snapped the towel at me, indicating that I should get off the table. "All done, Flash. Hope that cream works for you."

* * *

"... And if Morgan takes that job in the Atlanta office, that will leave an open position," Shiri said excitedly. "Because Tate will move up to take Morgan's place."

Shiri and I lay, face-to-face, on her leather sectional. Digital satellite was tuned to her favorite light jazz station, setting the mood with smooth tunes. Her head rested in the crook of my arm. My leg was tossed over her hip as she drew lazy, invisible lines up and down my arm.

It was the end of the summer. Now that the football season was over, we could spend much-needed, much-deserved time together. A frantic pace had kept us moving in and out of Birmingham, stealing moments when we could.

When Shiri wasn't in Birmingham, helping her mother with her family reunion plans, I was here, with her, in Jackson—taking time away from managing my sports training centers to recharge, reenergize.

Shiri's apartment was a second home to me, though it took a little getting used to her odds-and-ends eclectic choice in furniture, the lack of a decent workout facility near her home, and the stacks of fast-food cartons.

"Won't someone else take this Tate's place?" I asked. I had no earthly idea who these people were. Just names from Shiri's workday world. But I listened and asked all the appropriate questions because it seemed to matter to her.

"The only person qualified to take Tate's position is Carrolton. And she won't move."

"What makes you so sure?"

"Because," Shiri said impatiently as if the answer should be obvious to me, "it would be a lateral move for her. She won't want to give up her comfy position for a lateral with more responsibility. That leaves the field wide open for me. Don't you get it, Jack?"

"*Umm*, not really," I said lazily.

"Weren't you listening?" she asked.

"Of course I was!" I protested. "It's just that you're making it hard to pay attention."

"Would it help if I did this?" she murmured, pressing her lips to the hollow of my throat.

"Nuh-huh. Just made it harder." I guided her hand to my groin, showing her exactly what effect she was having on me.

"Do you think I should—" she began.

"Absolutely," I cut her off.

"You didn't let me finish!" Shiri protested, laughing at my impatience.

"Darlin', we're just getting started."

"I was going to ask you if I you thought I should say something now before Morgan's promotion became official. To show how motivated I am?"

"Very motivated," I echoed, contracting my leg to draw her closer.

"Or should I wait until Morgan makes the official announcement and then make a move? That'll show some respect for the length of time he'd been in that position." Her hand squeezed, drawing a moan from me.

Speaking of length and positioning!

"You could do that, too," I whispered. Her massage continued absently, tightening her circle while raising my blood pressure.

"I could submit my résumé now and pretend to be surprised when Tate addressed us." She considered that option as she slid her fingers under my waistband and belt buckle. She pressed down, the flat of her palm cupping and containing the heat emanating from my body.

"Yes," I hissed. "Do that."

I lifted my hips against her hand, timing my motion with the rhythm of her caress.

"I don't know," she continued on a sigh. She rested her cheek on the other hand as she sat up on her elbow. "I don't want them to think that I'm a fake, that I'm not really upset by Tate's leaving. He was a mentor to me. He was one of the few employees to take time to explain what I was supposed to be doing. Everybody else was too busy covering their own behinds to care. If it wasn't for him . . . At the same time, when that position opens, I can move back to Alabama, be close to my family. Closer to you.''

"Umm. Closer,'' I echoed like a broken tape recorder.

Finally, unable to stand her indecision, and the hesitation it caused, I pulled her toward me and up over me until she fully straddled me. Her knees sank into the soft-as-butter leather of the sectional.

"Maybe I'm not ready to move up,'' she continued. "I haven't been in my position for very long. Do you think the others might think I'm moving too fast?'' She punctuated her question with a slow, deliberate rotating of her pelvis.

"Or not fast enough,'' I managed to gasp. "You don't want them to underestimate the full power of your potential, either. You need to be assertive. Show them that you're up for the job.''

"But I need to move carefully,'' she said, unclasping my belt and pulling it away from its loops in one smooth motion. "I wouldn't want to blow it . . . the job, that is.''

"You can handle it,'' I assured her, at the same time giving her permission to touch me, to pleasure me, with the not-so-hidden undertones of the conversation. It was as much about her work as it was about her getting me worked up.

I needed her. Couldn't wait another minute. Didn't want to. I hooked my fingers into the waistband of her panties as Shiri continued to move against me faster and faster, invoking in me a sense of primal urgency.

Her fingers raked across my bared chest, leaving scores across my abdomen, across my shoulders, and down my arms. She took her hands away long enough to remove her blouse and release the front clasp of her brassiere. When the cooler air touched her skin, I felt myself grow even more aroused as I watched the deep, chocolate-toned nipples tighten and rise.

She leaned forward, urging me to sample, to taste. When my tongue darted forward, she gasped in pleasure, then shifted down so that her cheek rested against my chest. She nipped at my skin, then drew circles around my own nipple with the tip of her tongue.

Laughter shook my sides. "That tickles."

But she didn't stop. "You big baby," she chastised, then turned her cheek so that she could treat the other to the same. She continued, tracing a moist line down the center of my abdomen, probing the indentation of my navel, stopping short at the waistband of my jeans.

My breath heaved, stomach collapsing almost to my spine as I wondered what she would do next, where she would go next. With leisurely, languid motions, Shiri pulled my jeans from around my waist, past my hips, and down around my knees. Her face was only inches from my thighs. Her hair fell forward, tickling me, torturing me.

Knowing that her lips were mere inches away made me strain toward her, but each time she moved away—keeping the agonizing distance.

"Did anybody ever tell you that you have the most amazing thighs?" she murmured, running her hands up and down my legs and digging into the defined cut lines of each major muscle group, made more prominent as my legs strained to keep from plunging into her.

"Not recently," I gasped.

"You do," she insisted. "Absolutely incredible. Like a sculpture of Adonis made flesh."

Her small hands encircled my girth and squeezed. I arched my back and moaned aloud as a few, precious drops of fluid oozed forth and moistened the tip.

Shiri's lips parted. An eagerness just shy of carnality glittered in her dark eyes. I placed my hands on her shoulders and applied subtle but insistent pressure.

"Please." It was as close to begging as I'd ever come in my life.

"Well, since you're being so nice about it," she said, a temptress in every word, every move.

I closed my eyes, reeling in sensation as molten honey dripped over me, around me, and covered me with delicious precision. She took me to the brink and held me there with her—hovering—until I begged again for a free fall.

Shiri lifted her head, her eyes shining with unabashed

humor. I didn't see what was so damned funny. I was a living volcano, threatening to erupt at the slightest provocation.

"So, what do you think of my qualifications?" she asked.

"I'll . . . I'll tell you when my toes stop curling."

Shiri laughed out loud, then stretched out next to me again, yawning.

"I thought I was supposed to be the one to drop off to sleep immediately after. Isn't that what you women are always complaining about in those magazines?"

"What kind of magazines have you been reading? You don't hold the monopoly on being tired," she reminded me.

"Are you tired, Shiri?"

"A little," she said, yawning again. "All of that thinking, strategizing. It wears a girl out, you know."

"Shame on me, then."

"What for this time?"

"I've been lying around here like a slug, letting you do all the work."

"Slacker," she agreed. "Since the season's over, you've been a virtual goldbrick."

"Maybe I should put forth a little more effort," I suggested. Still turgid, I wasn't quite ready to call it a night.

"More than a little," Shiri encouraged as I settled over her. I needed her so much, was so ready for her.

And then, without warning, I wasn't.

No warning. No explanation. Nothing. One moment I was inside her, filling her. From what I could tell from her movements and expression, giving her pleasure. But somehow, *I'd* lost the feeling. Not just the mental, emotional feeling that connected me to her. The physical sensation of coupling with Shiri was gone. Vanished.

I experienced a moment of panic. What the hell was going on? Why couldn't I feel my woman? I heard her sighs, her ultimate exclamation, even though my movements had become mechanical, obligatory, to finish what we'd started.

As my movements grew more pronounced, so did hers. I bent my knees, pressed the balls of my feet into the couch for leverage. I grasped Shiri's warm, round rear and thrust into her, maybe too roughly. She cried out, then bit her lip. But she gave no other indication that she wanted me to stop. I knew all of the signals by now . . . the subtle ones that let me know when she'd had enough. If she pulled away, pushed against me, or clenched her teeth. Subtle changes in her tempo—more like a dead stop—that told me that enough was enough.

Again and again I came to her, my pelvis colliding with hers. I kept moving, motivated as much by fear that I would never feel her the same away again as by desire. She grasped the back of my head and drew my face toward hers for a kiss. As our lips met, I plunged my tongue deep into her mouth, probing, reveling in the joy that I could feel her kiss. I swallowed the surprised moan.

"Jack . . . Jack, what is it?" Shiri asked, sensing my urgency, my desperation.

"Shh . . ." I silenced her with another kiss, doubly passionate, doubly harsh. Almost manic. I rocked against her, again and again. Each stab an interrogation. Why couldn't I feel her? Why? Why? Why couldn't I? What was wrong with me? Raw, unfettered, unbridled. Again and again I drove myself into her, and nearly to the brink of despair.

Suddenly, I cried out as molten liquid shot from my groin, collected safely by the condom.

As we lay there, breathing deeply, I wished for the day when we didn't have to take these precautions. I lived for the day when careful was a word we'd use around the baby lying between us, instead of the thin sheath of rubber that kept the baby away.

But that was still some time away. Our wedding date was almost a year away, in August. And Shiri was adamant that there would be no waddling down the aisle. No whispers behind her back—is she or isn't she? Pregnant, that is. No wondering whether our baby was premature or full-term. She wouldn't give satisfaction to small-minded people who had nothing better to do than count backward from the wedding to the delivery date of the first child.

She'd already picked out her dress and she said, in no

uncertain terms, there would be no alterations. Not on the plus side, that is. Now, if she had to take in for losing a couple of inches because of her mother's rigorous diet and exercise regimen, that was a different story.

Her family had been waiting a long time, almost two years since the last reunion, for a family wedding. She was the one target this time; she was going to do it—and do it right.

NINETEEN

Something was wrong. I could feel it. Though it took me some time to notice that there was a problem. Nothing in Jack's behavior gave me any indication that anything was bothering him. Not at first. He was as kind and as attentive as ever. He took all of my constant interruptions of his work with my wedding-related questions in stride.

When I was ready to scream over minute details such as German chocolate cake over double fudge, bloodred carnations over white magnolias, tea-length hems over minis, he took it all in stride, making decisions quickly and decisively. I didn't know whether to bless him for helping me out of my endless loop of analysis paralysis or curse him for his ability to make a snap decision and never look back.

I should have trucked merrily along, blissful in the knowledge that soon I would be Mrs. Jack Deneen. I should have been ecstatic now that it was certain I would be the married one for the next reunion. My well-meaning aunts would turn their creative energies elsewhere. The selection of the "target" had happened so quickly, they had plenty of time left over until the reunion to go for a double-banger—two weddings before the next reunion. Brenda and Essence must have been sweating big time now.

I was, too. For the past few weeks, I'd had this feeling of unease that I couldn't put my finger on. Maybe that was it. I was the one putting all the fingers on. That is, whenever I reached for Jack, he always responded passionately. But lately, I was the one doing all the reaching.

At first, I thought it was the conclusion of Jack's football season stressing him out. Even though the Steeldogs had come off a winning season, they hadn't been able to bring the championship home to Birmingham. The coveted ArenaCup had eluded them, as they'd been plagued by mistackles, some questionable referee calls not in their favor, and plain ol' poor execution. All of the mishaps had taken their toll on the team the last few games.

Jack was concerned that his own performance wasn't up to his team's expectations. He'd trained just as hard, or harder, than anyone else. He'd studied plays until he could repeat play patterns in his sleep. Yet no matter how much effort he put into preparing for the game, none of that helped when the ball slipped unexplainably through his fingers. Or when defenders ran him down. Or when the opposing team got around him to break up a play in the backfield.

As much as I loved to watch him play, I hated what that stupid game was doing to him emotionally. I watched helplessly while frustration led to careless errors, and care-less errors led to missed opportunities. Jack took each loss of a down, each loss of a game, to heart. Secretly, I was glad when the season was over. For during those low periods, there was nothing I could do to console him. I was worried that that idiotic game would send him into a depression. But when I asked him about it, he assured me that everything was all right. Everything would be fine.

If it weren't for the sports training centers that he'd opened with his friend and teammate Mike, I think he would have driven himself nutty trying to figure out what he could have personally done to drag the Steeldogs to the championship.

When I tried to console him with the fact that there was

always next year, he looked at me as if I were the one who'd gone off the deep end. That's when I knew, beyond a shadow of a doubt, that something was wrong with Jack.

I'd often looked into Jack's eyes and been absolutely enthralled by the range of emotions those tigerlike eyes could convey. He'd looked at me with pride and possession, annoyance and amusement. I'd seen passion reflected there and preoccupation. I'd seen him sleepy and seductive. Trashed after an all-night party, introspective after an all-night heart-to-heart. Motivated by success, manic in front of adoring fans. Most times, I was right there. But when I'd suggested that he could always play again next year, that was the first time I'd ever seen fear in his eyes. Fear and doubt. I didn't understand, could not fathom why my simple show of support would frighten him. Jack Deneen was afraid of nothing. No one. That's what I would have said several weeks ago.

Now, I wasn't so sure. It was mid-February. Six months before the wedding and the family reunion. Plenty of time. Plenty to do. I was still starting to panic. Thank God for my family and their expertise with planning both.

As I sat at Mama's kitchen table, swatches of cloth, bridesmaids' patterns, and invitation samples spread out in front of me, I wondered how I was going to get it all done. I wondered how I was going to keep it all together, stay sane, until the big day came.

"So, what do you think of this one?" I held up a lemon-yellow swatch for Mama's approval.

"Essence would hunt you down and kill you if you made her wear that color," Mama said promptly.

"And Brenda thinks the green looks like baby puke." I discarded another sample. "What do you think about this one?"

"I like it," Mama agreed, fingering the deep maroon satin. "I think it's a color that will flatter both of them."

"Whew! Glad that's over with. Now all I have to do is decide on a pattern."

"Not that one," Mama said, turning over the Simplicity pattern that had enough ruffles to span the globe twice.

"Since it's going to be a summer wedding, I was thinking about something sleeveless, but tasteful. Or spaghetti straps like this one." I pointed to another pattern.

Mama and I went through a few more samples and considered a few more options, until we heard a car honking in the driveway.

"That should be Karen and Pammie," Mama predicted.

"And Jack," I said. "He said he was going to try to make this meeting, too."

"I have to wonder about that man's smarts. Hasn't he realized that every time he shows up for one of these meetings, we put him to work?"

"Even when he doesn't show up, you put an action item down by his name."

"To be more technical, since you're the official minutes keeper, you put the action item down," Mama corrected me.

"Details, details."

I flung the door open and crossed my arms as a wet, chill wind blew inside. "Y'all hurry up," I encouraged, waving for my aunts to gather their belongings. Jack's SUV pulled in directly behind them. He waved at me as I blew him a kiss.

"Ah, young love." Aunt Pam sighed as she kissed me on the cheek in greeting. "Shiri, your face is cold."

"It won't be for long," Aunt Karen commented slyly. "As soon as Jack steps through that door, there will be enough kindling going on in here to roast marshmallows."

"Mama's in the kitchen," I said pointedly, tilting my head.

"So, what are you trying to say?" Aunt Pam teased. "That you want to be alone?"

"You're lucky that it's me and your aunt Pam," Aunt Karen added. "If it had been Aunt Rosie and your grandmother, you wouldn't have a moment's peace to yourselves."

"No wonder she's keeping that apartment in Jackson," Aunt Pam said.

"I still work there, you know."

"I thought you'd gotten some big-time promotion?"

"Not until the summer," I said.

"Seems like everything's falling in place for you at the same time."

"Uh-huh," I said distractedly. Jack still hadn't climbed out. I was starting to get curious as to what he was doing. "Lucky me."

Finally, I heard the door slam and the chirp of the alarm engaging. Jack trudged up the walkway with his hands tucked into his leather, bomber-style jacket. A baseball cap was pulled low over his eyes. The weather wasn't cold enough for a freeze, but the water on the stone path still made speed walking treacherous. I guess that's why he took his time getting to me.

"Hey, baby," I said, helping him shrug out of his jacket.

He rubbed his hands briskly together. "It feels good in here."

I wrapped my arms around his waist, squeezing tightly. "It feels good in here, too," I murmured. "How did it go today?"

"Pretty good," he said, smiling down at me. But there was a hesitancy in his voice. He reached out, not to hold me, but to pull my arms away from him. When I pinned him with a curious, disappointed stare he said, "Be nice. We're at your mama's house."

"She's not going to disown me for hugging you, Jack. Besides, we're practically married already. Everybody says so."

"Uh-huh."

"So, how did the meeting go today?"

"Pretty good," he repeated. "The numbers look good enough. I think we can open a third center."

"You keep this up and you won't have to play football next season," I teased.

Jack stopped in midstride. "What do you mean by that?"
The hand on my shoulder clenched.

"What do you mean, what do I mean? It was just a joke."
I twisted out of his grasp. It was the first time I could ever
remember not wanting him to touch me.

"Why would you say something like that to me, Shiri?"
His voice was low and tight. He cut his eyes toward the
kitchen, where he could hear my relatives, but they remained
out of sight. Their voices rose and fell with their conversation, their laughter. But out here in the foyer, the conversation
had turned as crisp and chilly as outdoors.

"It was a joke, Jack. Geez! Lighten up."

"It wasn't funny."

"I'm sorry. If I'd known you'd take it that way, I wouldn't
have . . . that is . . . forget it. Forget I said anything."

He took a deep breath, exhaling through his nostrils. "No,
I'm the one who should be sorry. I didn't mean to jump on
you, Shiri. It's just . . . uh . . . it's been a long day, okay?
I'm tired."

I bit my lip, wanting to say more but uncertain how he
would take it. "No problem. I understand."

Give me an Academy Award. My best portrayal of the
sympathetic fiancée ever. I didn't understand. Not really.
We'd had disagreements before, differences of opinion. But
I always knew where he stood, where he was coming from.
Where this sudden surge of surliness was coming from, I
hadn't a clue. "Come on in and take a load off, Jack. Mama's
cooked her world-famous beef-tip stew and homemade biscuits."

"I'm not very hungry."

Now I *knew* something was wrong. Jack could come off
of a twelve-course eating binge and still have room for
Mama's cooking.

"Jack, are you all right?"

"Yeah," he said simply, then headed for the kitchen with
me, dazed and confused, in tow.

"Pull up a chair, Flash. Tell us, what's new in the world
of sportsmania?" Aunt Pam greeted him.

I watched in total astonishment as the man who seconds before could barely spare two words for me became Mr. Garrulous. He'd even kissed Aunt Karen and hugged my mother.

So fake, I couldn't help thinking. A second ago, he was biting my head off. And now, in front of my family, in front of me, he was putting on a show—being Mr. Amiable when it was obvious to me that he was feeling anything but chatty.

The fact that he could switch personas so easily didn't surprise me. I knew that Jack had a public and a private side. And then there was the side, somewhere in between the two, that he only showed to me. Sweet and vulnerable, powerful and passionate. Calm and sometimes kinda kooky.

In front of me, he never felt compelled to show that public face. He could drop the star-player persona and be the man he wanted to be, not the one everyone expected him to be. When we were together, I always knew that he could express himself openly, honestly, without worrying that I would think any less of him for all of his imperfections and human frailties. I loved him. All of him. And hoped that he understood that he never had to pretend with me.

I sat at the table across from him, watching in stupefied silence while he yukked it up with my family. Who was that man? I asked myself that question several times during the evening.

I'd cleared away most of my wedding planning materials to make room for the reunion planning stuff—brochures for the Orlando activities, sample chamber-of-commerce freebies, AAA maps. However, a stray wedding invitation had mixed in with the reunion materials. Aunt Karen came across it, oohed and aahed with delight, then passed it across the table for Jack to admire.

"Feel the texture on this raised print, Jack," she encouraged, thrusting it into this hands.

Jack handled the paper as if it were a snake about to bite him, then let it fall to the table.

"Sorry," he muttered. He started to reach for the invitation again and wound up knocking his coffee cup onto the floor. Mama winced as the cup shattered into a thousand pieces, but was quick to assure him that it was okay.

Jack stood up abruptly from the table, tucking his hands into his pants pockets. The chair scraped across the linoleum as he stood.

I went to the kitchen sink for paper towels to sop up the mess. It didn't occur me that Jack would leave until I heard the front door open.

"Jack!"

I barely made it to the door before I heard his engine start. I saw him, one arm draped over the passenger-side seat, the other hand making tiny adjustments to the steering wheel as he backed out of the drive. He would have left me, without as much as a good-bye, if it hadn't been for the car passing in front of our drive just as he reached the main road. Jack stomped on the brakes, bringing his SUV to a sliding halt. He then threw the vehicle into park and sat inside with the engine idling.

I hurried around to the driver's-side window and banged on the glass with my fist. "All right, Jack. Open up."

The window whined as he pressed a button to lower it.

"What the hell is going on?" I demanded.

He shook his head. "Nothing."

"Bull. Don't give me that. I want to know what's the matter with you and I want to know right now." I used my take-no-prisoners voice that I used at work when I needed to get something done quick, fast, and in a hurry.

Jack turned tortured eyes to me and I felt my anger deflate a notch. "I have to go, Shiri."

"Go? Go where? Why do you have to leave, Jack?"

He moved as if he was about to put the truck back into reverse. I couldn't believe it. He would rather run over my foot than talk to me. What kind of mess was that? Anger ratcheted back up a notch. I reached inside and grabbed the keys out of the ignition with a quick twist and jerk of my wrist.

"You're not going anywhere until you tell me what's going on."

"Damn it Shiri. Give me the frigging keys."

I blinked, completely caught off guard. I wanted to believe he'd said *frigging,* but I was fooling myself. He'd cursed me. He'd actually cursed me! I'd heard him use the word before. His use of the expletive didn't shock me. Used in a certain context, whispered into my ear at just the right moment, he'd even used it to arouse. But something told me that he wasn't thinking about making love to me when he'd used it. He was deliberately trying to make me mad.

Guess what?

He'd succeeded.

"Fine," I said, dropping the keys into his lap and stepping back. "Take them."

I had enough on my mind to worry about without his mood swings. I wasn't going to stand there and let him curse me. My own family didn't curse me.

Later, after I got over being mad, I'd be concerned. No . . . I'd be mad, then pissed, then annoyed, then concerned. And maybe, if I thought about it some more, I'd work my way back to mad. If he didn't want to talk to me, I could accept that. He was a big boy and didn't need my coddling and cajoling.

"I'll . . . I'll call you later," he promised.

"Whatever." I flipped my hand to show him that I'd heard but didn't care. Another Academy Award–winning performance. If I didn't care, why was I hurting so much? This was our first big fight as a couple. And for the life of me, I didn't know what we were fighting about. Was he getting cold feet? How could he? The wedding was still months away.

Was the stress of making his sports centers a success driving a wedge between us? Perhaps. But unless he wasn't being truthful when he said that business was doing well, I didn't see why he'd suddenly turn sour on our relationship.

I stood in our driveway, my arms folded across my chest, watching him back out of the drive. In my head, a refrain from a Mary J. Blige song kept running through my head.

I wasn't going to cry. Just because my eyes turned red

and water leaked down my face and snot dripped to the tip of my nose . . . that didn't mean I was crying.

I watched Jack until his SUV's taillights disappeared into the night; then I stomped back into the house. What could have made him so moody all of a sudden? If he'd been a woman, I would have blamed it on PMS. I was about to start my period. Maybe, since we'd spent so much time together, he was picking up on my vibes, my emotional cycle.

Closing the door behind me, I leaned against it, trying to collect my thoughts. Actually, my thoughts were about as collected in my head as I was going to get them. I was really trying to come up with a plausible excuse for why Jack had bolted like that. I couldn't even come up with an excuse that sounded good to me. I knew that it wouldn't satisfy my folks.

I worked up enough bravado to tell myself, *Why should I have to tell them anything? Do they have to know all of my business?*

Setting my face into a hard mask, I rejoined Mama and my aunts in the kitchen. Without a word, I slid into my chair and pulled up to the table. I didn't speak for several seconds. In fact, the lack of conversation spoke loudly. It was so quiet, I could hear the lid rattling on top of Mama's Dutch oven as steam escaped from the stew left simmering. The drip of the leaking faucet, the hum of the refrigerator, the occasional clink as the ice maker dropped another load of ice into the tray filled the air with non-noise.

"Pass the biscuits, Aunt Karen," I said.

"Here you go, hon." She held the basket out to me.

Aunt Pam passed me a bowl of stew, then licked her fingers as the overflowing bowl dribbled a little on the sides.

"So," Mama said, helping to break the uncomfortable silence. "Anybody have any idea what the weather's supposed to be like Labor Day weekend?"

"It had better be nice," Aunt Karen said, as if threatening Mother Nature herself. "We've got a whole lot of activities planned for outside. Friday's the tour of Orlando, every morning breakfasts by the pool, and Sea World. . . . It had better not rain on this Johnson parade.''

"If it does rain, we could always use those fancy address books and calendars we've got for souvenirs to cover our heads,'' Aunt Pam suggested.

"As the finance committee chairperson, I'm here to tell you that at three dollars a pop for printing, you'd better grab a newspaper to cover your head,'' I replied in derision.

"How are we doing with the budget?'' Mama asked.

"So far, so good. We're still well under our estimates.''

Aunt Pam snickered. "We knew what we were doing when we appointed Shiri to the finance committee. The way this child holds on to a dime, you'd have to wrestle her to the ground to get it out of her tightfisted fingers.''

Smiling wanly at the offhanded compliment, I lifted my arm and flexed my biceps. If only I could hold on to Jack as strongly as I could hold on to a dollar.

TWENTY

I was hoping that she would have the strength to end it. I thought she'd get tired of me cutting her off, shutting her out, and decide for the both of us that we'd made a terrible mistake. Maybe, if I was cold enough toward her, cruel enough, she would decide that being the wife of a public figure wasn't all that it was cracked up to be.

If we ended it now, before too much time, money, and emotional effort had been expended, maybe no one would get hurt. Or was I just fooling myself? There was no getting around the pain. We'd come too far, too fast, for me to pretend that I could perform a clean, surgical break. It would hurt. That is, the hurt would be sharp and painful for a brief while, then would fade just as quickly as our relationship had begun.

If I believed that, then I was dumber than I must have looked when I'd bolted out of Shiri's home. When was it . . . three days ago? Four? I'd lost count, burying myself in work, avoiding her calls, turning off my cell phone. I'd put myself in a twilight zonelike kind of existence where time didn't matter. It didn't matter because I didn't care what happened to me now. I'd lost Shiri. No, not lost. I'd given her away.

I couldn't help leaving as I had. I couldn't stay. I just couldn't. Once that invitation had slipped through my fingers, I'd known what would come next. And I'd been right. There'd been no way for me to control myself. The coffee cup had come next. And if I hadn't done something fast, they would all have seen me degenerated. They would all know. I wasn't ready for that. Not yet.

So I'd taken off. As much as it had hurt me to see her expression, I'd had to keep going. She would be all right, I'd convinced myself. She'd run back to her relatives. They would probably sit around the table, console her, *advise* her as only the women in a close-knit family could. I could hear their voices in my head—distinct and detrimental to our relationship.

Their words might not have started out that way, because I truly believed that the Johnsons had taken me into their family as one of their own. I'd breached the Johnson stronghold and had become one with them. Their words to her would have started off kind, solicitous, wondering if I was all right.

And as their collective rancor at my ill treatment of her had grown, as each unkind word, or offhanded gesture I'd ever given her (real or imagined) had come to light, my estimation in their eyes would have grown dimmer and dimmer. She deserved better, they would have told her. If nothing else had come out of that conversation, that much was true.

I've heard it said that when someone was talking about you, your ears would burn. Well, I'd been carrying around smoldering cinders on the sides of my head for days. If I had a dollar for every time I whipped around, thinking I'd seen one of her brothers stalking me, ready to beat some good sense into me with a tire iron . . .

I'd never felt this way, a fugitive in my own city. But I

had to sever all contact if I was going to make her hate me. By the time I'd managed to make myself call her, I'd been ready to face the combined wrath of the entire Johnson clan.

It had never come to that. Too proud to beg, Shiri had saved me from botching the break by telling me that the room deposit was in the mail. She'd come to the conclusion that was best for all of us. She'd called the wedding off—valiantly citing instances of differences too deep to bridge, lifestyles too set to change.

God, how I wished that it didn't have to be that way. How I wished that I could come right out and tell her why. But if I did, I knew what she would say. I knew what she would do. I knew my Shiri, what kind of woman she was.

If I told her why I wanted to part, she'd never leave me. She'd hang in there with me, stand by me until the bitter end. For better or for worse—and we hadn't even exchanged vows yet. That's why I loved her so. I knew that Shiri would never willingly abandon those she loved. She might stray, but she would always return. I knew the worst was yet to come and she'd still be there. Five years. Ten years. Twenty. How long would it be? How long would she remain chained to me—suffering, as I would suffer, because of her love and commitment? I would rather kill her love for me now than commit her life to that.

And if I lingered on, slowly degenerating in health and vitality, what kind of life would that be for her? What kind of man would I be if I selfishly kept her to her marital vows, knowing that I could not honor and cherish her as I'd sworn to do?

This malady attacking my body would eventually kill my soul. Shiri was that soul. And I refused to take her down with me.

She was the first thing I thought of when I left my doctor's office for an unscheduled physical. It had gotten to where I could no longer explain or wish away the random numbness in my extremities, the headaches. The games were over. Even though I was still working out, I wasn't putting my body through the grueling punishments of the games. Something else had to be wrong.

To ward off any potential problems for next season, I'd scheduled an appointment with my family physician, Dr. Mathers. He was a general practitioner. A good one. But couldn't quite pin down what was wrong with me.

One appointment turned into two. Two turned into three, which blossomed into several more appointments with various specialists while I endured a series of tests to rule out obvious causes. Pinched nerves, migraines, even gout had crossed my mind.

Even then, I wasn't too worried. My doctor continued to assure me that for the most part, I was in perfect health. It wasn't until he suggested a neurological scan and a spinal tap that I started to get concerned. Concerned, hell. The word was *scared.*

I *hated* needles. The very thought of someone sticking a giant pin into my spine makes me quiver. I'd sooner take a full body block from Big Dog than face a steel rod jabbed into my back. As far as the closed-in space of the MRI chamber, forget it! As I lay there, trying to be still while some lab geek shot radiation into my brain, all I could think of was clawing my way out of there. Some big, strong football hero I turned out to be.

Maybe I should have given Shiri the benefit of the doubt. Maybe I could have gotten through the tests better if she'd been there to hold my hand. But after the first MRI scan, and the dizziness and nausea that followed, I didn't want her to see me weak and puking. Not a pleasant image for a husband-to-be at all.

In fact, when my doctor informed me that he suspected multiple sclerosis, every way I'd ever imagined myself flew out the window. Hale. Hearty. None of those pictures seemed to fit me anymore. I kept seeing myself, sitting in a wheelchair, bound for life, no longer able to do any of the things that I loved most—playing football and making love to my woman.

At that point, any assurances Dr. Mathers gave me fell

on deaf ears. Oh, he gave me lots of information on MS. He set me up with support groups. He even claimed that people in my condition lived long, productive lives with the advances in medicine and alternative treatments. But I wasn't hearing any of that. Didn't want to hear it. Would not believe it.

I couldn't believe that my life would ever be anything but normal or productive. I don't mind admitting that I went through a series of emotional roller-coaster rides—bouts of anger and denial. How could this happen to me? I didn't abuse my body. Didn't smoke. Didn't do drugs. I was a poster child for the responsible drinker. I ate my veggies, stayed away from red meat. How could I have developed multiple sclerosis?

And if I couldn't believe my life would ever be the same, there was no way I was going to make Shiri believe it. And I loved her too much to watch her try to put on a brave face when I couldn't.

Am I a coward for cutting out on her? Maybe. Am I lonely? Definitely. Now that I've made the decision to push her out of my life, all I can think of is how much I really need her now. Me. Jack Deneen—the needy. It cut me to the quick just thinking about it.

"Flash, you got a minute?" Mike popped his head in the door to our northside sports training center.

"Whassup, Mike?" I lifted my chin to greet him.

"Are you busy?"

I looked at the mountain of paperwork on my desk and spread my hands as if in answer. Truth was, I hadn't picked up a scrap in over an hour. "What do you think?"

"Do you think you could tear yourself away? There's some folks outside asking to see you."

"Who is it? What do they want?"

"Some lady. And she says that she wants you."

"About?"

"She wouldn't say. But I think she means business. She's got some rough-looking jokers trailing her. Biker dudes." Mike leaned on my desk.

My head snapped up. Biker dudes? I didn't think Shiri's brothers rode. But she had zillions of cousins. Any one of them would probably be willing to crush my skull in retaliation for what I'd done to her heart.

"I thought you told me the loan to open this place was through conventional means. If I'm about to get my legs broken—"

"Then you'd be in the perfect place for rehabilitation," I retorted, shuffled some of the papers around my desk to stall for time, then pushing them unceremoniously in a drawer.

I stood slowly, deliberately, holding on to the desk. I was very careful about my movements these days. Very conscious of the fact that at any moment, they might betray me. Sometimes, it was as simple as losing enough feeling in my hands to drop whatever I might be holding. Other times, it might be my legs—giving out from under me to make walking an exercise in uncertainty. The attacks were scattered, unpredictable, sometimes not manifesting for weeks. Other times, the symptoms were always with me, tingling in my extremities. Or the opposite—numbness. I couldn't even hold Shiri without fearing that though my love for her remained, my desire, my physical ability to satisfy her would ebb and flow at a moment's notice. That was no way to start a marriage.

And hiding out at my job was no way to start the rest of my life. If the bikers were here for me for what I'd done, then so be it. Let them come. I may have been ashamed of the way I'd handled Shiri, but I had no doubt that my heart was in the right place. Somehow, I had to make them see that steeling my heart against her was the only way to give her a chance of ever loving again.

"Where are they?" I asked.

"I left her at the front desk. The biker dudes are checking out the workout equipment."

"What's the matter with you, Mike? Haven't you ever been taught that you don't keep a lady waiting?"

Mike grinned at me. "Yeah, Barb's been schooling me on that fact every night."

It was the first time I could remember being jealous of Mike. He and Barb were like rabbits—going at each other with enough vigor and frequency to keep experimental labs flush with test specimens for years.

"I guess I don't need to ask how things are going on between you?"

"Forget training camp," Mike assured me. "I'll be in great shape by the time next season starts."

"Bully for you," I muttered and closed the door to my office.

The administrative offices of the sports center were on the upper floor. From the balcony, we could see the entire layout of the building. The strength and conditioning weights were grouped in the center of the building and a padded track ran around the outer perimeter. Off to the right, two large rooms were sectioned off for the aerobics and Tae-Bo classes. To the left, a basketball court. The rear of the building contained the lockers, showers, and sauna. On staff were twelve personal trainers, a nutritionist, and a part-time sports doctor.

Out of the three facilities that Mike and I owned and managed, this was the largest facility and my favorite. Two others contained most but not all of the same offerings. This was the one I was most proud of, being the closest to my vision of what a sports training center should be.

Unlike some health clubs I'd scouted in research before opening our first center, the equipment was top-notch enough to draw professional, full-time athletes but open and friendly enough to encourage regular folks who just wanted to work up a good sweat. Once you were in, you wouldn't be bothered. No part-time sales folks disguising themselves as trainers.

"There she is," Mike pointed out to me as he headed down the stairs.

I waited for a moment, grasped the railing, then started down. It was only a short flight, but already I considered putting in an elevator. I didn't relish the idea of taking a tumble down the stairs. It would be really bad if I embarrassed myself in front of the big, bad biker dudes. If they had come to get me, I wasn't going to make it any easier for them by rolling down the stairs at their feet.

I didn't recognize the woman at first. She had her back to me and was dressed in full leather gear—jacket, pants. A bloodred motorcycle helmet with a sword-bearing angel emblazoned on the back dangled from her fingers. She stood at the reception desk, flipping through several leaflets.

"Can I help you?" I called out, approaching the desk. I took a startled step back when Shiri's aunt Rosie turned around to greet me.

"Mrs. Kincaid!"

"Well now, Flash." She smiled at me with sparkling dark eyes so much like Shiri's. "You seem to be doing pretty well for yourself."

"I can't complain," I said, clasping her to me in a brief hug.

"Martyrs never do," she replied cryptically and kissed me on the cheek.

"What are you doing here?"

"You have to ask?"

"Did Shiri send you?"

"Now, you know better than that. I'm here because I'm not one to stand by when a member of the family is trying to make a jackass out of himself."

"I'm not family anymore, Mrs. Kincaid. . . . That is . . . she gave the ring back."

"Takes more than a hunk of rock to make family, son," she said stoutly. When she noticed the front desk receptionist edging closer to listen, she said loudly, "Can we go somewhere and talk, Flash? What happens in the family stays in the family."

"Upstairs. In my office." I indicated the way I'd come, then gestured for her to proceed ahead of me.

"What a wonderful facility you have here, Flash," she

said, turning around to address me as I reached for the railing.

At that traitorous moment, my hand trembled, spasmed so that I had to clench the rail for support. I think she noticed, but she didn't say anything, just continued up the stairs chatting pleasantly about the sports training center.

"My partner, Mike, and I have dreamed of running something like this since we were kids."

"Nothing like having your childhood fantasy come true to propel you into a second childhood."

"Is that what your gear is all about? Living out some kind of fantasy life?"

"Oh, this?" Aunt Rosie laughed and spun around for me to get the full effect. "This isn't fantasy. But it is fun."

"What are you doing? Tooling around the countryside?"

"For a good cause," she insisted, wagging her finger at me. "There's nothing like mixing fun and function."

"What do you mean?"

"I'm on a cross-country charity ride. I've got pledges backing me with dollars for every mile that I ride."

"You? Riding a Harley cross-country?"

"Not actually me driving. Diablo doesn't let anyone touch his hog."

"Diablo?"

"The tattoo artist that worked on me. Didn't Shiri tell you that I have a tattoo?"

"I think she may have mentioned it."

"Anyway, he asked me if I wanted to participate in a cross-country ride to raise money for some unfortunate kids."

"And you said yes."

"I practically jumped at the chance. I'd do anything for the babies, Jack. Which is why I'm here. You're messin' with my chance to do something for Shiri's babies."

My heart froze in my chest. What babies? How could there be babies? We'd been so careful.

"No, she's not pregnant," Aunt Rosie said, reading my panicked expression. "No thanks to you."

"I'll bet Mrs. Johnson doesn't share your views," I wagered. She was adamant that Shiri was a good girl. And should be treated as such.

"Don't worry. If I can't make you see reason, you'll soon be getting a visit from her, too. And if that doesn't work, it'll be her aunt Karen. And then her aunt Pam. And her uncles. And her cousins. So, you see, Jack, you might as well cave in."

"You don't understand," I began wearily.

"How long?" she asked.

"Excuse me?"

"The tremors. How long have you had them?"

"I don't know. It's hard to say."

"What does your doctor say?"

I snorted in derision. "Gave me a lot of nonsense about how I could expect to live a long, productive life. How the quality of life of people with multiple sclerosis is improving in leaps and bounds. All they have to do is pump themselves with a lot of artificial steroids or other, manufactured drugs, and they can go about their merry way as if nothing ever happened."

"You don't have to take the drugs, Jack." I knew she was serious because she'd called me by my given name. "There are alternative treatments."

"Don't you think I know that? But you have one group of experts who say that they're a load of crap, another equally reputable group who say that drugs are the way. And the fence-sitters, squatting in the middle, telling you to try a cocktail. Try a little of this. Try a little of that. Biofeedback, acupuncture, copaxone . . . in the meantime, while my doctor's running around like a chicken with his head cut off trying to figure out what's best for me, I've put my life on hold—letting the best things in my life slip away. I can't play football worth a damn. Can't love my woman like I want to. You tell me what the hell I'm supposed to do."

Aunt Rosie's face reflected sympathy for all of thirty seconds. "You selfish son of a bitch."

"Excuse me?"

"You heard me. Read my lips. I called you a selfish son of a—"

"I heard you, I heard you. How am I being selfish? I've given up everything that ever mattered to me. How can wanting to protect Shiri be selfish?"

"First of all, did you even tell her that you were ill?"

I shook my head.

"She was bound to notice something was wrong. Did she ask you?"

"She did."

"And I'll bet you told her everything was fine, didn't you? Looked her right in the eye and told her that everything was hunky-dory fine."

"Of course I did. I didn't want to worry her."

"So you're selfish *and* a liar."

"Isn't there some kind of rule or law or something about a man being beaten down in his own place? I told you. I didn't want to hurt her."

"Let me see if I can get this straight," she said, folding her arms across her chest. "You lie to her. You curse her. And then you dump her. Yeah, I can see how that would prevent a hurtin'."

She grasped my shoulders and shook me until my teeth rattled.

"Jack, you and Shiri love each other. What did you think marriage was, if not sharing the bad with the good? That means all of it. You can't make a one-sided decision and expect her not to hurt. You say you love her; but you don't trust her enough to make the decision whether she wants to weather this storm with you. You took her love, all of it, and left her alone. Empty. You can't get any more selfish than that."

"I love her so much, Aunt Rosie. I didn't want to see her hurt."

"Horsefeathers! This isn't about her. It's about you. You didn't want her to see you hurting. The big, bad football hero brought to his knees. There's nothing standing between you and Shiri but pride and vanity."

"You don't know what it's like!" I snapped back, jerking out of her grasp. That vanity crack hurt.

"Don't I?" she said softly. She walked away from me, staring out the window onto the floor below. Her voice was sadly introspective as she said, "Jack, I'm over eighty years old. For my sixtieth birthday, do you want to know what I got? Not an anniversary party like George and Lela. I got a mastectomy. That's right. Breast cancer. Rather than run the risk of having that evil destroy the rest of my life, I cut it out of me. Did it affect me emotionally as well as physically? You bet it did. Cutting off my breast struck at the very core of womanhood. You see, I'm not a bad-looking gal. But who was going to look at me with only one breast? Implants leaking silicone into my body? No thanks. Not an option. If it weren't for my family's support, I don't think I could have survived. The follow-up chemotherapy that made me sick as a dog, the fear that they didn't get it all, going hairless for months ... it was Shiri who helped me regain a sense of who I was. You want to know what she told me?"

When she turned to face me, her eyes glittered with tears. "She said, 'Aunt Rosie, you could be an Amazon!' An Amazon, of all things. Strong, warrior woman. That's how she saw me. Legends say that Amazons deliberately cut off a breast to make it easier to draw back their bowstrings. Whether that was true or not, that's how I wanted to be. Because of that spirit of support in her, I'm the kind of woman that I am today. I'm still alive. And I'm going to keep on living until I die."

She walked up to me again and placed my face between her warm hands. "Give her a chance to do the same for you, Jack. Give her a chance to let her keep you in the land of the living ... and the loving."

I shook my head, then leaned down to kiss her cheek. "You are one incredible woman, Rosie Kincaid."

"There's more of us out there than you think, Jack Deneen. Now, you go get yours."

EPILOGUE

"Here you go. I believe this one is yours, Grandpa." I handed out reunion packets to my relatives as they approached the hospitality table set up in one of the Orlando Wyndham Resort conference rooms.

It was only five o'clock. According to the reunion schedule, registration wasn't officially supposed to start until six. So I had my hands full trying to set up the table and appease my travel-weary relatives who'd arrived early. Good thing I'd had all of that volunteer time at the botanical gardens with Mama. That had taught me how to smile and keep smiling, even when I was ready to toss a few people into the hotel pool.

"Wait a minute now. Who shrunk my shirt?" Grandpa George pulled out a large, purple family reunion T-shirt from the huge manila envelope and held it up to his chest.

Jack and I exchanged amused glances. Who was going to be the one to tell him that there was nothing wrong with the shirt? In almost a year's time since we'd taken T-shirt orders and sizes, he'd gotten a little thicker around the middle.

"There must be a mix-up somewhere," Jack said

smoothly. "I'll see about getting you a larger . . . that is, the right size for you."

"You're a good man, Jack. Glad to have you in the family."

Grandpa stood at the table, rummaging through the reunion packet—dumping out maps, bus passes, name tags, and other reunion materials on the table as I tried to set out the table decorations.

"Maybe you want to go through that upstairs in your room, Grandpa?" I suggested gently, tugging the envelope from his hands and sweeping his materials back inside.

"Look at her. The girl gets a little rock on her finger and she turns into everybody's boss. Just like those Johnson women. You sure you want to get tied to this family, Jack?"

"Oh, *nowwww* you tell me." Jack shook his head in mock annoyance. "You should have mentioned that before that lavish ceremony at your church."

"You two are so not funny," I grumbled as I handed Jack another stack of envelopes to alphabetize. It made searching for the names that much easier when my relatives came up to claim theirs. "Here. Make yourself useful."

He took the envelopes and leaned forward to kiss my cheek. "You weren't complaining about my usefulness when we . . ." He continued the conversation in a whisper, making me blush and my grandfather clear his throat loudly.

"It's a good thing we got you two married off fast," he muttered, heading for the bank of elevators to retire to his room.

I punched Jack in the arm. "See there? You're going to get me into trouble."

"That's the general idea," he replied, raising his eyebrows at me. "After all, what's a honeymoon for if you can't stir up a little trouble?"

Smiling reluctantly, I wrapped my arms around his waist. "There's a time and a place for everything, Jack."

"And before this reunion weekend is over, I hope we make love in every single one of them. Ever make love in the Sea World whale tank with Shamu as our only witness?"

"Have you?" I challenged.

"Gives a new meaning to the word *blowhole*."

"Oh, you!" I lifted my hand, ready to punch him again, but wound up giving him a halfhearted swat instead. What could I say? How could I punish a man who made me feel as I did? I was cherished by his love and challenged by his wit, seduced and serenaded by love's sweet song. Annoyed by overeager fans, exhausted by the rigors of helping him run his business, I was a public figure's wife. The picture wasn't always pretty.

However, at the moment, we were in a fairy-tale setting. Surrounded by the lavish resort amenities and support of my family, I knew that the start of this marriage could lead a less grounded person to believe that our lives would always be this perfect.

Though my heart soared in the clouds, my head and feet were held firmly on the path of reality. I knew with Jack, there would be some good days and some bad days. We understood the limitations that his illness placed on him and vowed to face them together.

For better or for worse.

Those weren't just words we'd obediently echoed because the traditional ceremony required us to. Those were words that we'd taken to heart. And In repeating them, face-to-face, the solemn words had strengthened us, fortified us, bonded our lives together—bright, shining, and as tough as steel.

Dear Readers:

This book is dedicated to you—for all your continued support and encouragement. I hope that you'll enjoy reading about the Johnson family and come to love Shiri and Jack's story as much as I have. As always, I welcome your comments and suggestions. If any part of the Johnson family story touches your heart, let me know. I'd love to hear from you; you can e-mail me at geri_guillaume@hotmail.com.

Sincerely,
Geri Guillaume

ABOUT THE AUTHOR

Geri Guillaume is the pseudonym for an author who lives in Texas. A technical writer, she is also the mother of two children and raises horses.